MR. WOLF'S CLASS

LUCKY STARS

ARON NELS STEINKE

graphix
AN IMPRINT OF
■SCHOLASTIC

For Marlen

Library of Congress Control Number: 2018953582

ISBN 978-1-338-04789-9 (hardcover)
ISBN 978-1-338-04783-7 (paperback)

10 9 8 7 6 5 4 3 2 1   19 20 21 22 23

Printed in China   62
First edition, September 2019

Edited by Cassandra Pelham Fulton
Book design by Phil Falco
Publisher: David Saylor

CHAPTER ONE

Writer's Workshop

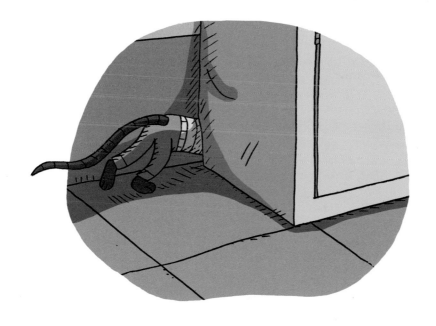

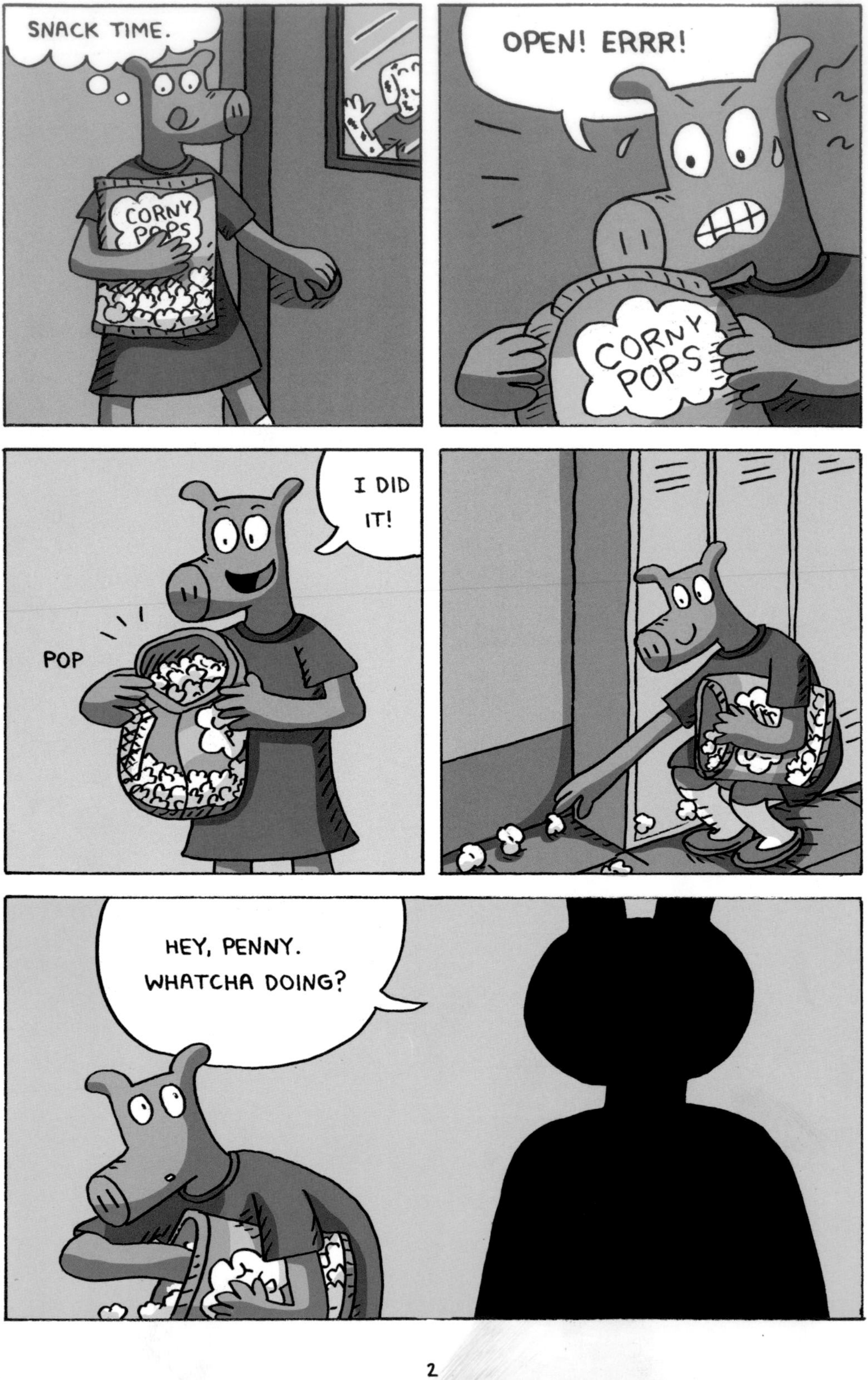
SNACK TIME.
CORNY POPS
OPEN! ERRR!
CORNY POPS
I DID IT!
POP
HEY, PENNY. WHATCHA DOING?

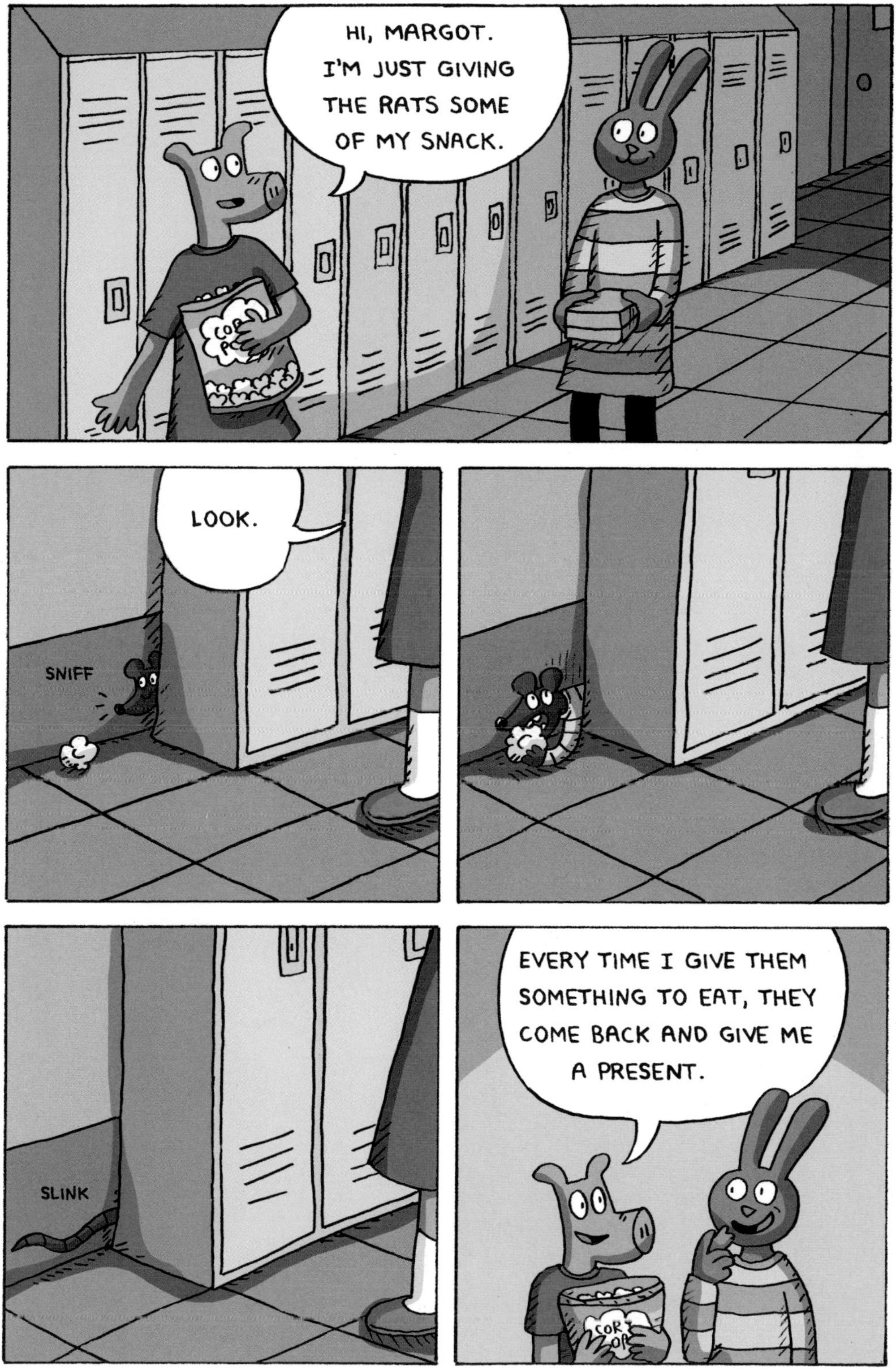
HI, MARGOT. I'M JUST GIVING THE RATS SOME OF MY SNACK.
LOOK.
SNIFF
SLINK
EVERY TIME I GIVE THEM SOMETHING TO EAT, THEY COME BACK AND GIVE ME A PRESENT.

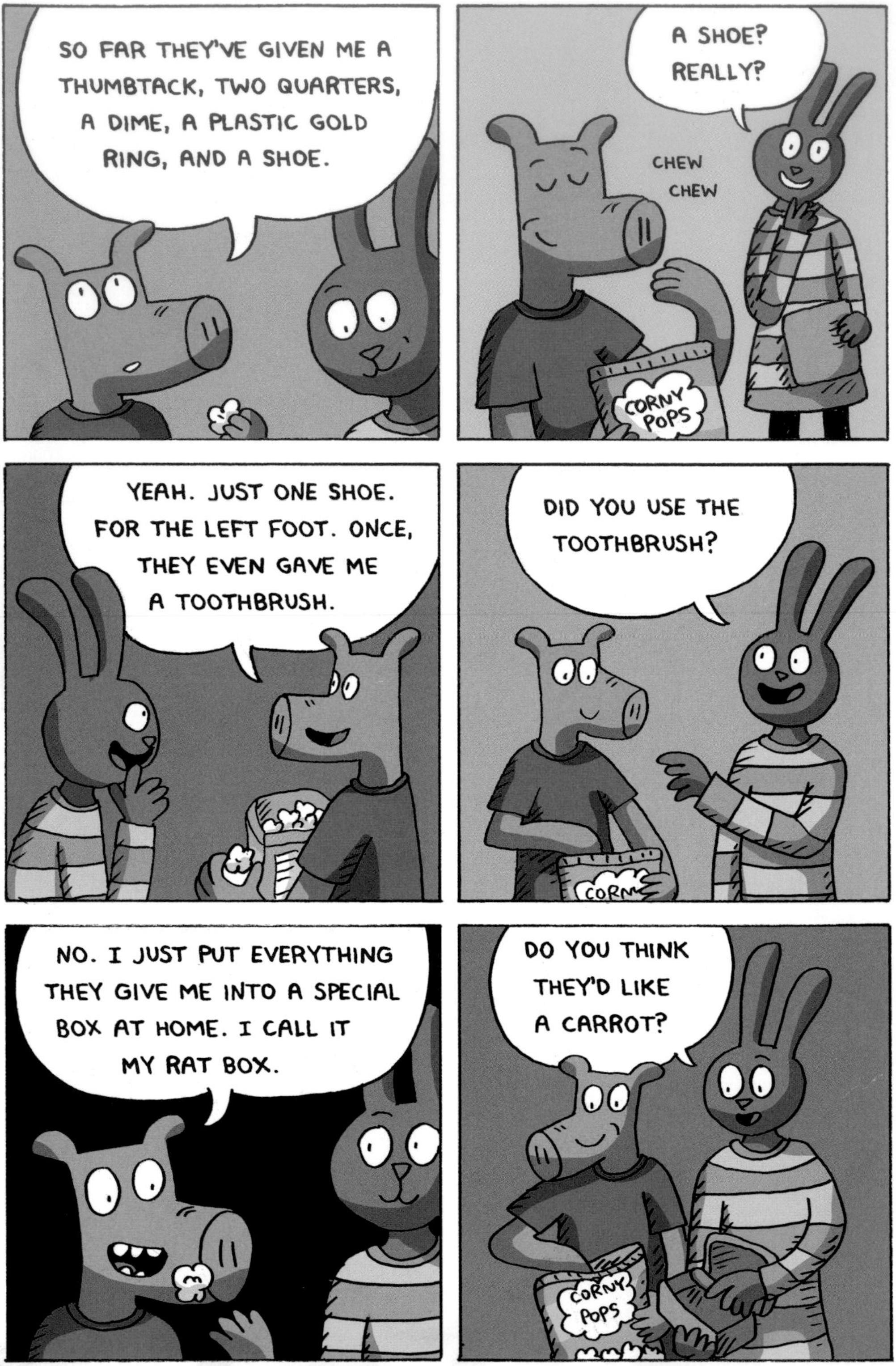
SO FAR THEY'VE GIVEN ME A THUMBTACK, TWO QUARTERS, A DIME, A PLASTIC GOLD RING, AND A SHOE.
A SHOE? REALLY?
CHEW CHEW
CORNY POPS
YEAH. JUST ONE SHOE. FOR THE LEFT FOOT. ONCE, THEY EVEN GAVE ME A TOOTHBRUSH.
DID YOU USE THE TOOTHBRUSH?
NO. I JUST PUT EVERYTHING THEY GIVE ME INTO A SPECIAL BOX AT HOME. I CALL IT MY RAT BOX.
DO YOU THINK THEY'D LIKE A CARROT?
CORNY POPS

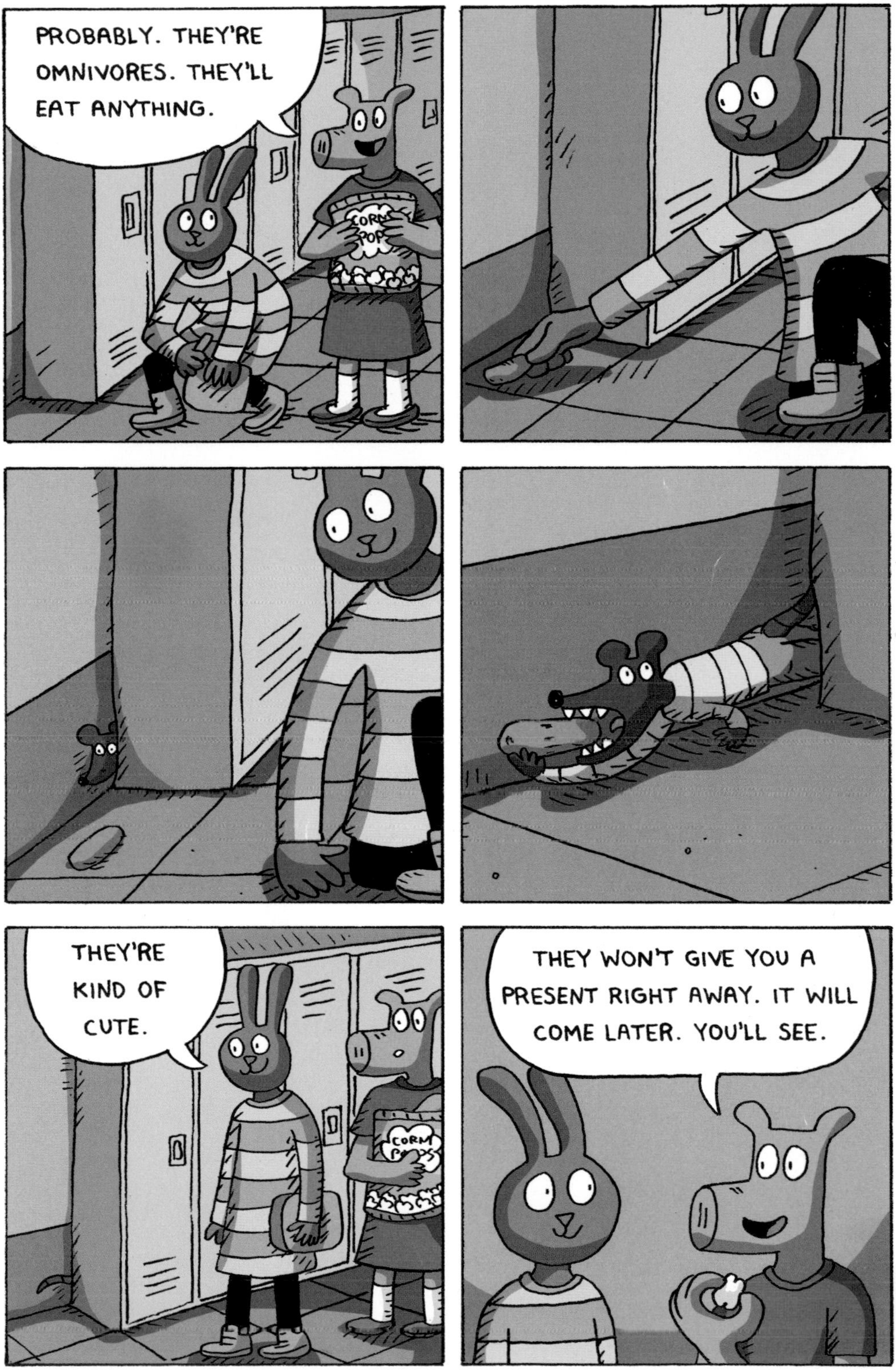
PROBABLY. THEY'RE OMNIVORES. THEY'LL EAT ANYTHING.
CORN POPS
THEY'RE KIND OF CUTE.
CORN POPS
THEY WON'T GIVE YOU A PRESENT RIGHT AWAY. IT WILL COME LATER. YOU'LL SEE.

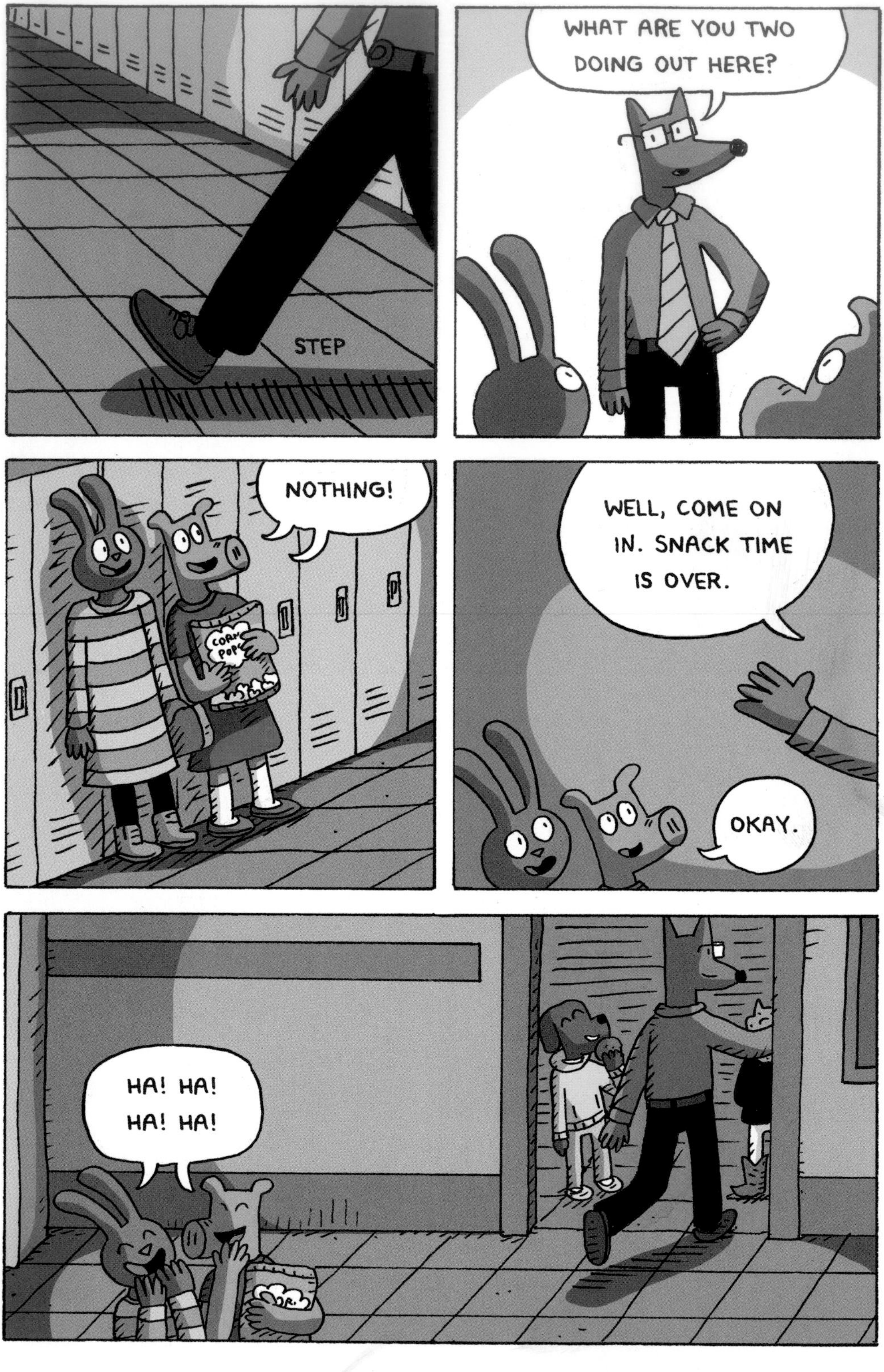
STEP
WHAT ARE YOU TWO DOING OUT HERE?
NOTHING!
CORN POPS
WELL, COME ON IN. SNACK TIME IS OVER.
OKAY.
HA! HA! HA! HA!

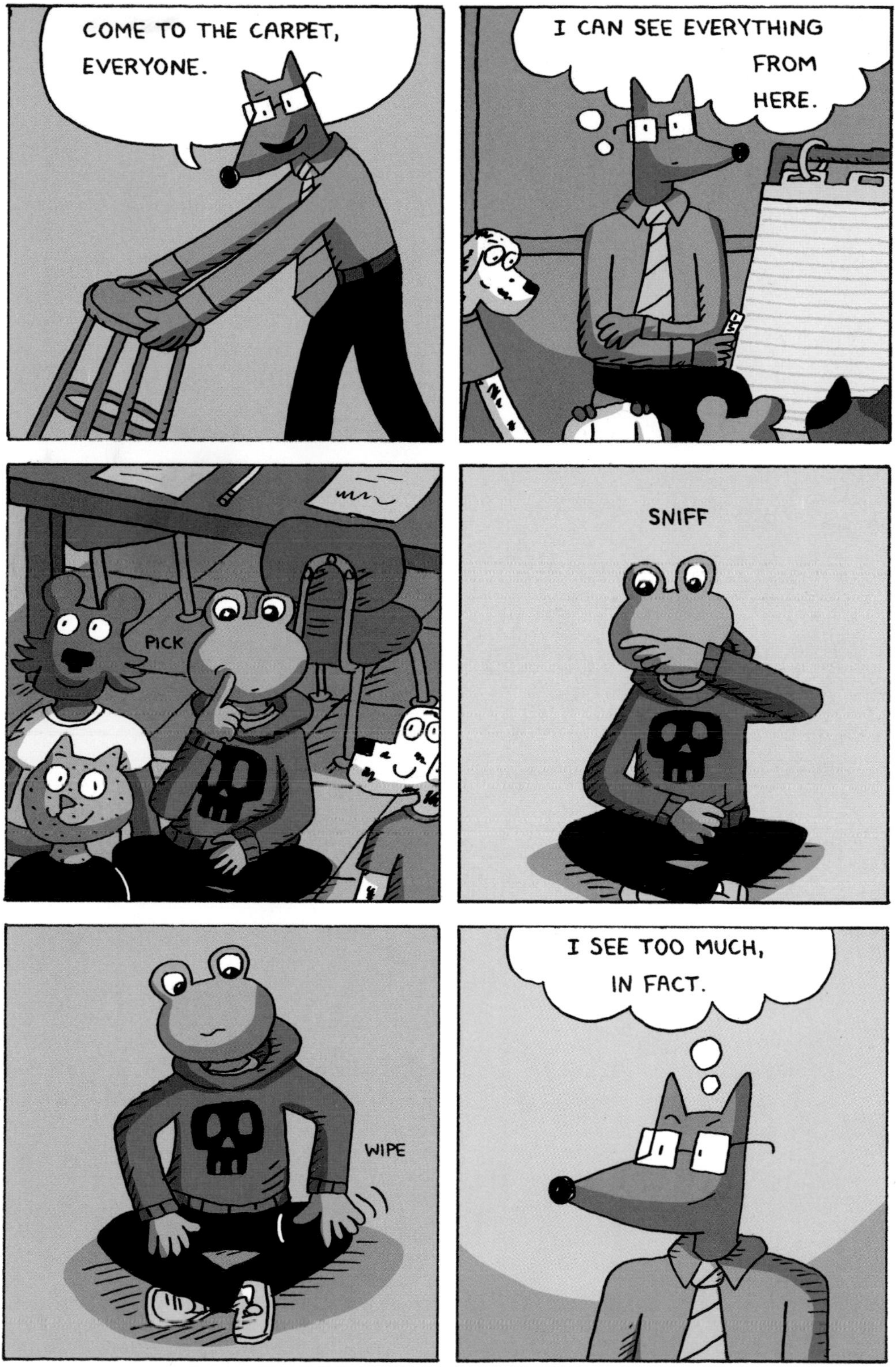
COME TO THE CARPET, EVERYONE.
I CAN SEE EVERYTHING FROM HERE.
PICK
SNIFF
WIPE
I SEE TOO MUCH, IN FACT.

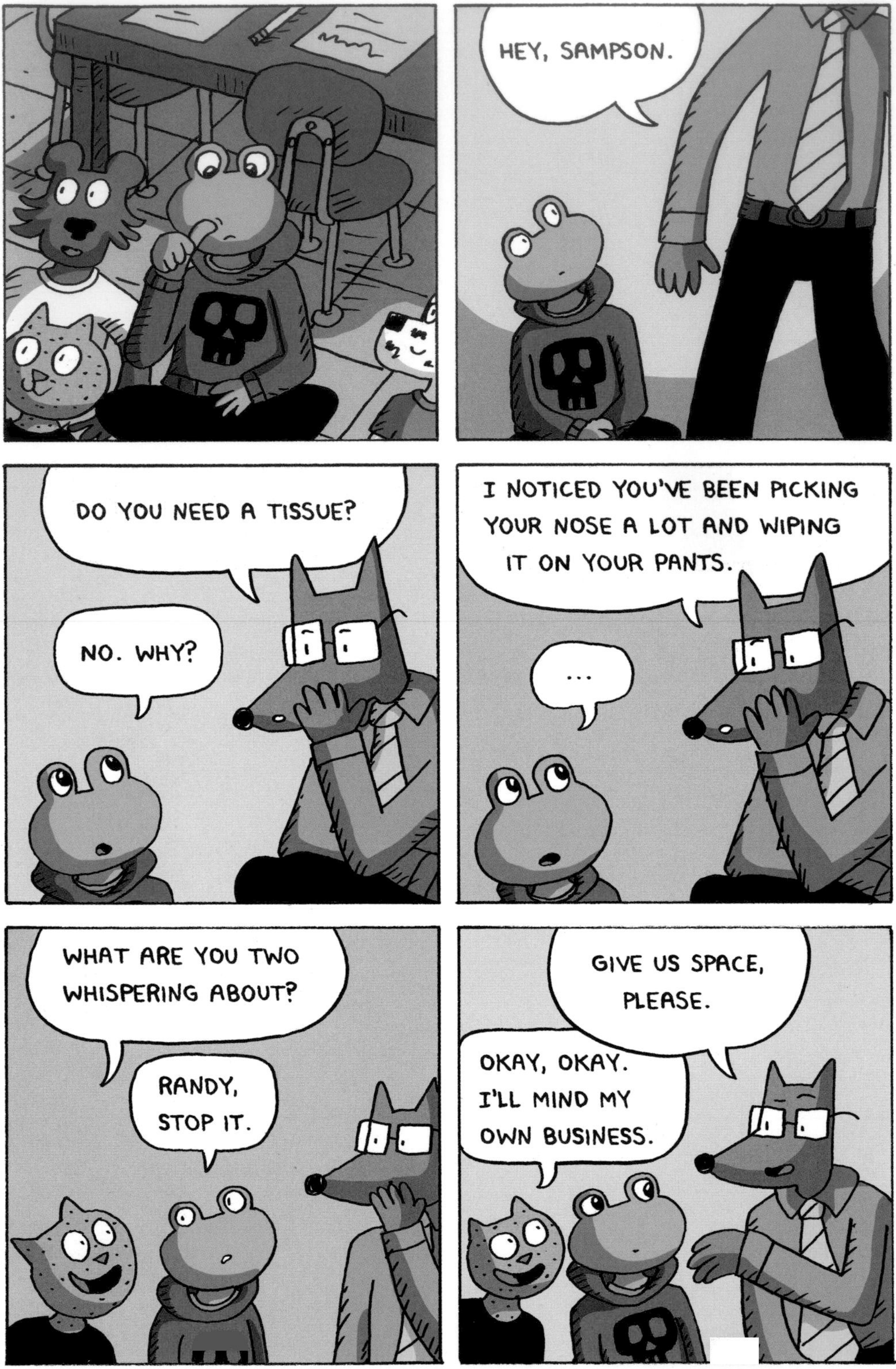
HEY, SAMPSON.
DO YOU NEED A TISSUE?
NO. WHY?
I NOTICED YOU'VE BEEN PICKING YOUR NOSE A LOT AND WIPING IT ON YOUR PANTS.
...
WHAT ARE YOU TWO WHISPERING ABOUT?
RANDY, STOP IT.
GIVE US SPACE, PLEASE.
OKAY, OKAY. I'LL MIND MY OWN BUSINESS.

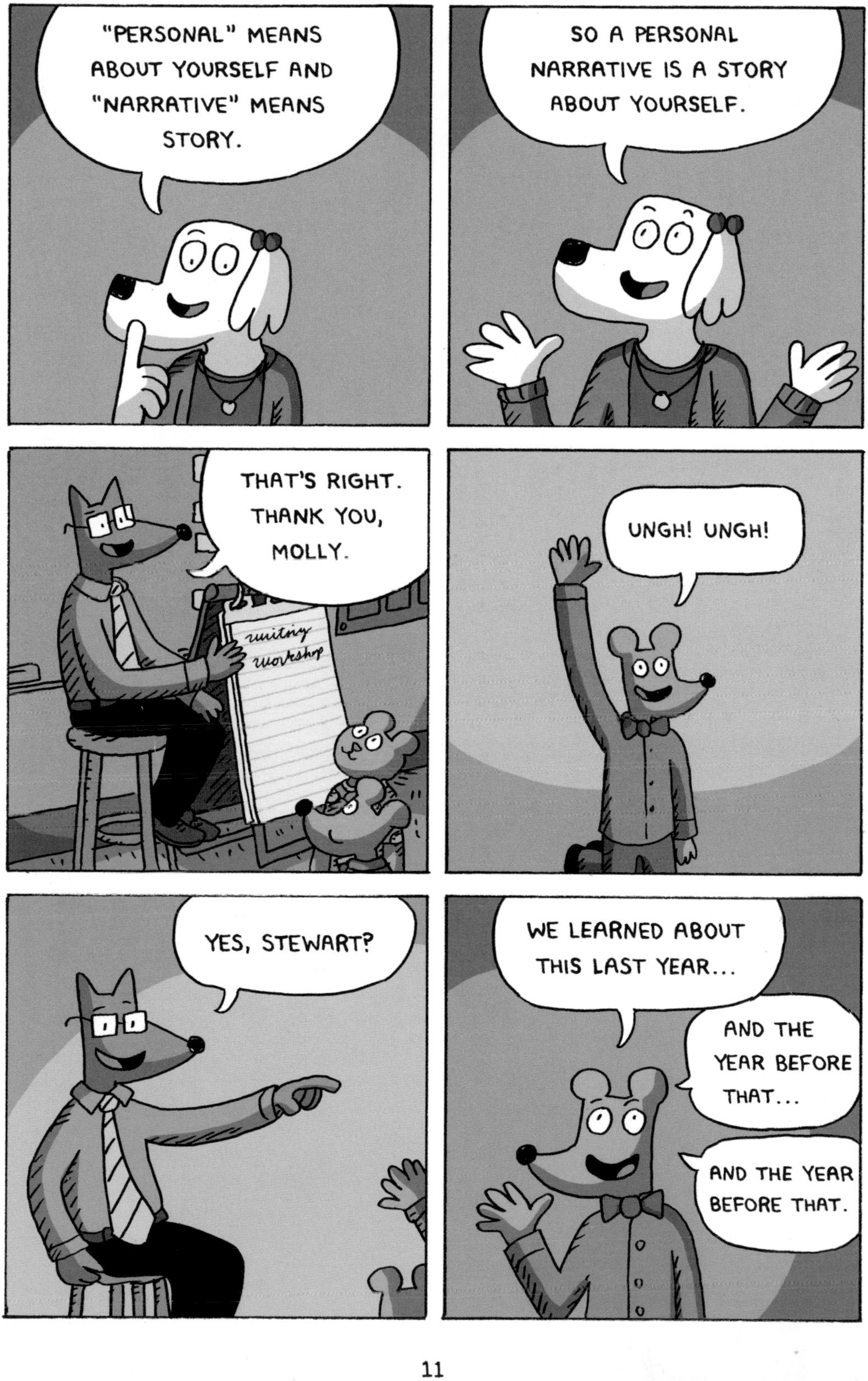
"PERSONAL" MEANS ABOUT YOURSELF AND "NARRATIVE" MEANS STORY.
SO A PERSONAL NARRATIVE IS A STORY ABOUT YOURSELF.
THAT'S RIGHT. THANK YOU, MOLLY.
writing workshop
UNGH! UNGH!
YES, STEWART?
WE LEARNED ABOUT THIS LAST YEAR...
AND THE YEAR BEFORE THAT...
AND THE YEAR BEFORE THAT.

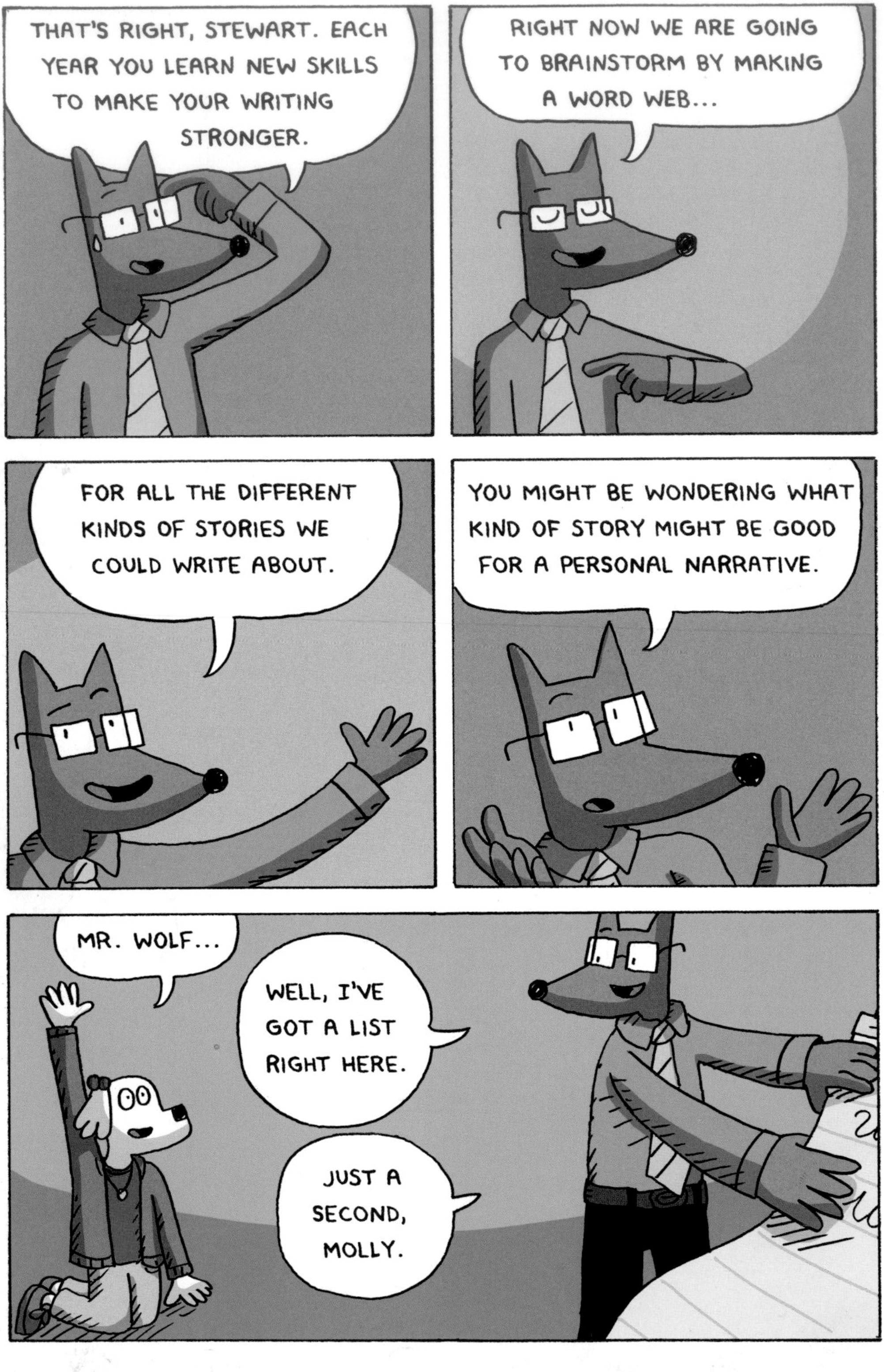
THAT'S RIGHT, STEWART. EACH YEAR YOU LEARN NEW SKILLS TO MAKE YOUR WRITING STRONGER.
RIGHT NOW WE ARE GOING TO BRAINSTORM BY MAKING A WORD WEB...
FOR ALL THE DIFFERENT KINDS OF STORIES WE COULD WRITE ABOUT.
YOU MIGHT BE WONDERING WHAT KIND OF STORY MIGHT BE GOOD FOR A PERSONAL NARRATIVE.
MR. WOLF...
WELL, I'VE GOT A LIST RIGHT HERE.
JUST A SECOND, MOLLY.

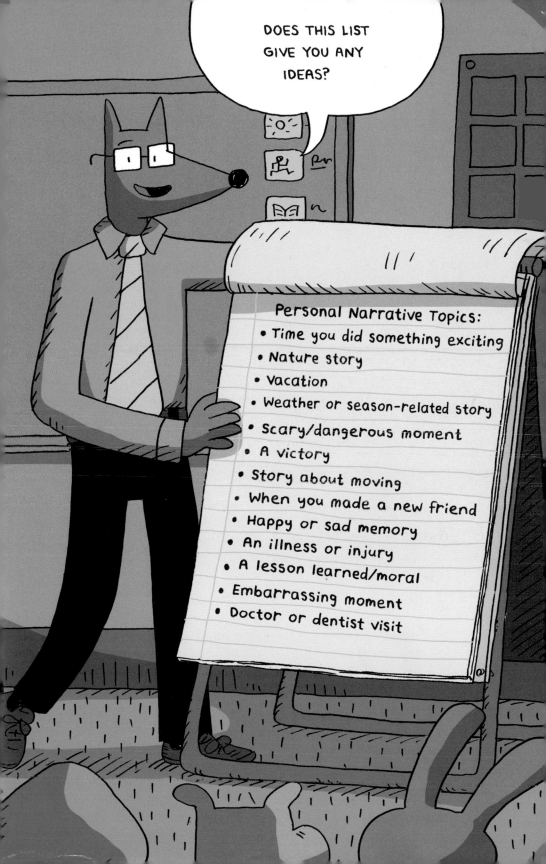

MOLLY, DO YOU STILL HAVE A QUESTION?

CAN I WRITE ABOUT THE TIME MY LITTLE SISTER WAS BORN?

YOU CAN.

RANDY?

CAN I GO TO THE BATHROOM?

SAMPSON, SHHHH!

IN JUST A MINUTE.

IF YOUR STORY DOESN'T END UP FITTING INTO ONE OF THESE CATEGORIES, THAT'S OKAY, TOO.

THIS LIST IS JUST A WAY TO HELP YOU COME UP WITH IDEAS.

Personal Nai
T u did
story
vacation
weather or
scary/dange

I'M BACK FROM THE BATHROOM...NOW CAN I GET A DRINK OF WATER?

CHAPTER TWO
Writer's Block

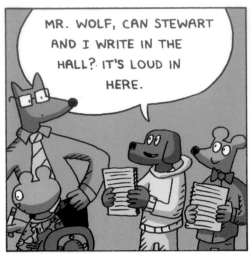

MR. WOLF, CAN STEWART AND I WRITE IN THE HALL? IT'S LOUD IN HERE.

SURE. I'M GLAD TO SEE THE TWO OF YOU GETTING ALONG.

I'M DONE.

SNIFF

CLICK
CLICK
CLICK

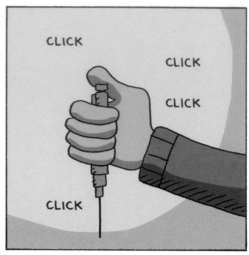

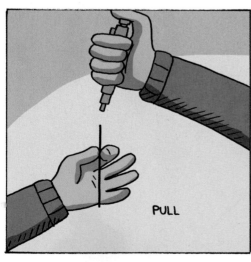

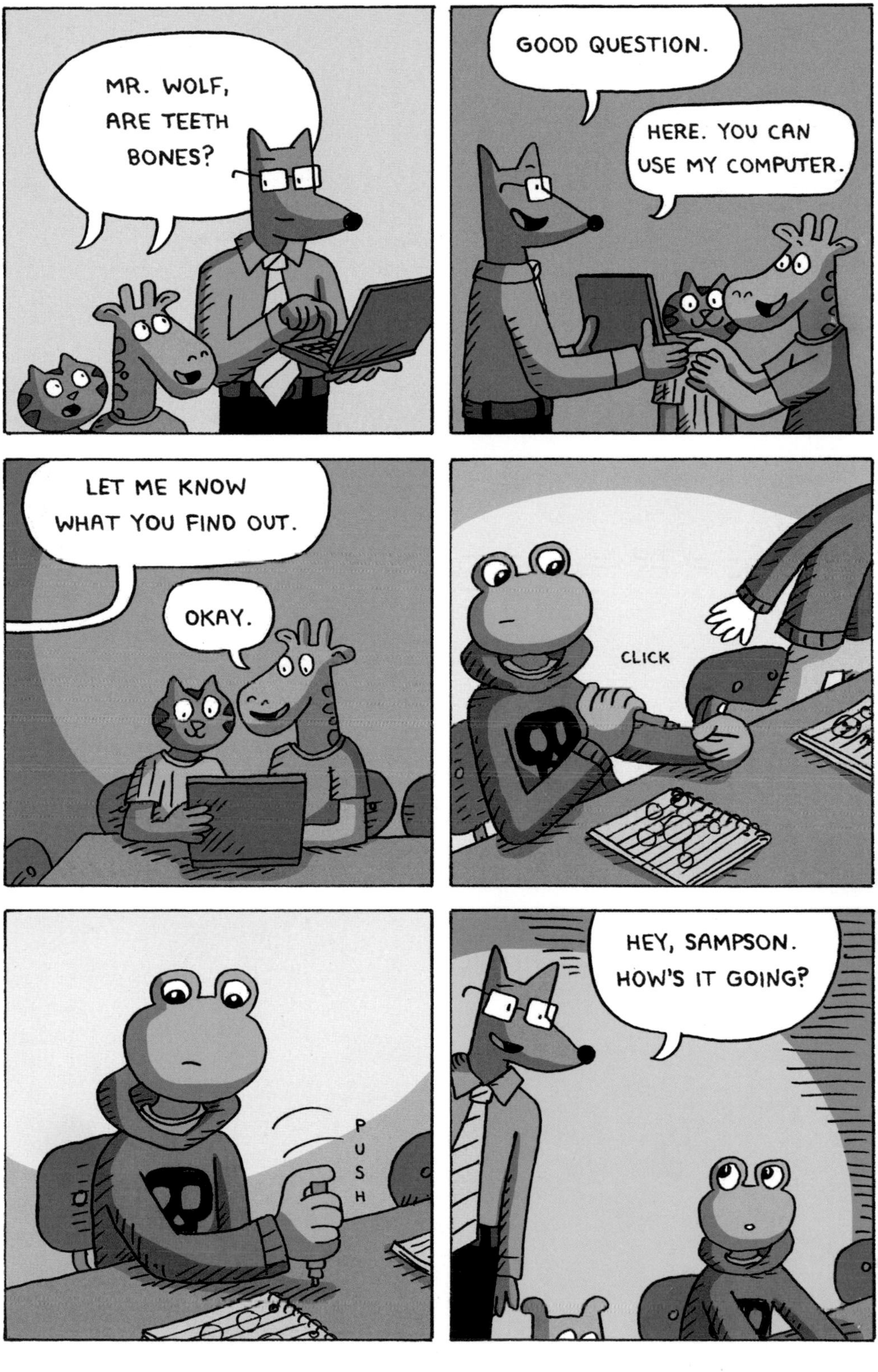
MR. WOLF, ARE TEETH BONES?
GOOD QUESTION.
HERE. YOU CAN USE MY COMPUTER.
LET ME KNOW WHAT YOU FIND OUT.
OKAY.
CLICK
PUSH
HEY, SAMPSON. HOW'S IT GOING?

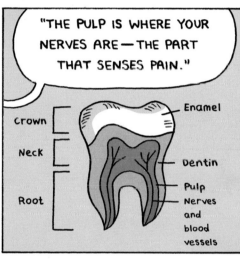

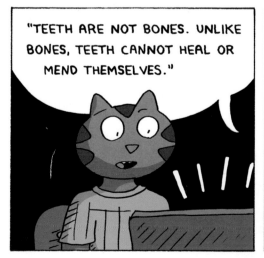

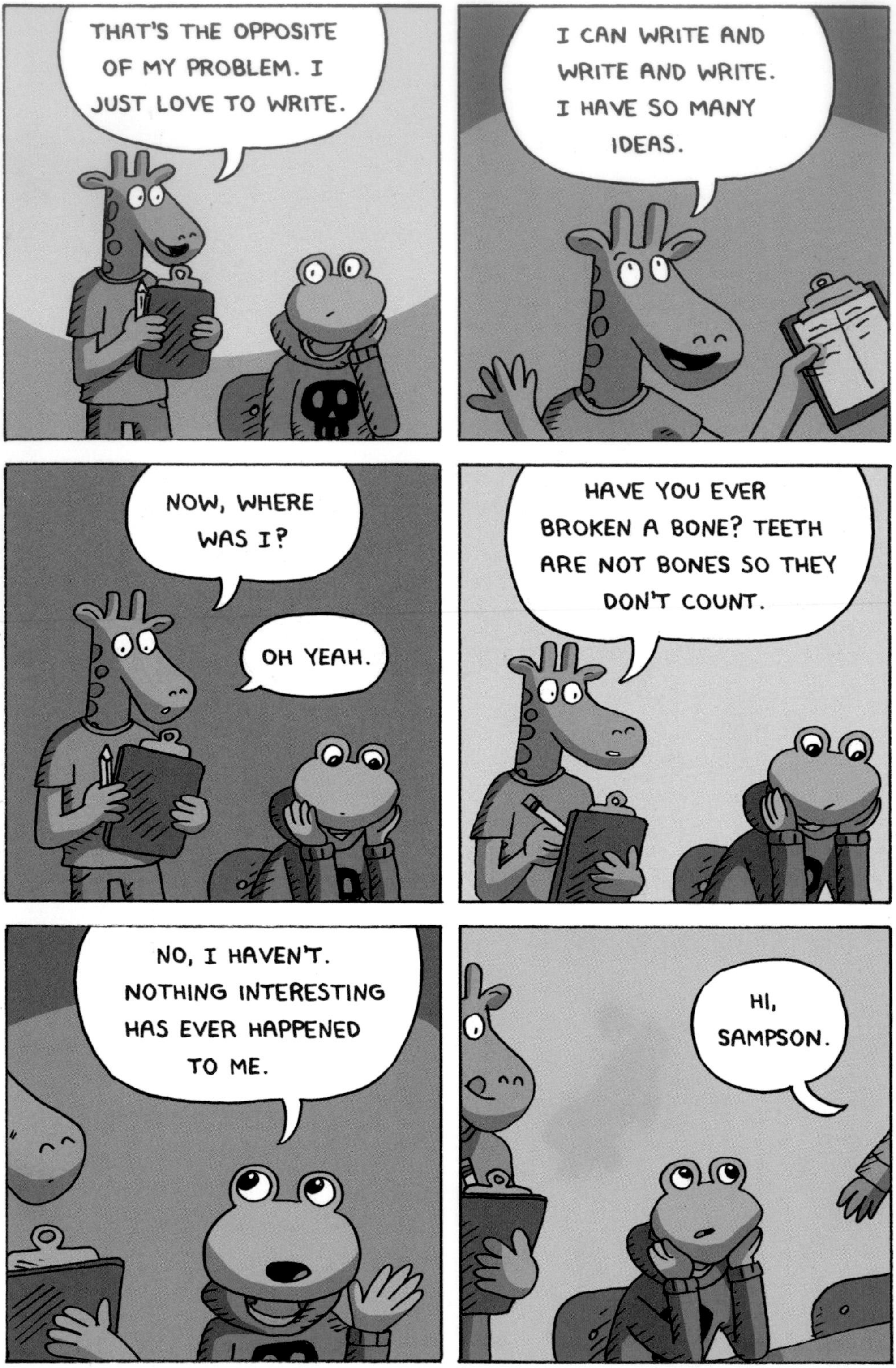
THAT'S THE OPPOSITE OF MY PROBLEM. I JUST LOVE TO WRITE.
I CAN WRITE AND WRITE AND WRITE. I HAVE SO MANY IDEAS.
NOW, WHERE WAS I?
OH YEAH.
HAVE YOU EVER BROKEN A BONE? TEETH ARE NOT BONES SO THEY DON'T COUNT.
NO, I HAVEN'T. NOTHING INTERESTING HAS EVER HAPPENED TO ME.
HI, SAMPSON.

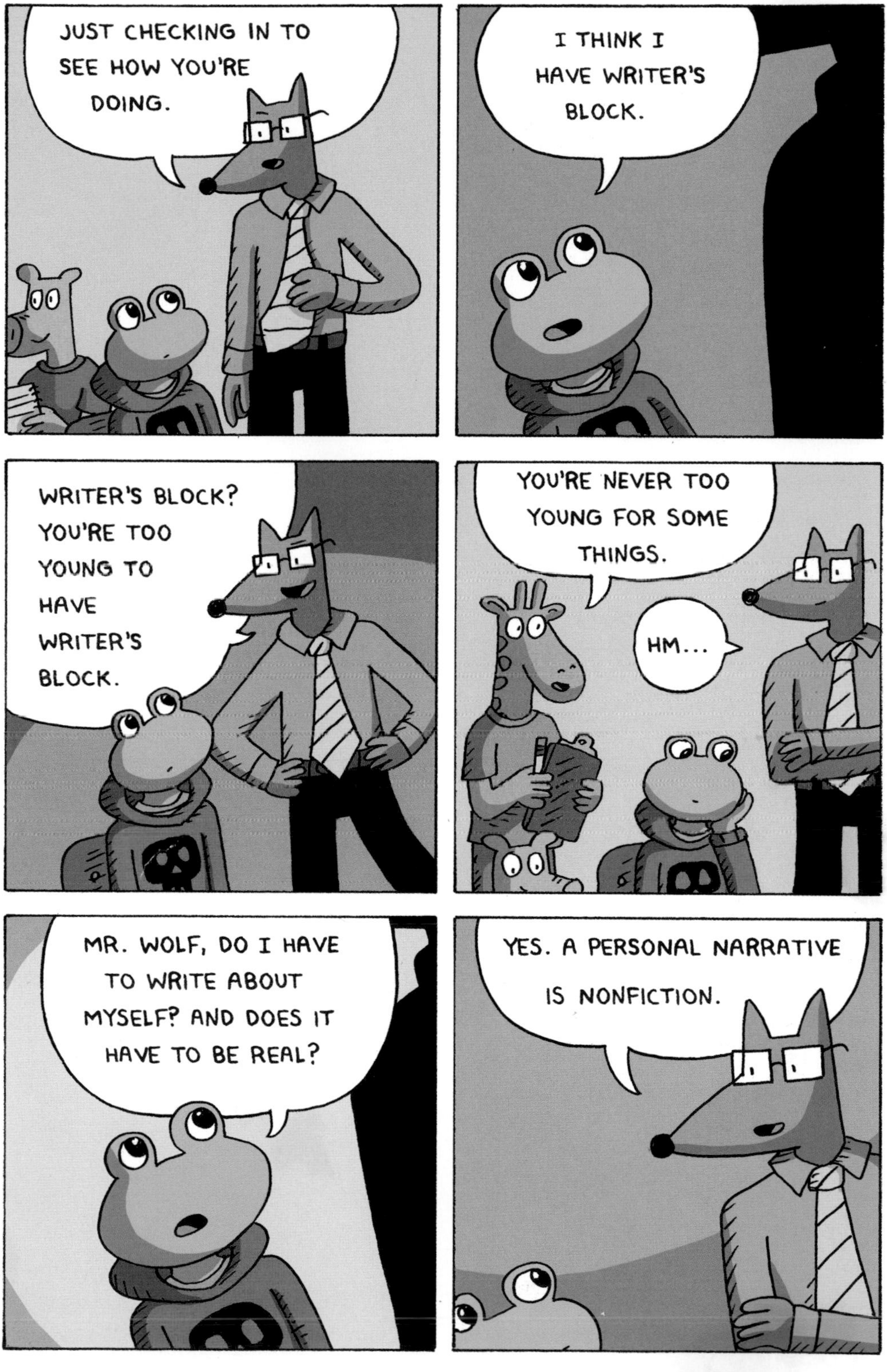
JUST CHECKING IN TO SEE HOW YOU'RE DOING.
I THINK I HAVE WRITER'S BLOCK.
WRITER'S BLOCK? YOU'RE TOO YOUNG TO HAVE WRITER'S BLOCK.
YOU'RE NEVER TOO YOUNG FOR SOME THINGS.
HM...
MR. WOLF, DO I HAVE TO WRITE ABOUT MYSELF? AND DOES IT HAVE TO BE REAL?
YES. A PERSONAL NARRATIVE IS NONFICTION.

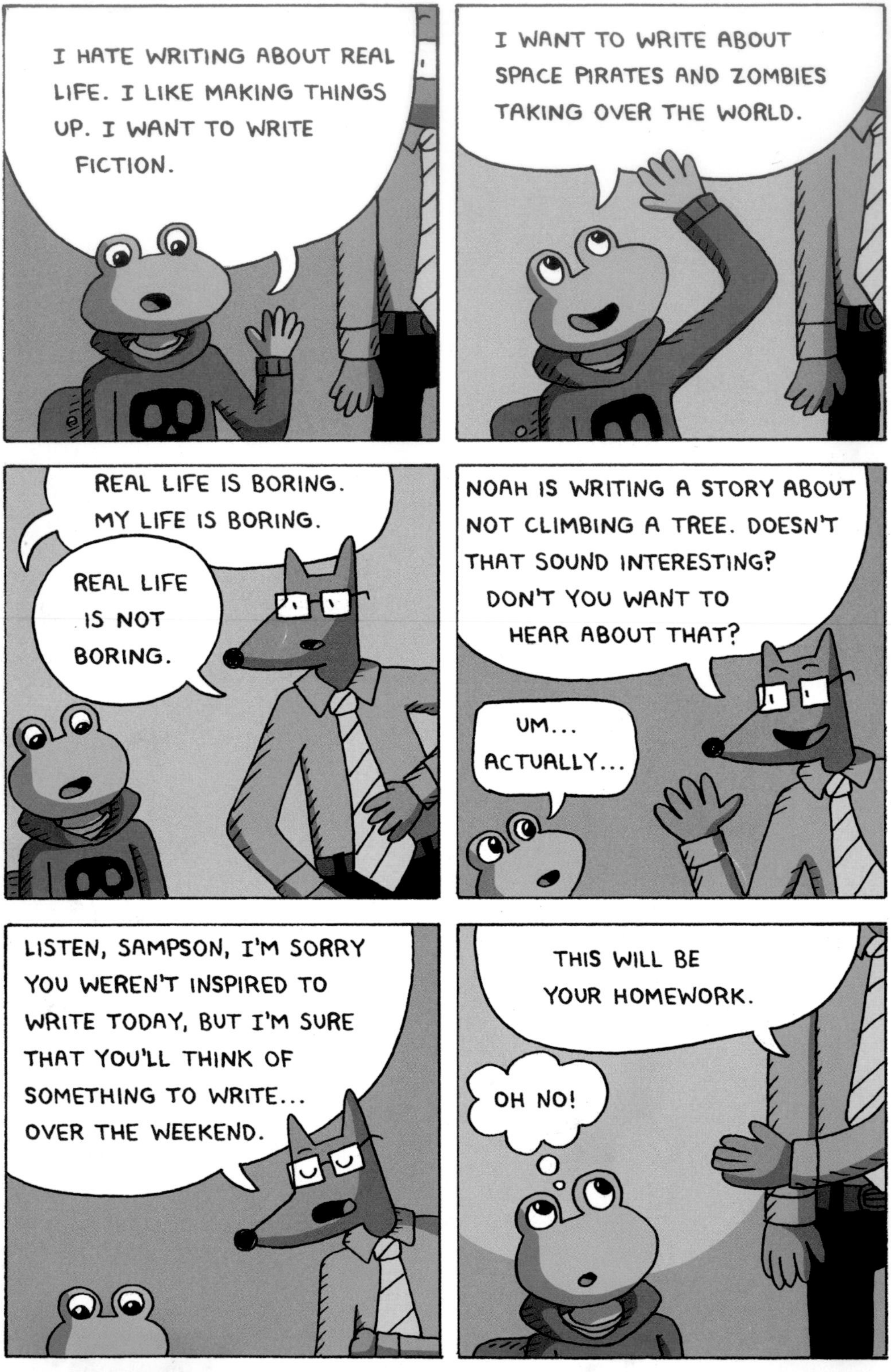
I HATE WRITING ABOUT REAL LIFE. I LIKE MAKING THINGS UP. I WANT TO WRITE FICTION.
I WANT TO WRITE ABOUT SPACE PIRATES AND ZOMBIES TAKING OVER THE WORLD.
REAL LIFE IS BORING. MY LIFE IS BORING.
REAL LIFE IS NOT BORING.
NOAH IS WRITING A STORY ABOUT NOT CLIMBING A TREE. DOESN'T THAT SOUND INTERESTING? DON'T YOU WANT TO HEAR ABOUT THAT?
UM... ACTUALLY...
LISTEN, SAMPSON, I'M SORRY YOU WEREN'T INSPIRED TO WRITE TODAY, BUT I'M SURE THAT YOU'LL THINK OF SOMETHING TO WRITE... OVER THE WEEKEND.
THIS WILL BE YOUR HOMEWORK.
OH NO!

CHAPTER THREE
Chicken Hill

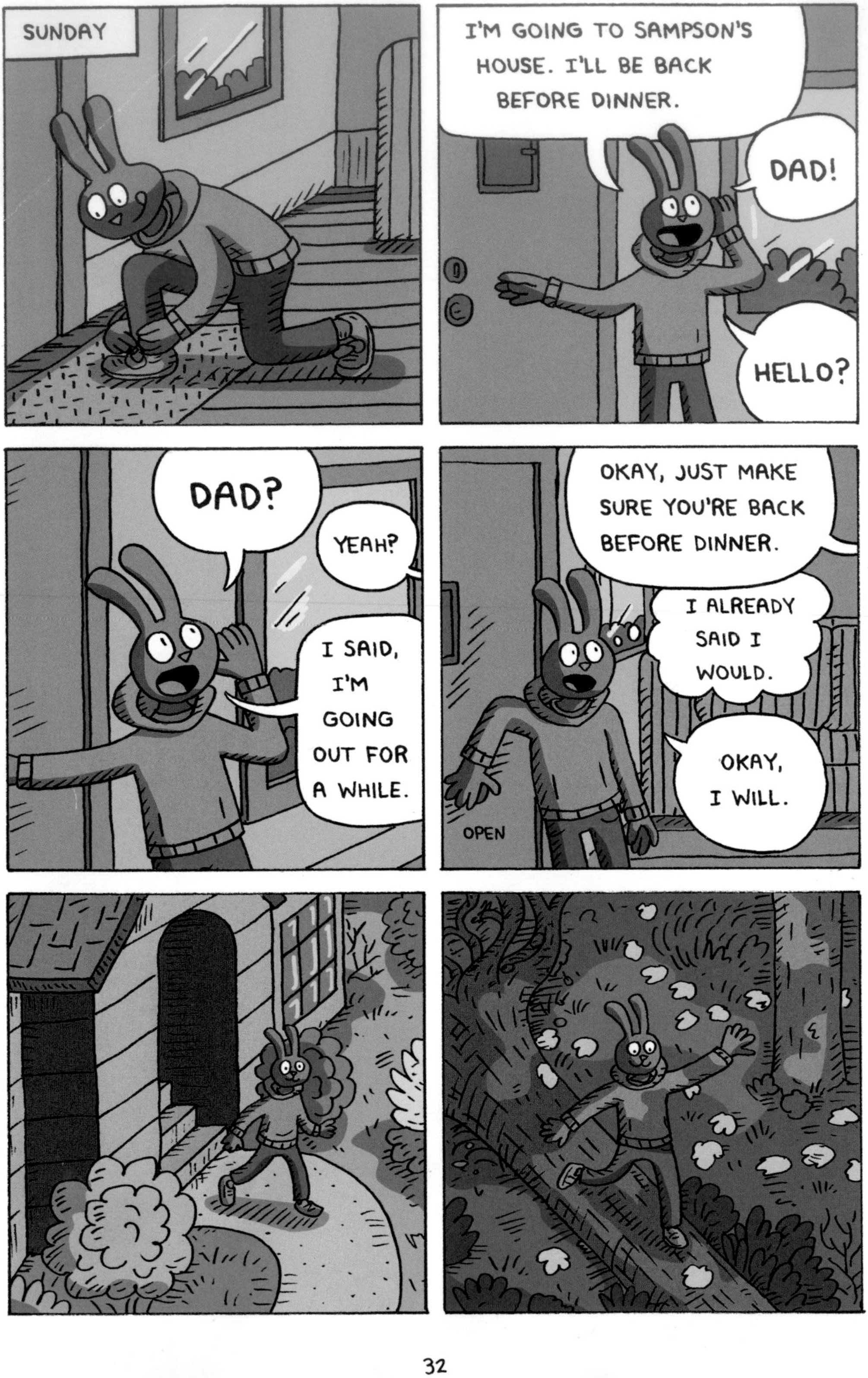
SUNDAY
I'M GOING TO SAMPSON'S HOUSE. I'LL BE BACK BEFORE DINNER.
DAD!
HELLO?
DAD?
YEAH?
I SAID, I'M GOING OUT FOR A WHILE.
OKAY, JUST MAKE SURE YOU'RE BACK BEFORE DINNER.
I ALREADY SAID I WOULD.
OKAY, I WILL.
OPEN

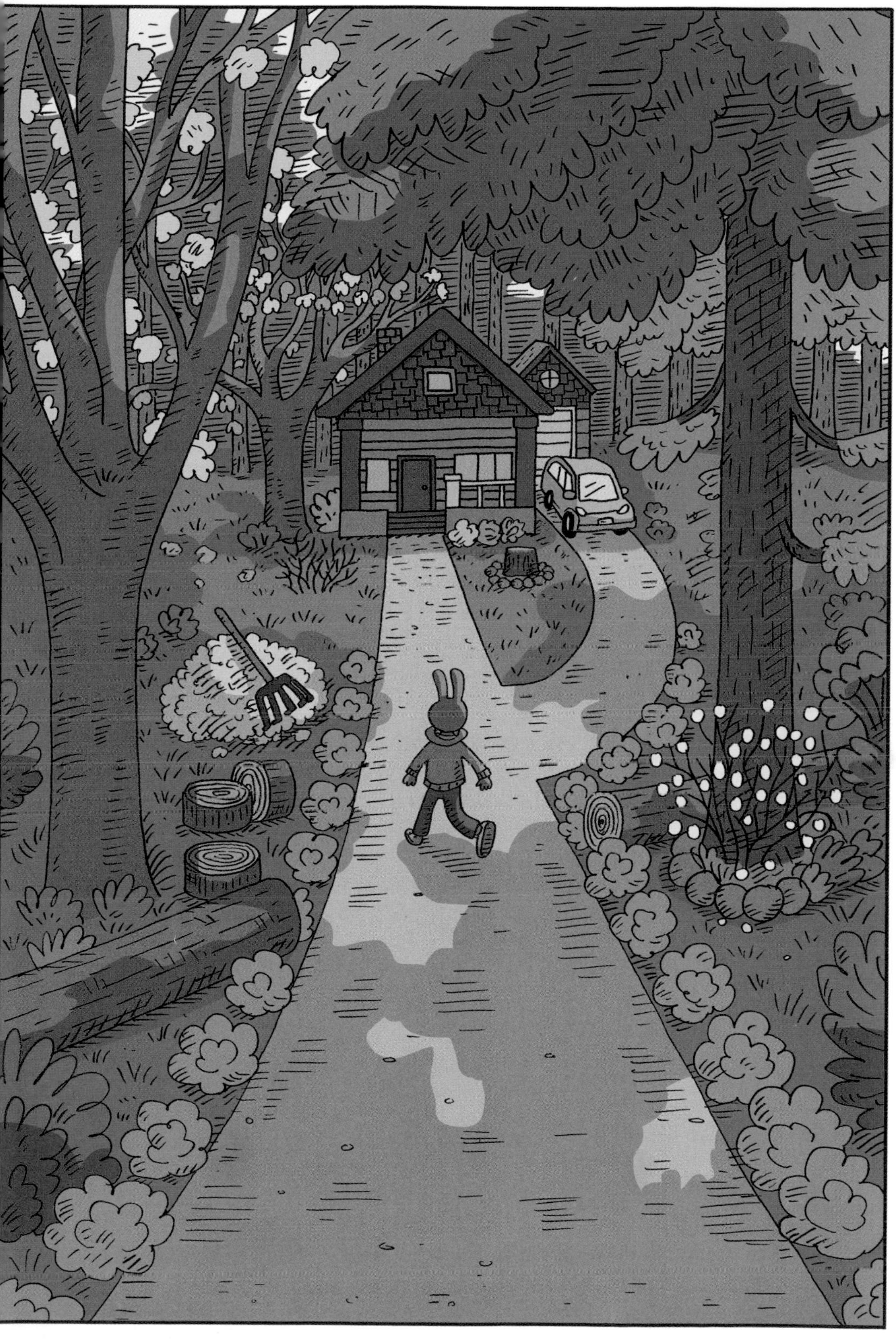

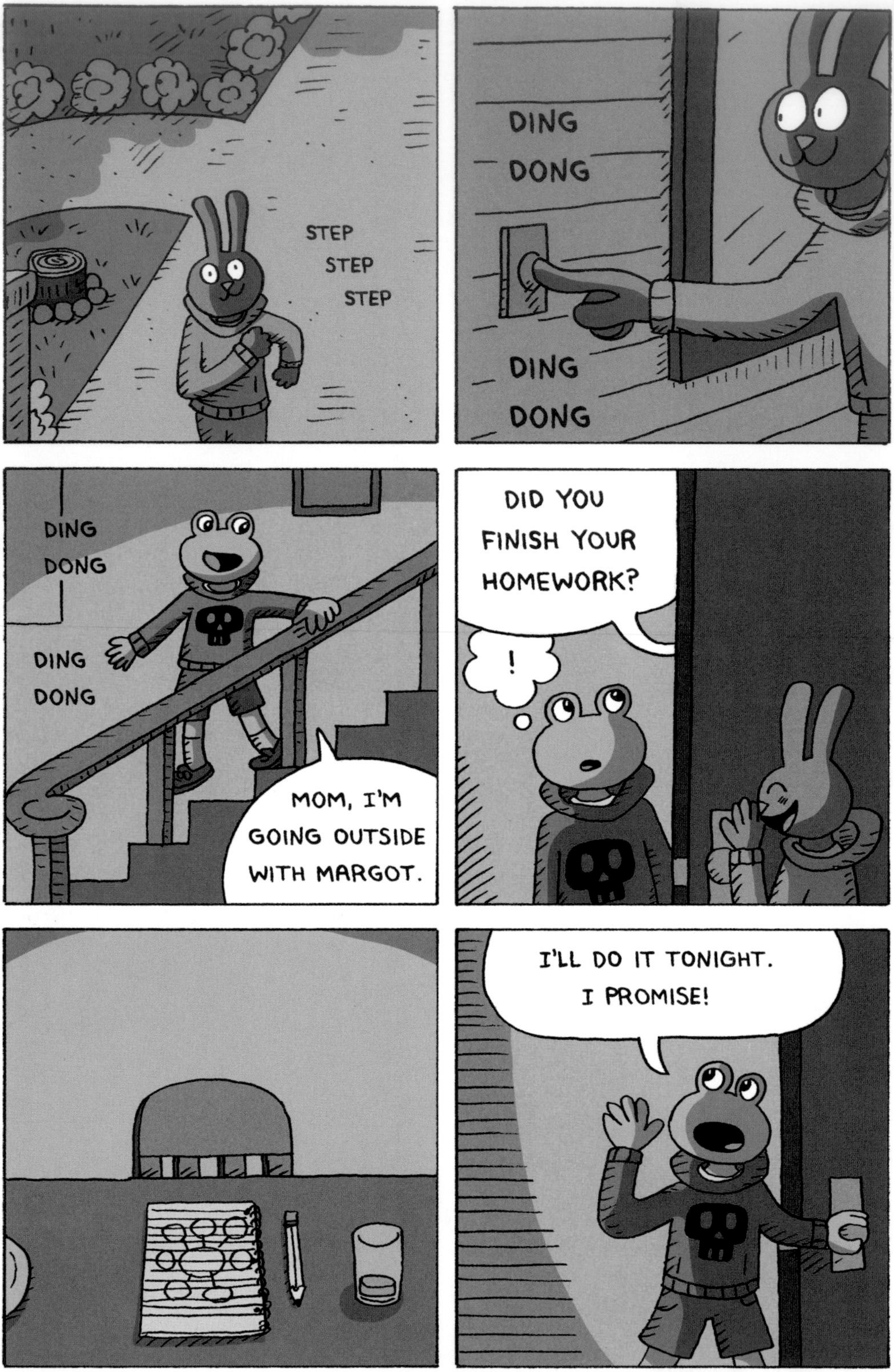
STEP
STEP
STEP
DING
DONG
DING
DONG
DING
DONG
DING
DONG
MOM, I'M GOING OUTSIDE WITH MARGOT.
DID YOU FINISH YOUR HOMEWORK?
!
I'LL DO IT TONIGHT. I PROMISE!

IF I'M GOING TO RIDE YOUR BIKE, WHAT ARE YOU GOING TO RIDE?

I DIDN'T KNOW YOU HAD A BROTHER.

ALEX IS EIGHTEEN. HE'S IN COLLEGE NOW.

HE SAID I COULD BORROW HIS BIKE WHILE HE'S AWAY.

IT'S A LITTLE BIG BUT I SHOULD BE FINE IF I JUST LOWER THE SEAT.

WHAT ARE YOU LOOKING FOR?

AN ALLEN WRENCH.

TA-DA! FOUND IT!

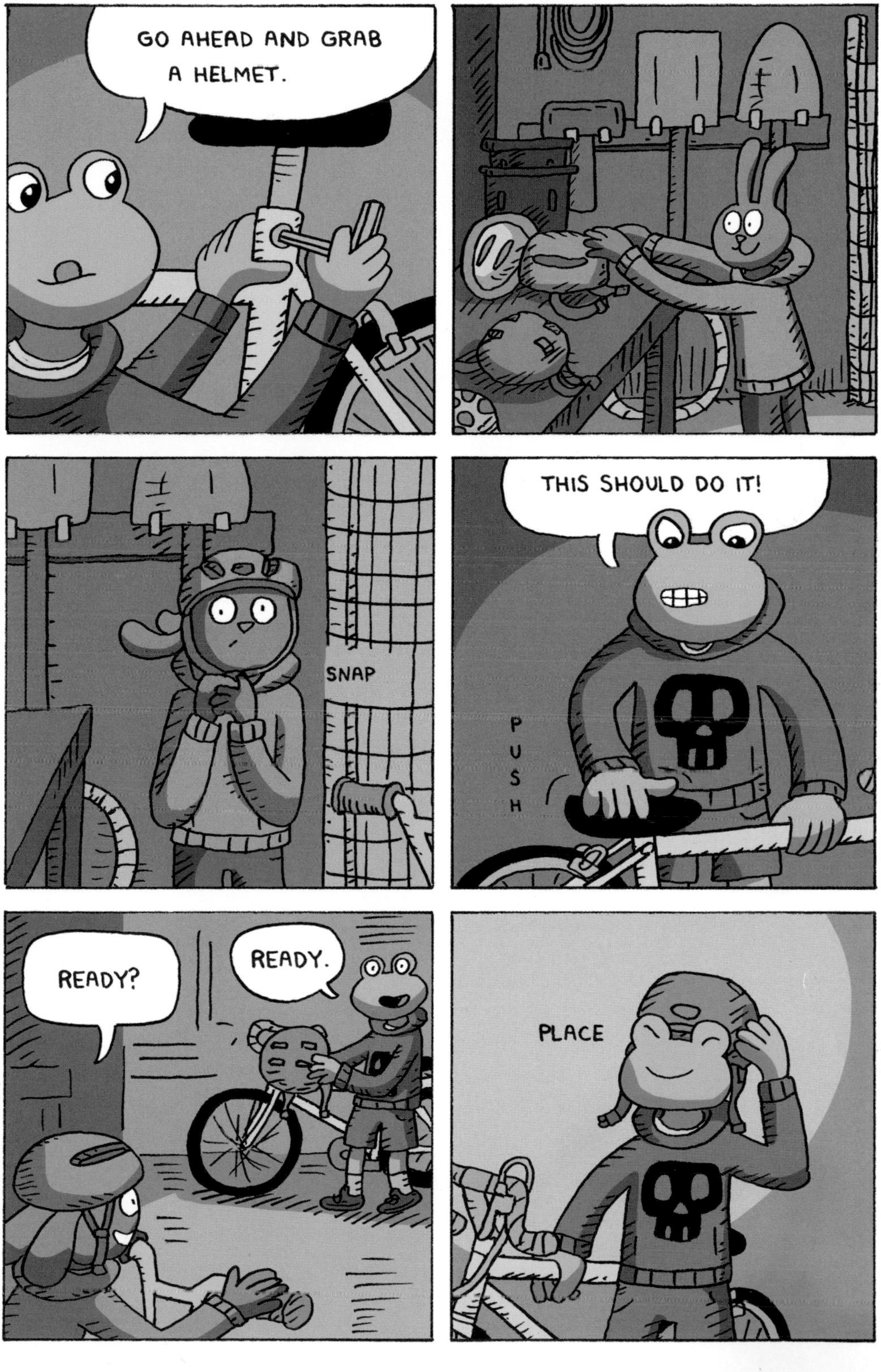
GO AHEAD AND GRAB A HELMET.
SNAP
THIS SHOULD DO IT!
PUSH
READY?
READY.
PLACE

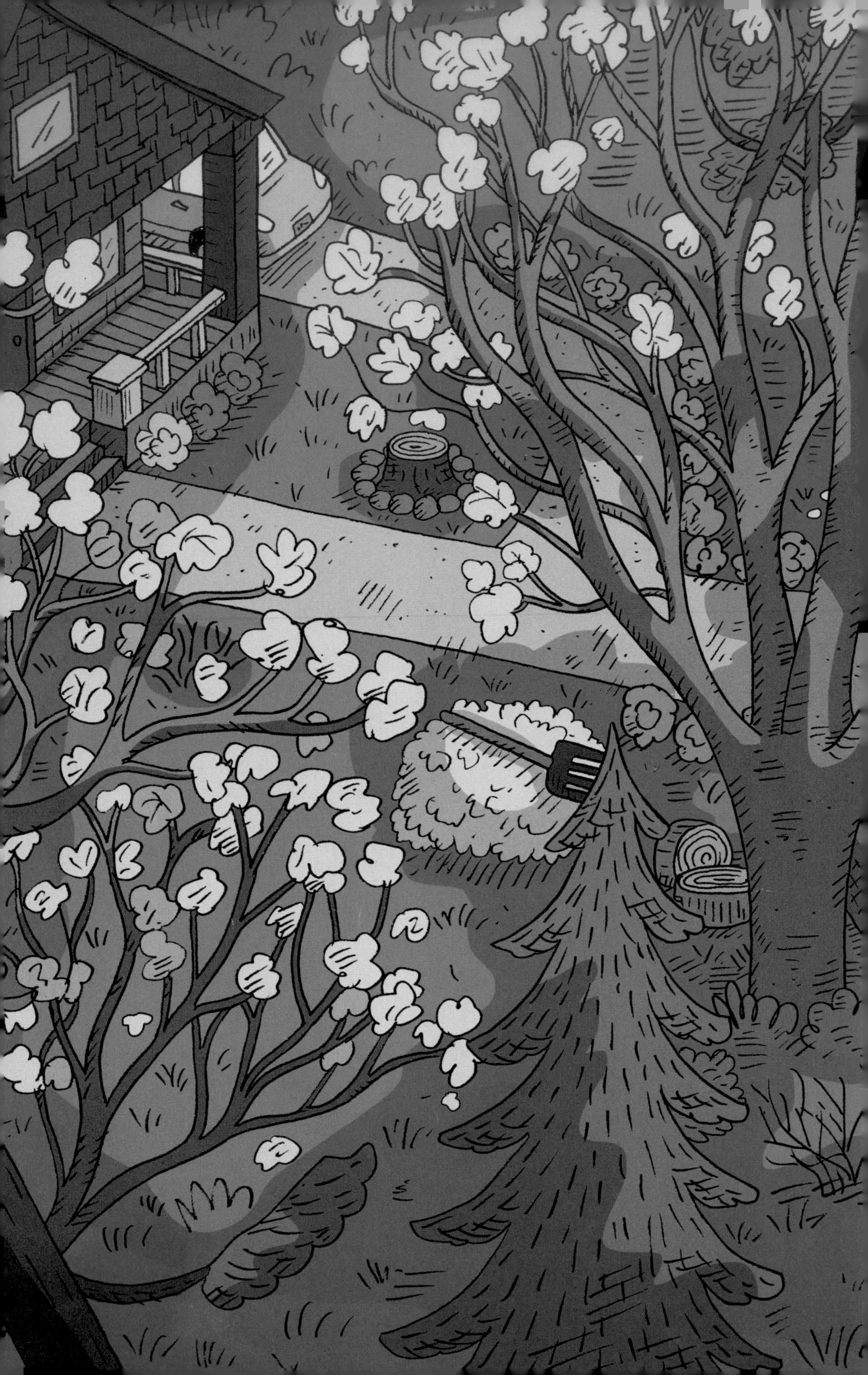

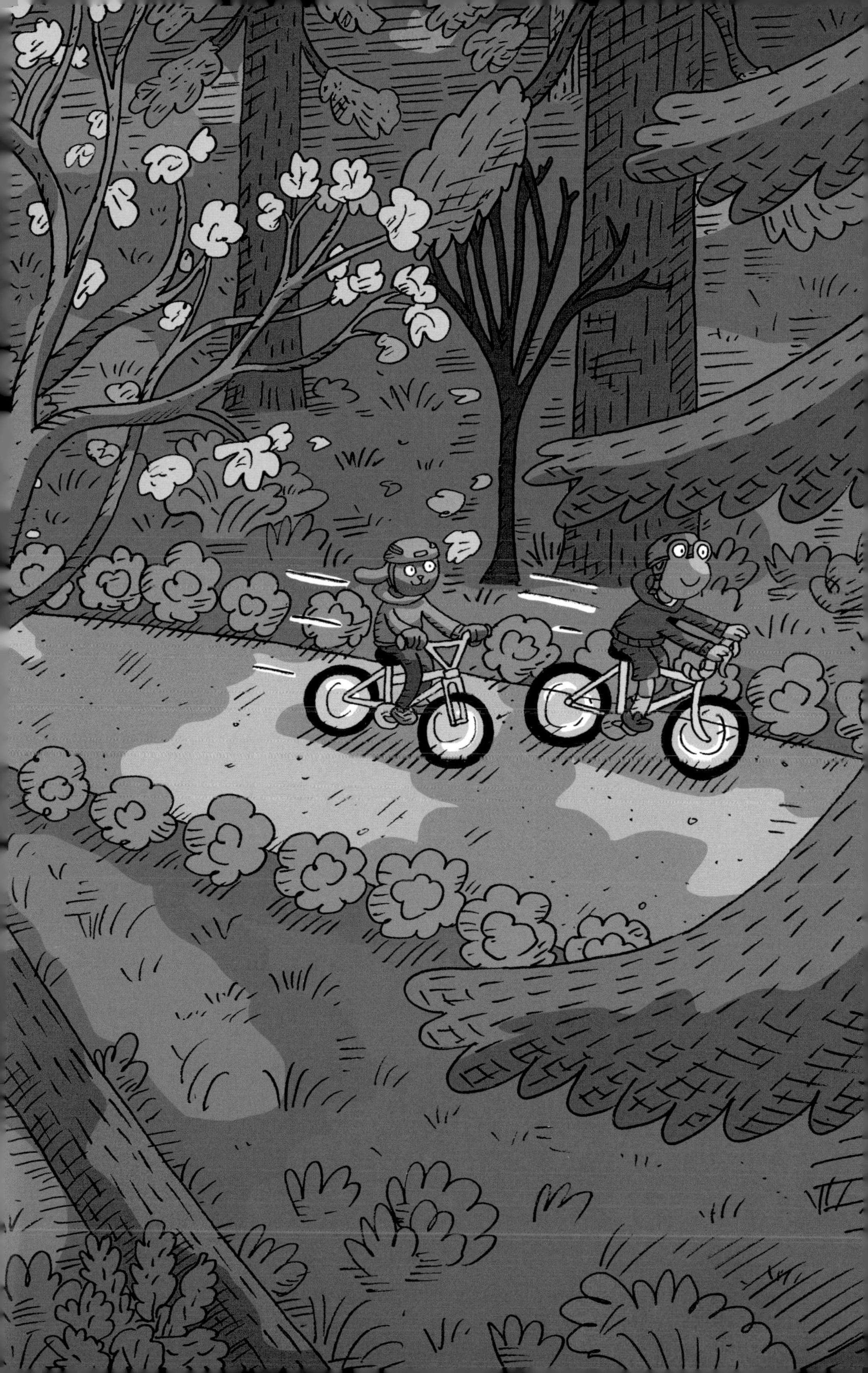

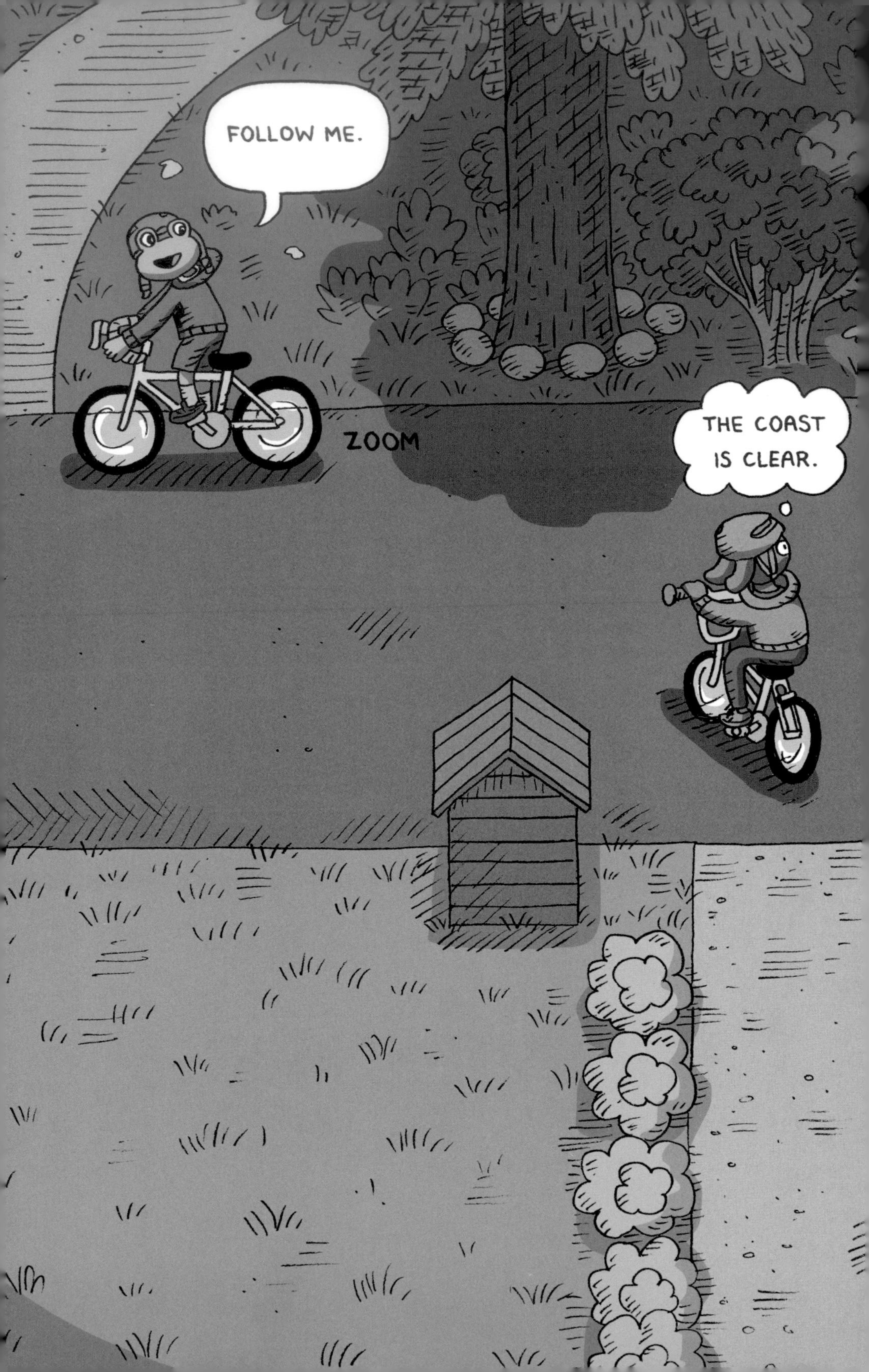
FOLLOW ME.
ZOOM
THE COAST IS CLEAR.

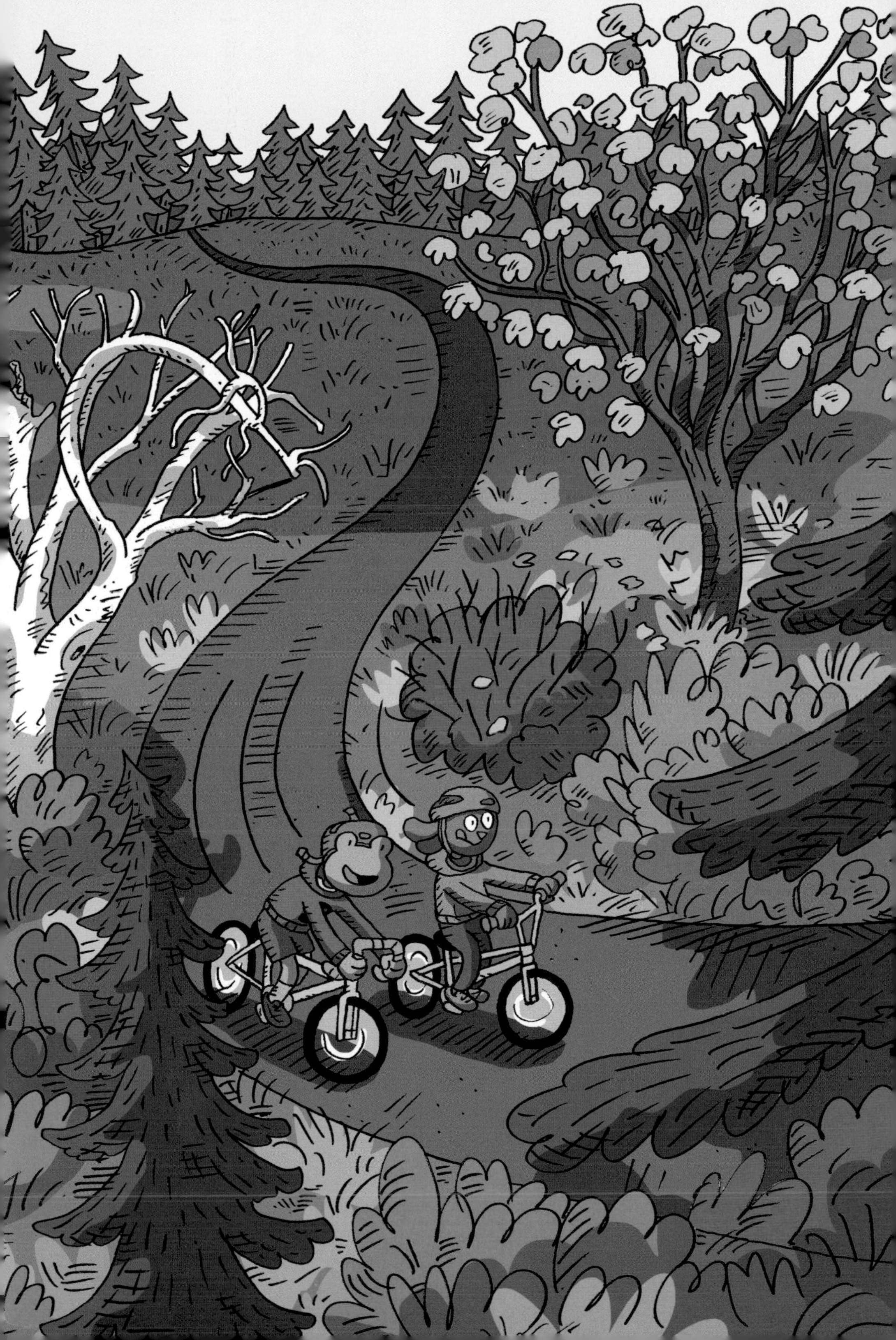

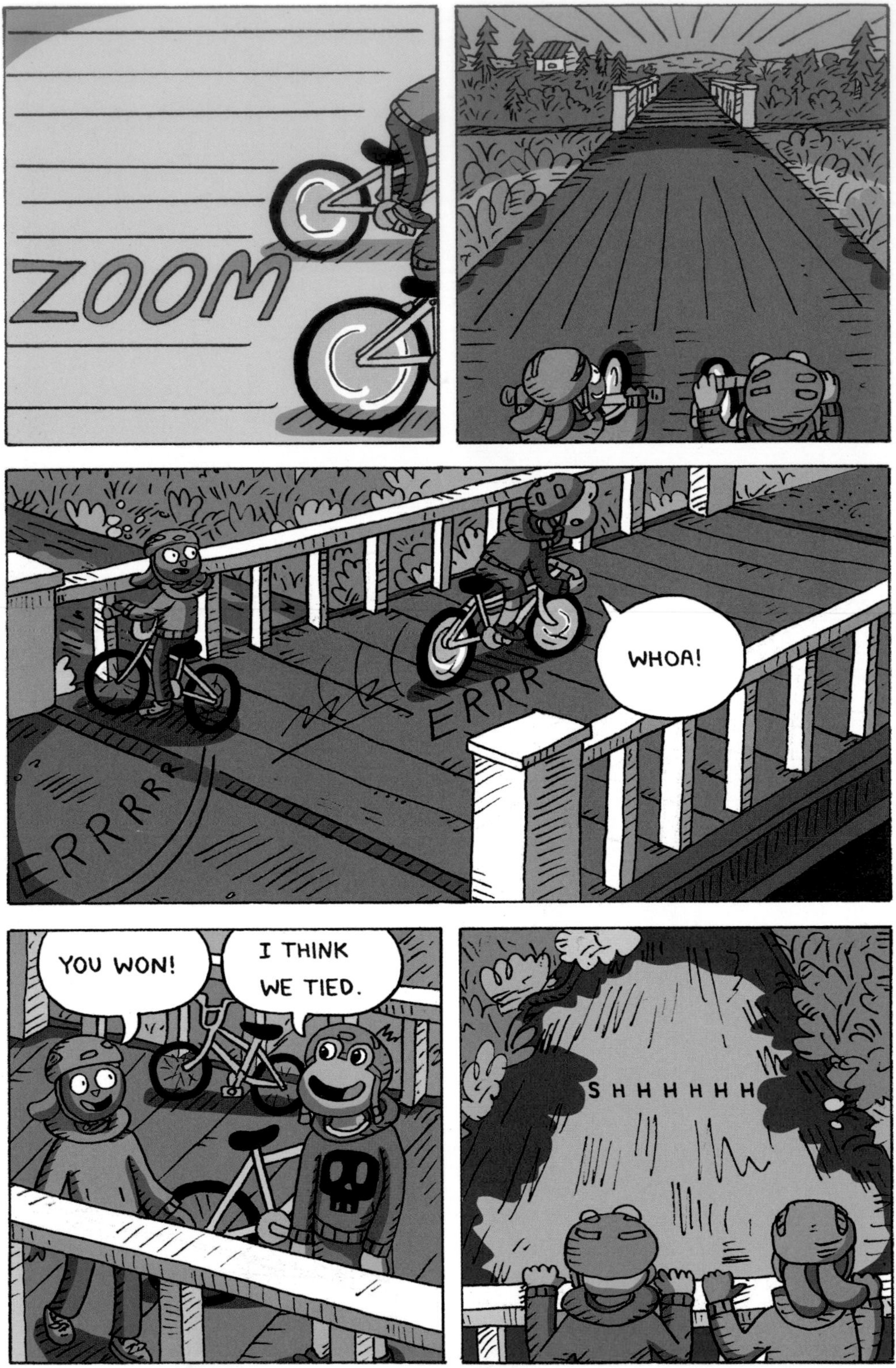
ZOOM
ERRRRR
ERRR
WHOA!
YOU WON!
I THINK WE TIED.
SHHHHHHH

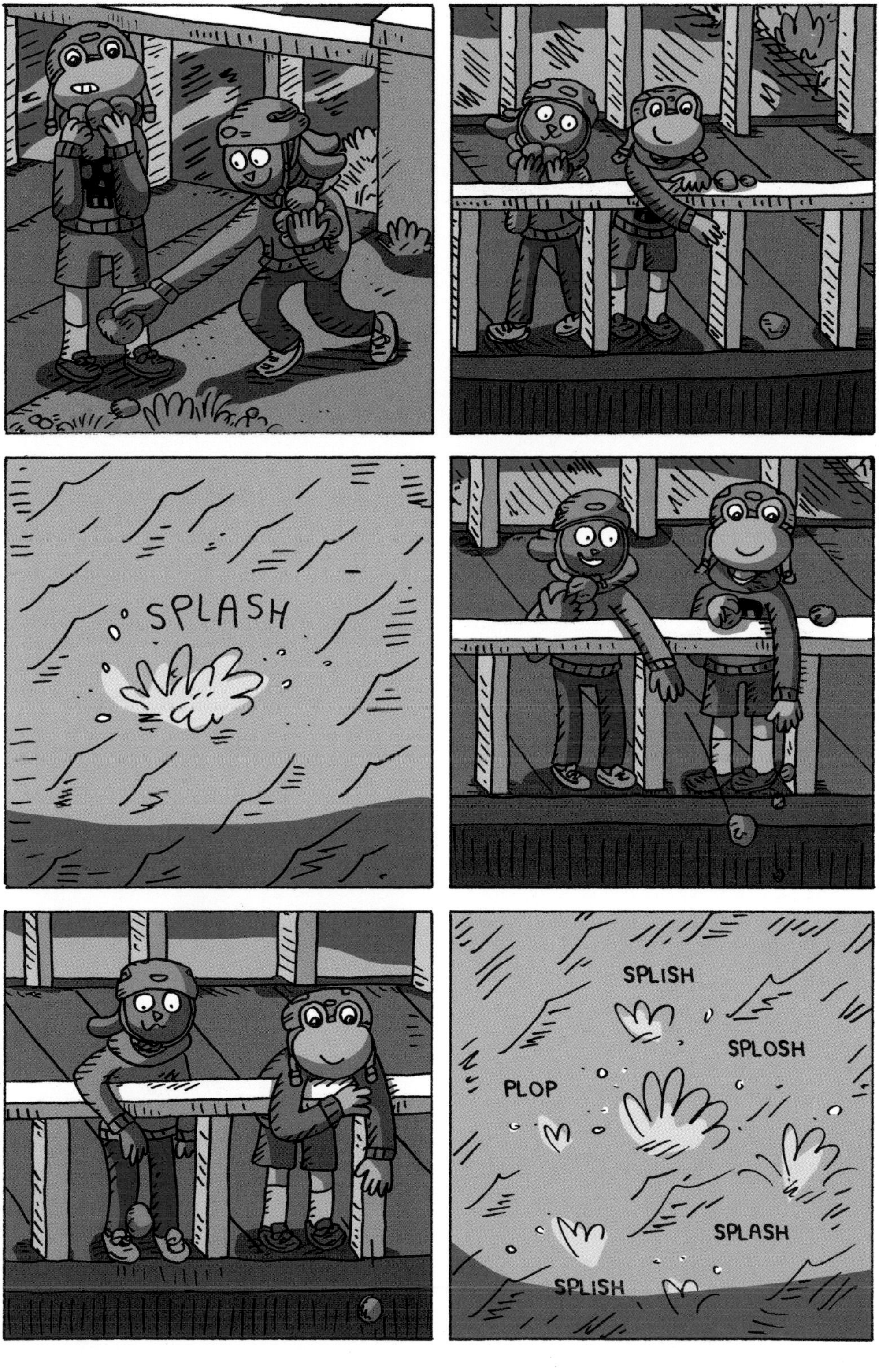
SPLASH
SPLISH
SPLOSH
PLOP
SPLASH
SPLISH

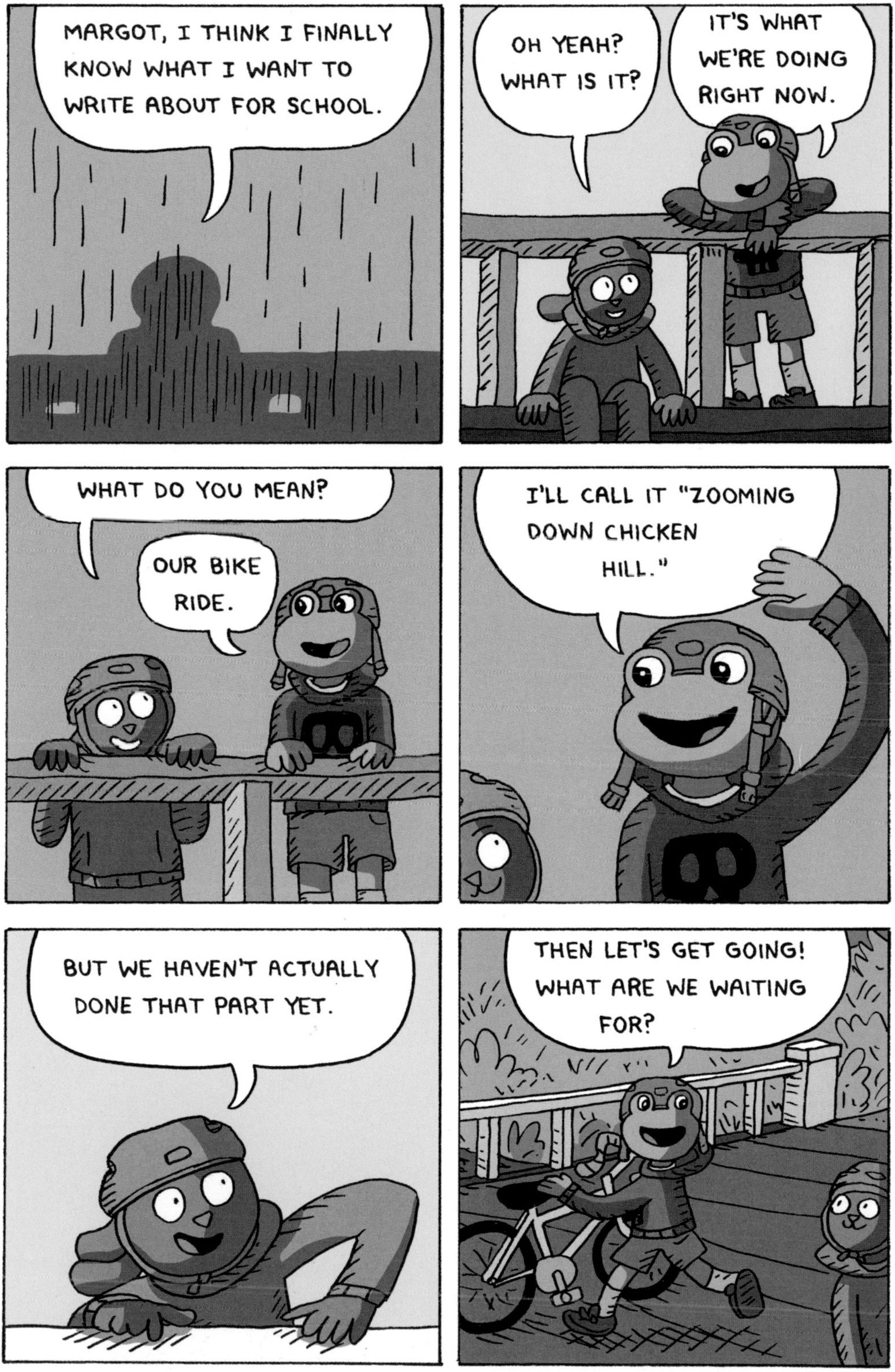
MARGOT, I THINK I FINALLY KNOW WHAT I WANT TO WRITE ABOUT FOR SCHOOL.
OH YEAH? WHAT IS IT?
IT'S WHAT WE'RE DOING RIGHT NOW.
WHAT DO YOU MEAN?
OUR BIKE RIDE.
I'LL CALL IT "ZOOMING DOWN CHICKEN HILL."
BUT WE HAVEN'T ACTUALLY DONE THAT PART YET.
THEN LET'S GET GOING! WHAT ARE WE WAITING FOR?

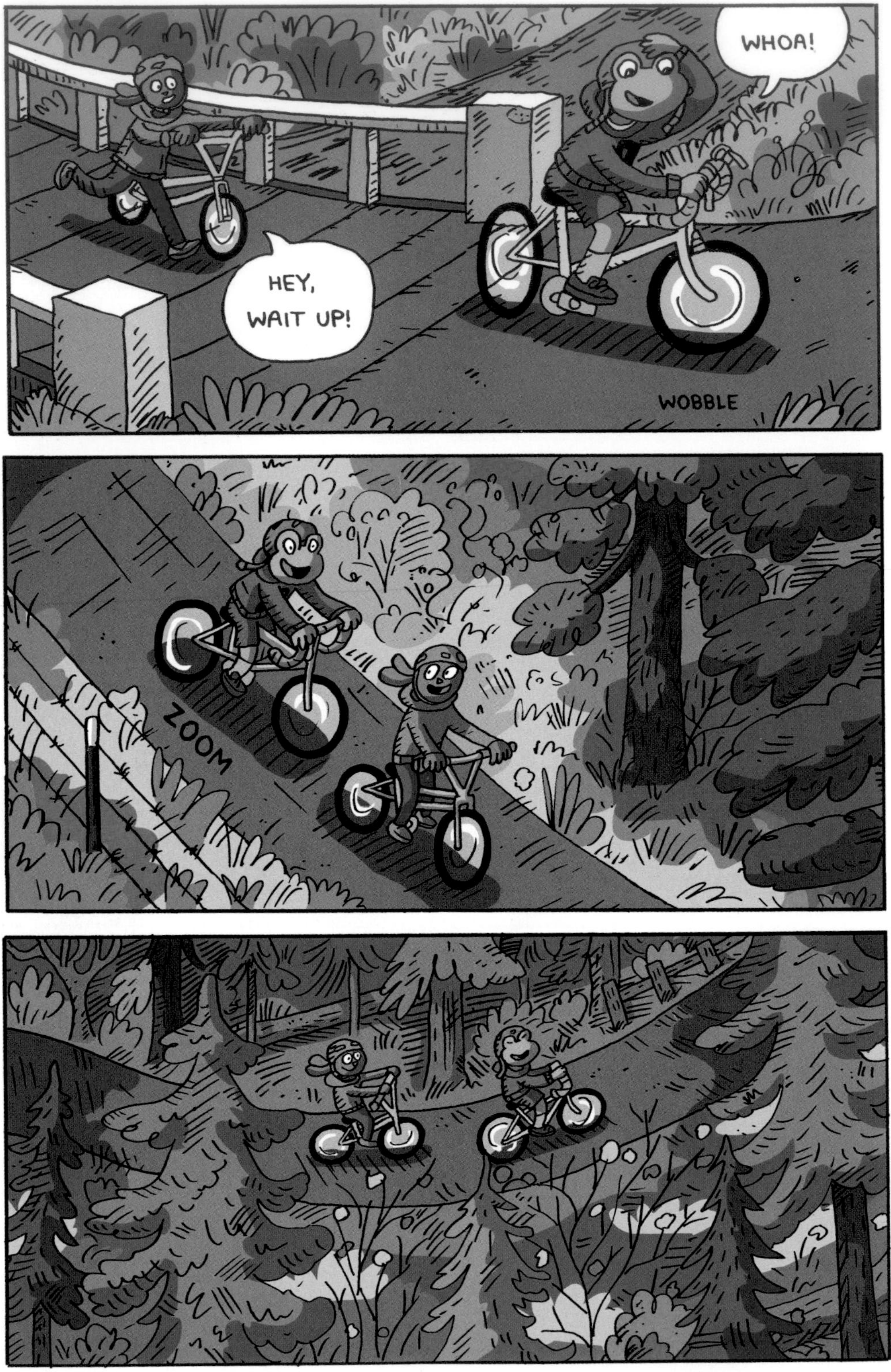
WHOA!
HEY, WAIT UP!
WOBBLE
ZOOM

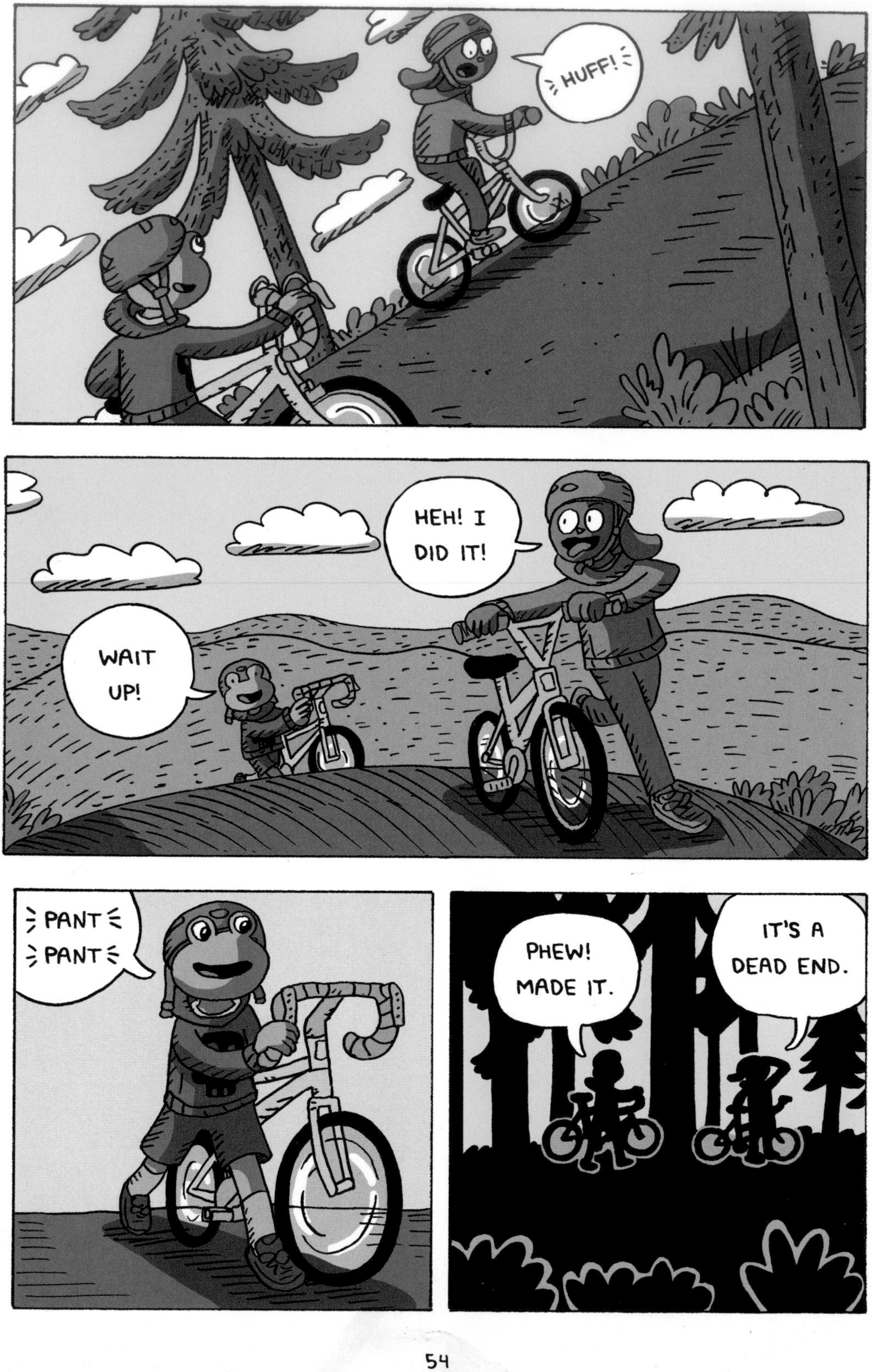
HUFF!
HEH! I DID IT!
WAIT UP!
PANT
PANT
PHEW! MADE IT.
IT'S A DEAD END.

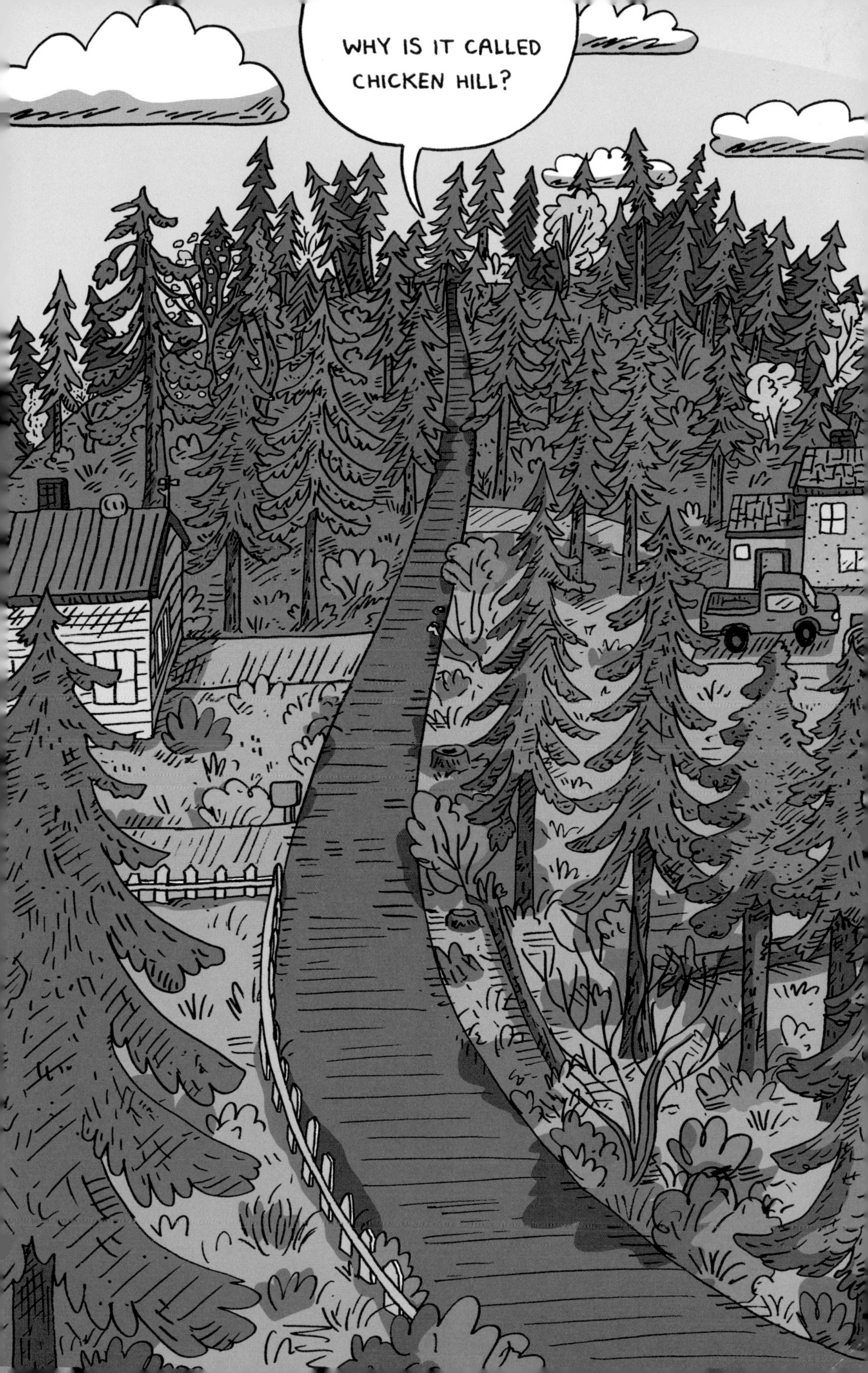
WHY IS IT CALLED CHICKEN HILL?

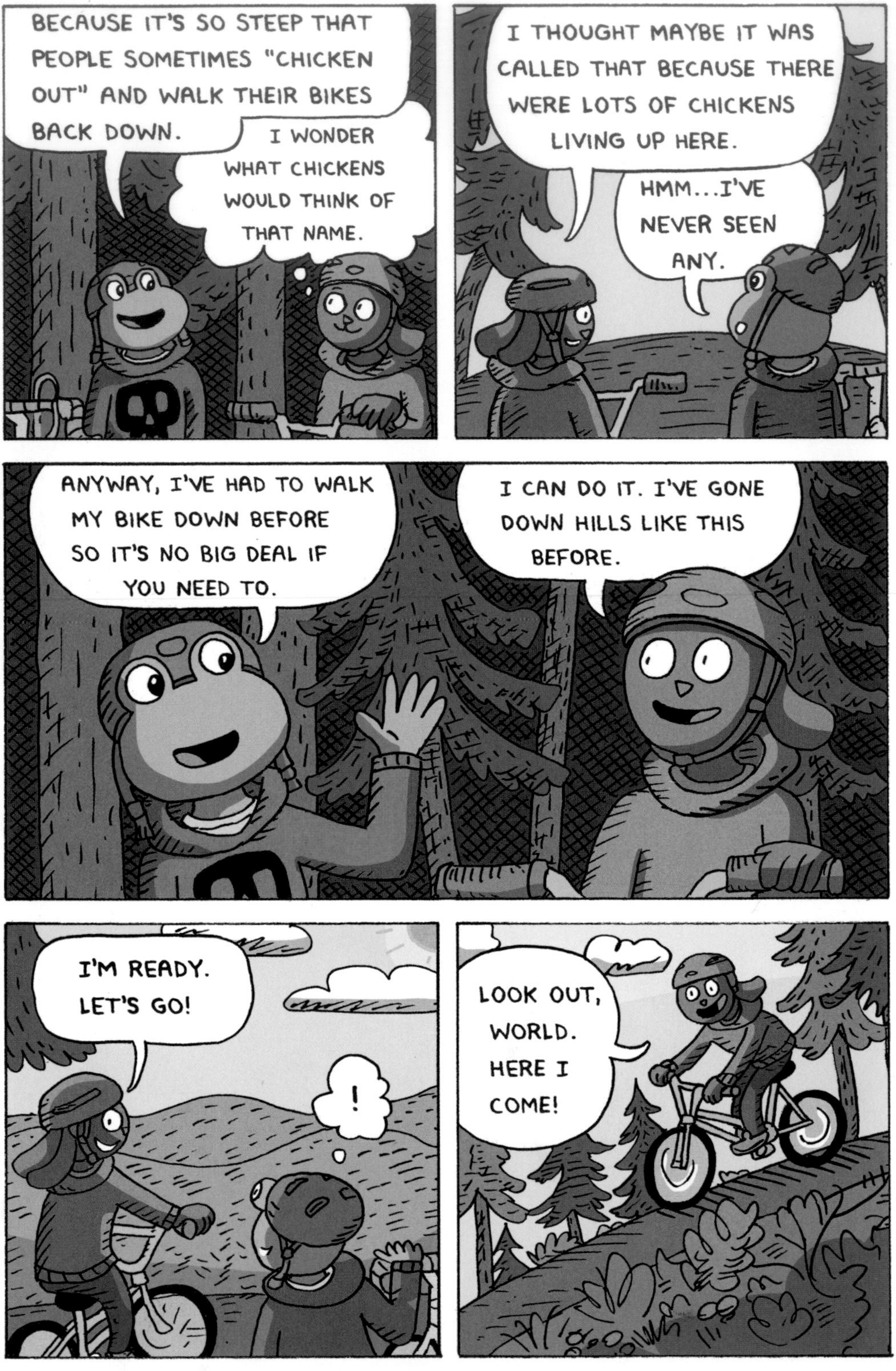
BECAUSE IT'S SO STEEP THAT PEOPLE SOMETIMES "CHICKEN OUT" AND WALK THEIR BIKES BACK DOWN.
I WONDER WHAT CHICKENS WOULD THINK OF THAT NAME.
I THOUGHT MAYBE IT WAS CALLED THAT BECAUSE THERE WERE LOTS OF CHICKENS LIVING UP HERE.
HMM...I'VE NEVER SEEN ANY.
ANYWAY, I'VE HAD TO WALK MY BIKE DOWN BEFORE SO IT'S NO BIG DEAL IF YOU NEED TO.
I CAN DO IT. I'VE GONE DOWN HILLS LIKE THIS BEFORE.
I'M READY. LET'S GO!
!
LOOK OUT, WORLD. HERE I COME!

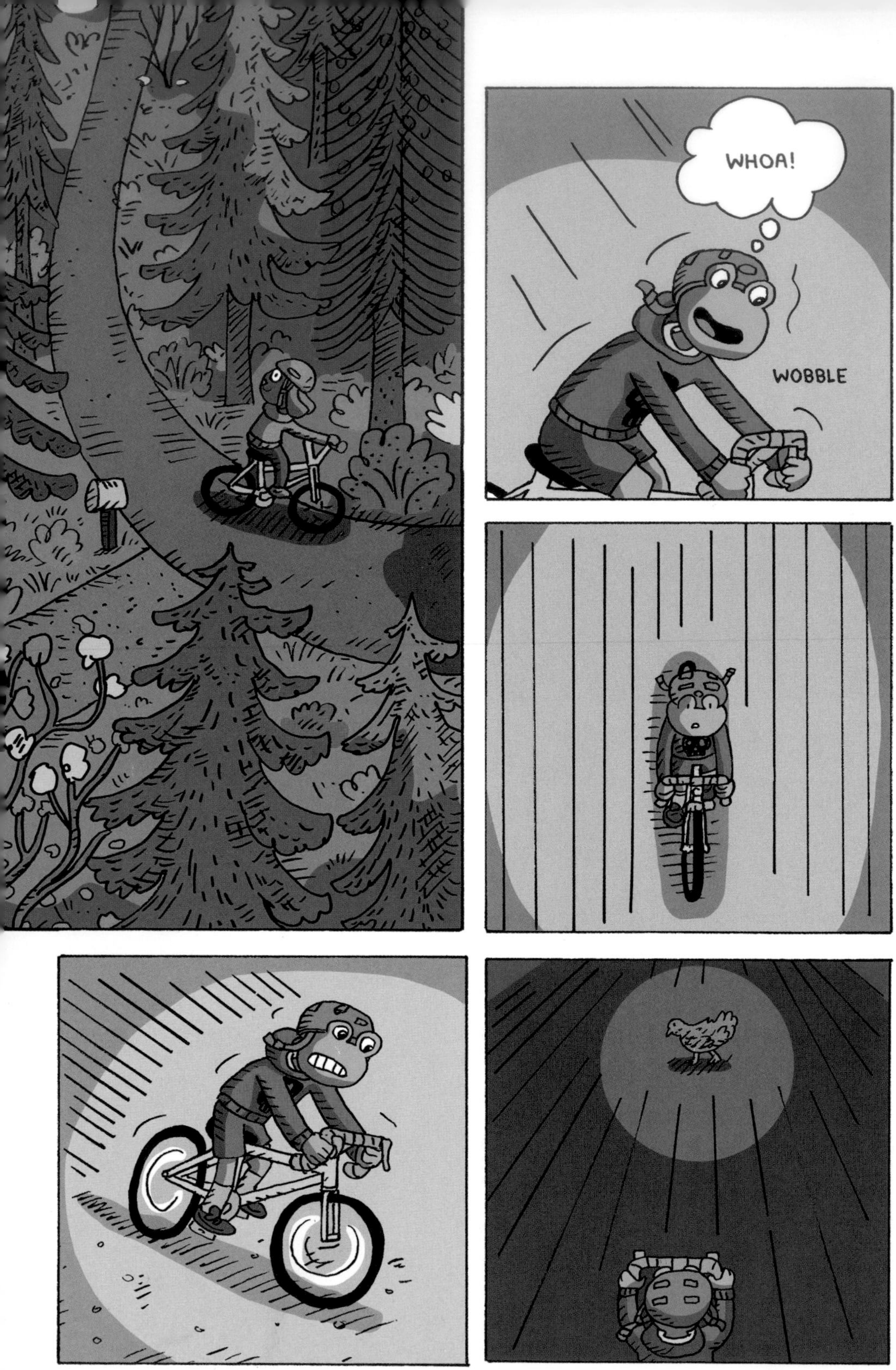
WHOA!
WOBBLE

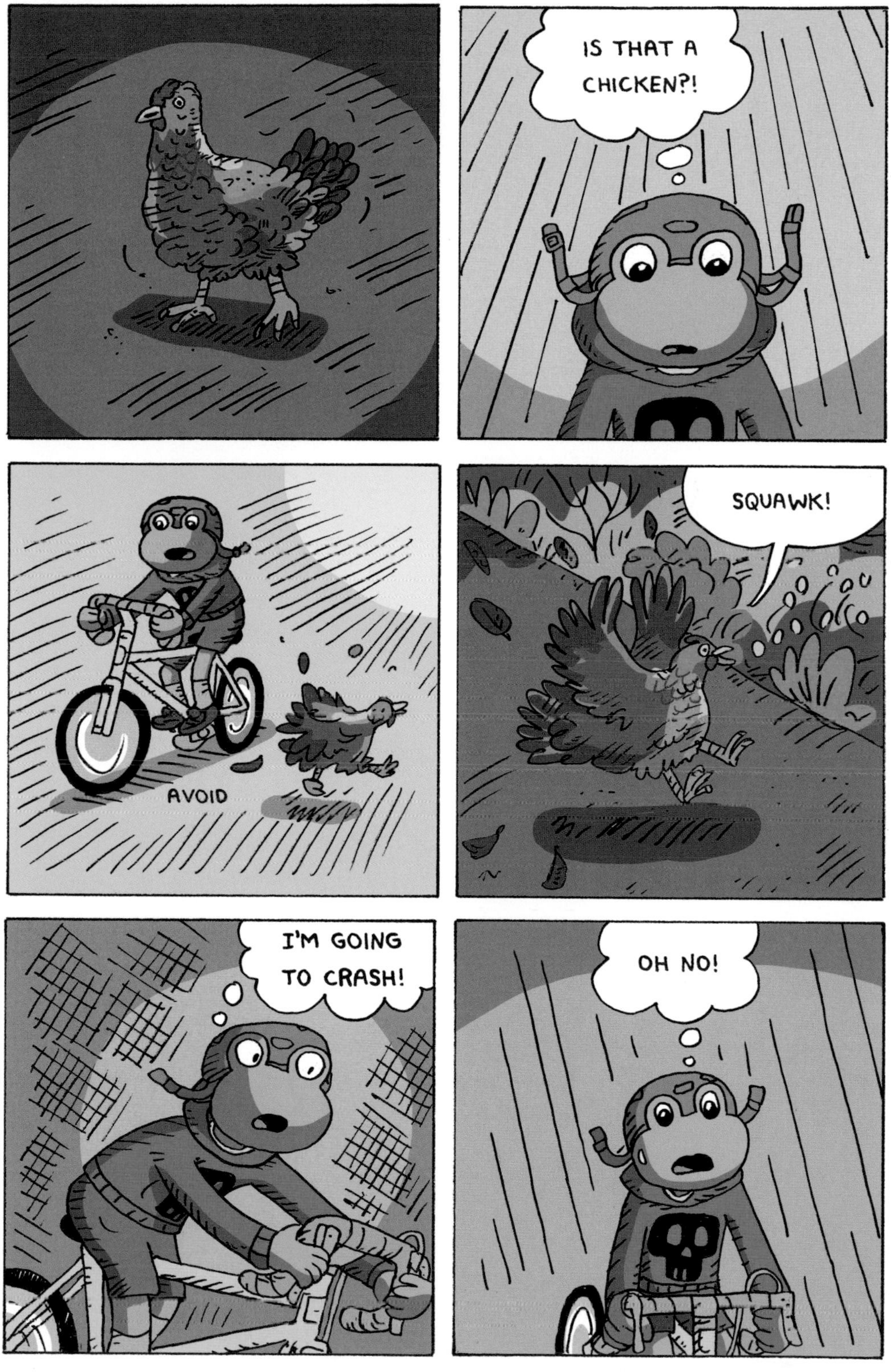
IS THAT A CHICKEN?!
AVOID
SQUAWK!
I'M GOING TO CRASH!
OH NO!

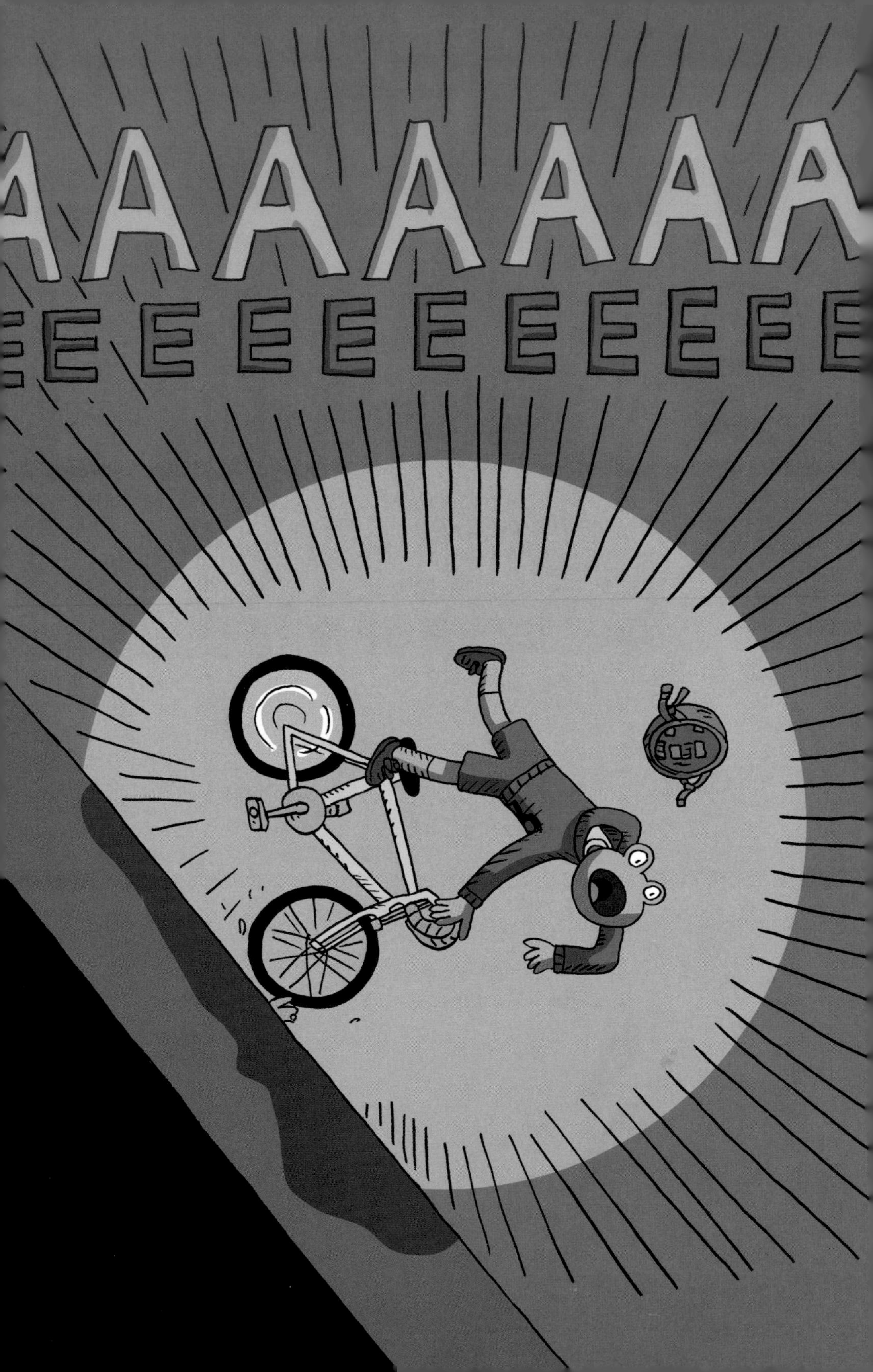
AAAAAAA
EEEEEEEEEEE

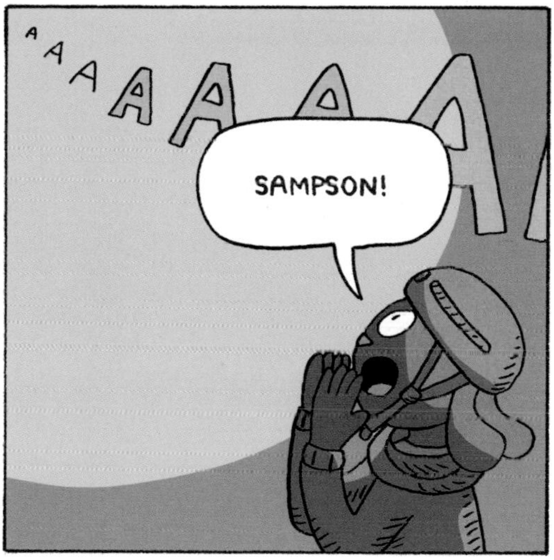
AAAAAAAA
SAMPSON!

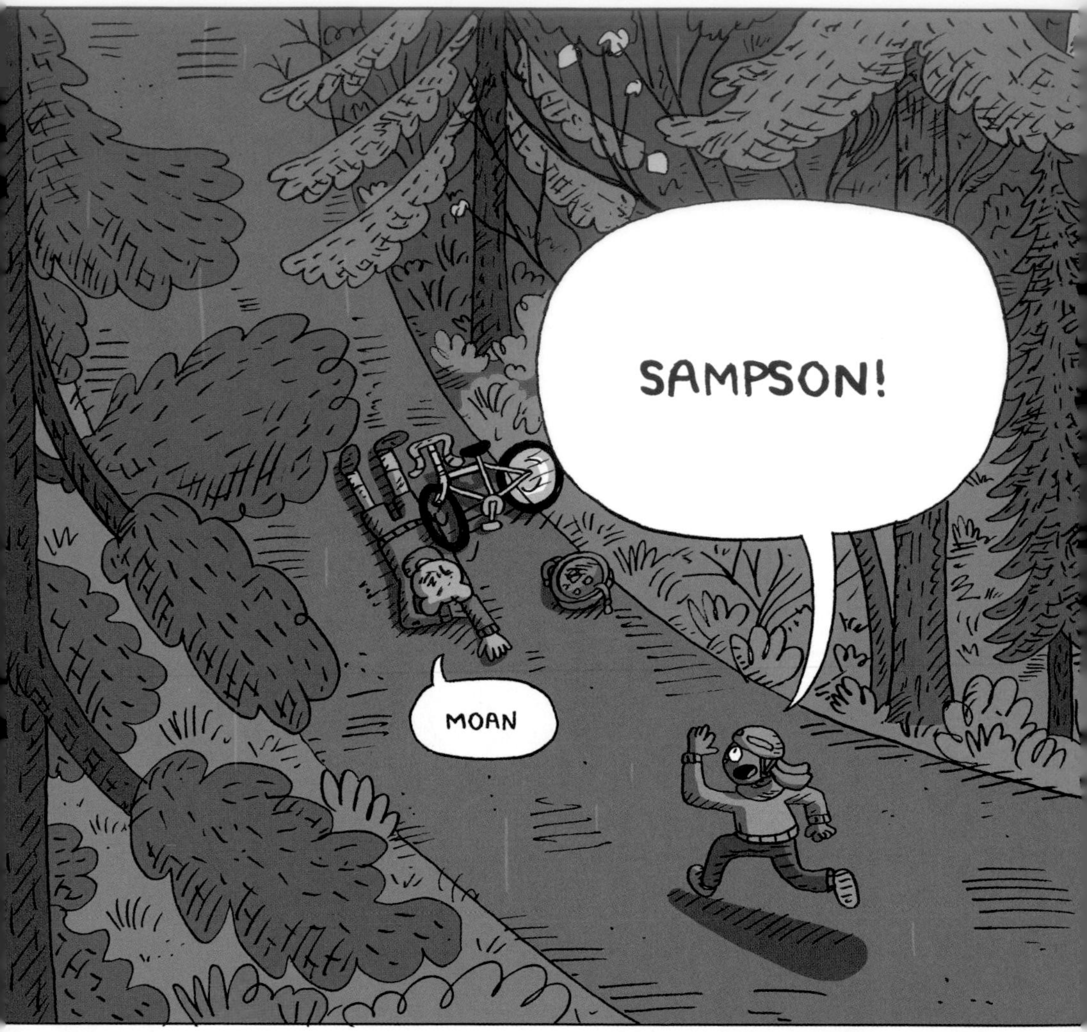
SAMPSON!
MOAN

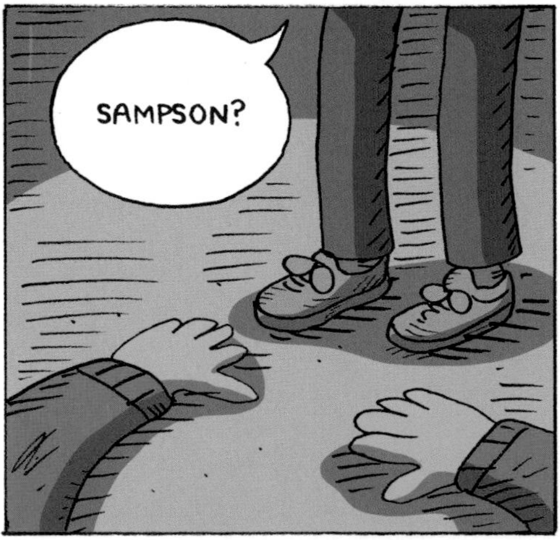
SAMPSON?

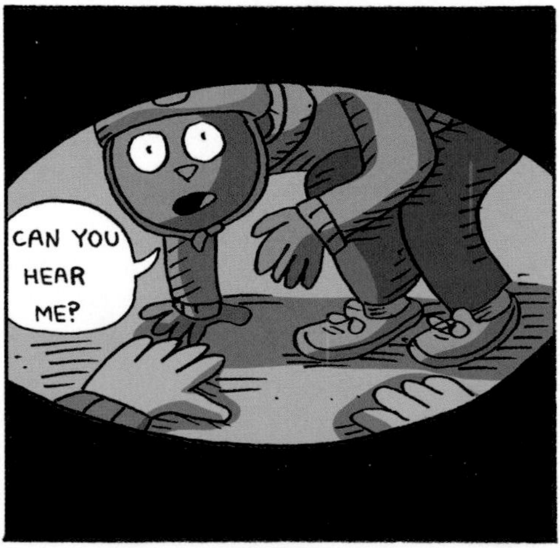
CAN YOU HEAR ME?

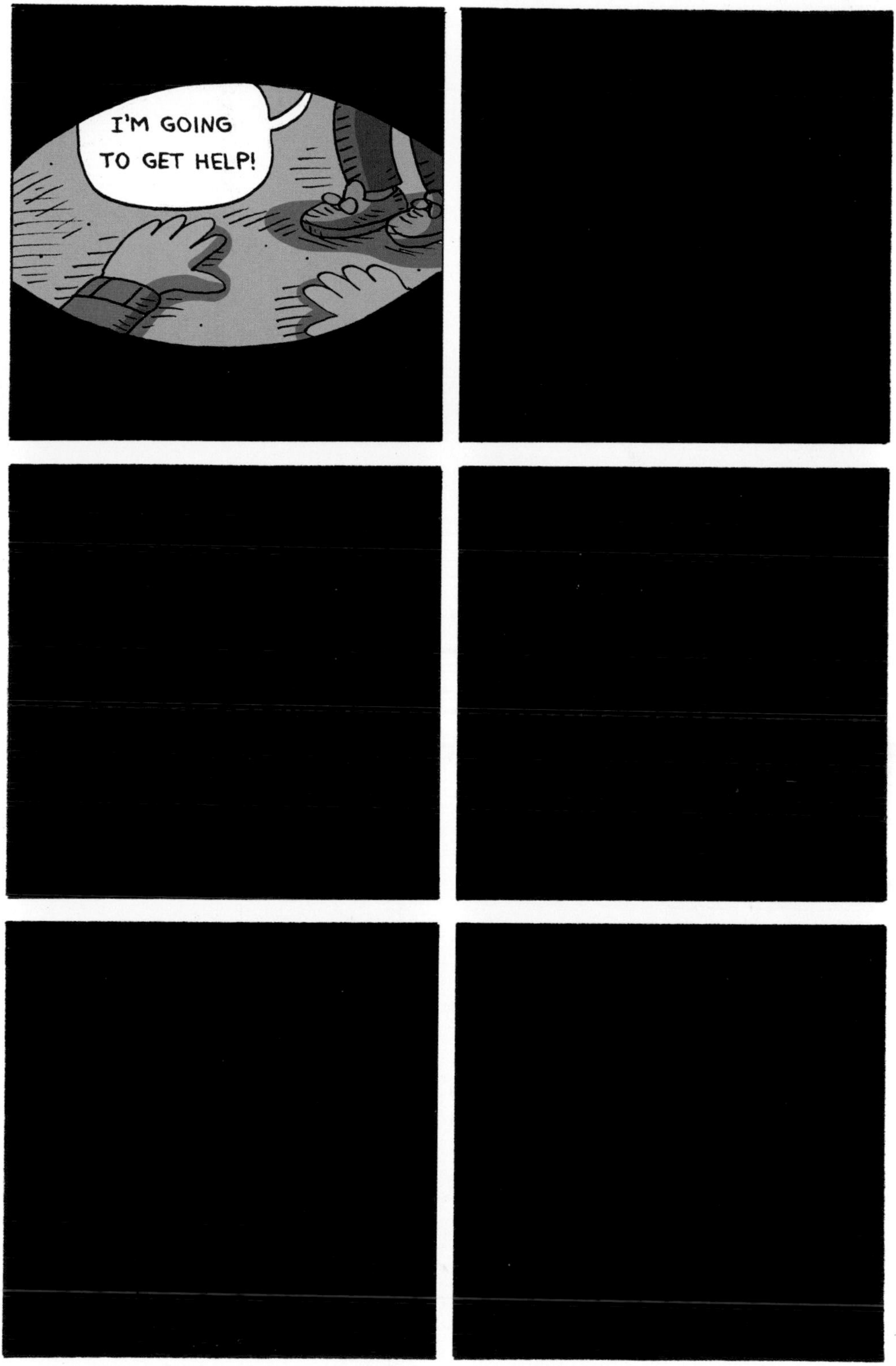
I'M GOING TO GET HELP!

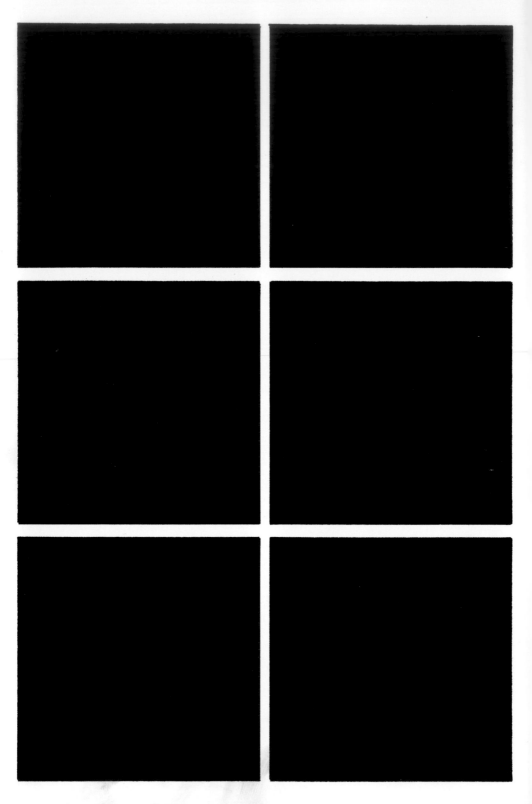

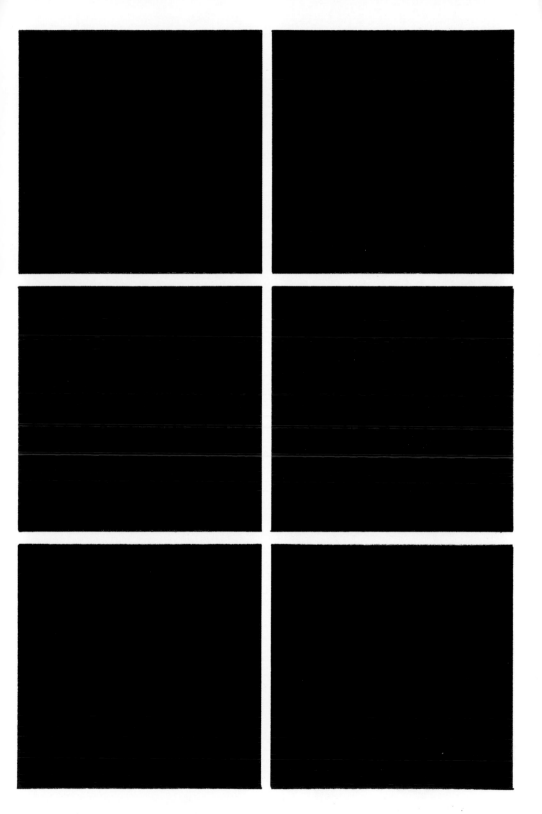

I THINK HE'S STARTING TO WAKE UP.

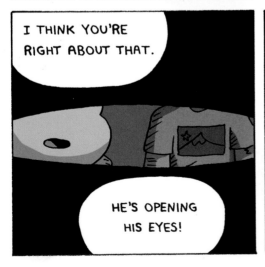

I THINK YOU'RE RIGHT ABOUT THAT.

HE'S OPENING HIS EYES!

HI, SAMMY. WELCOME BACK! HOW ARE YOU FEELING?

CHAPTER FOUR

Thank Your Lucky Stars

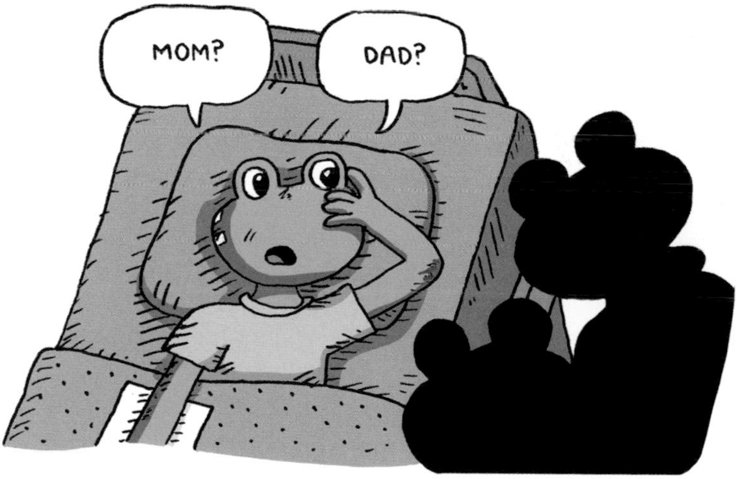
MOM?
DAD?

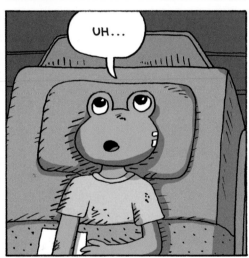

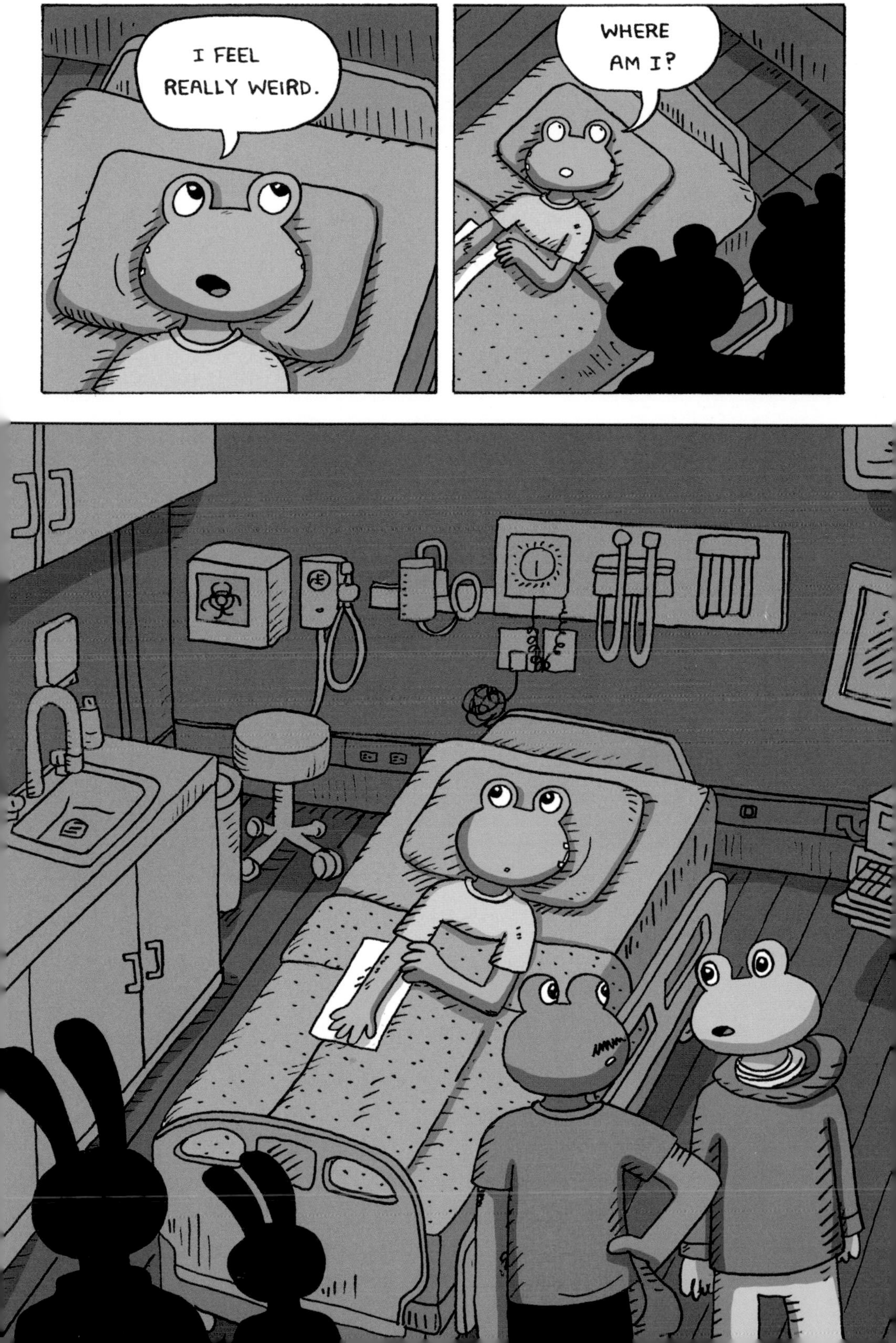
I FEEL REALLY WEIRD.
WHERE AM I?

YOU HAD A BAD ACCIDENT. WE'RE IN THE HOSPITAL.

OH...

OH YEAH.

I REMEMBER FALLING.

I WAS GOING FAST! I SAW A CHICKEN AND THEN I LOST CONTROL.

A CHICKEN?

YEAH. AND WHEN I CRASHED I SAW MYSELF IN THE THIRD PERSON.

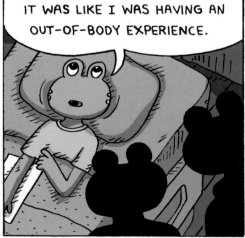

IT WAS LIKE I WAS HAVING AN OUT-OF-BODY EXPERIENCE.

I SAW A CARTOON VERSION OF MYSELF.

BOUNCING UP AND DOWN ON MY HEAD, OVER AND OVER AND OVER AGAIN.

CRASH

BOUNCE

CRASH

AND THEN I WAS BACK INSIDE MY BODY, LYING ON THE ROAD.

SAMPSON?

IT HAD JUST STARTED RAINING AND THE PAVEMENT SMELLED GOOD.

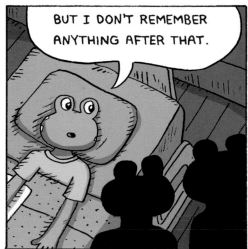
BUT I DON'T REMEMBER ANYTHING AFTER THAT.

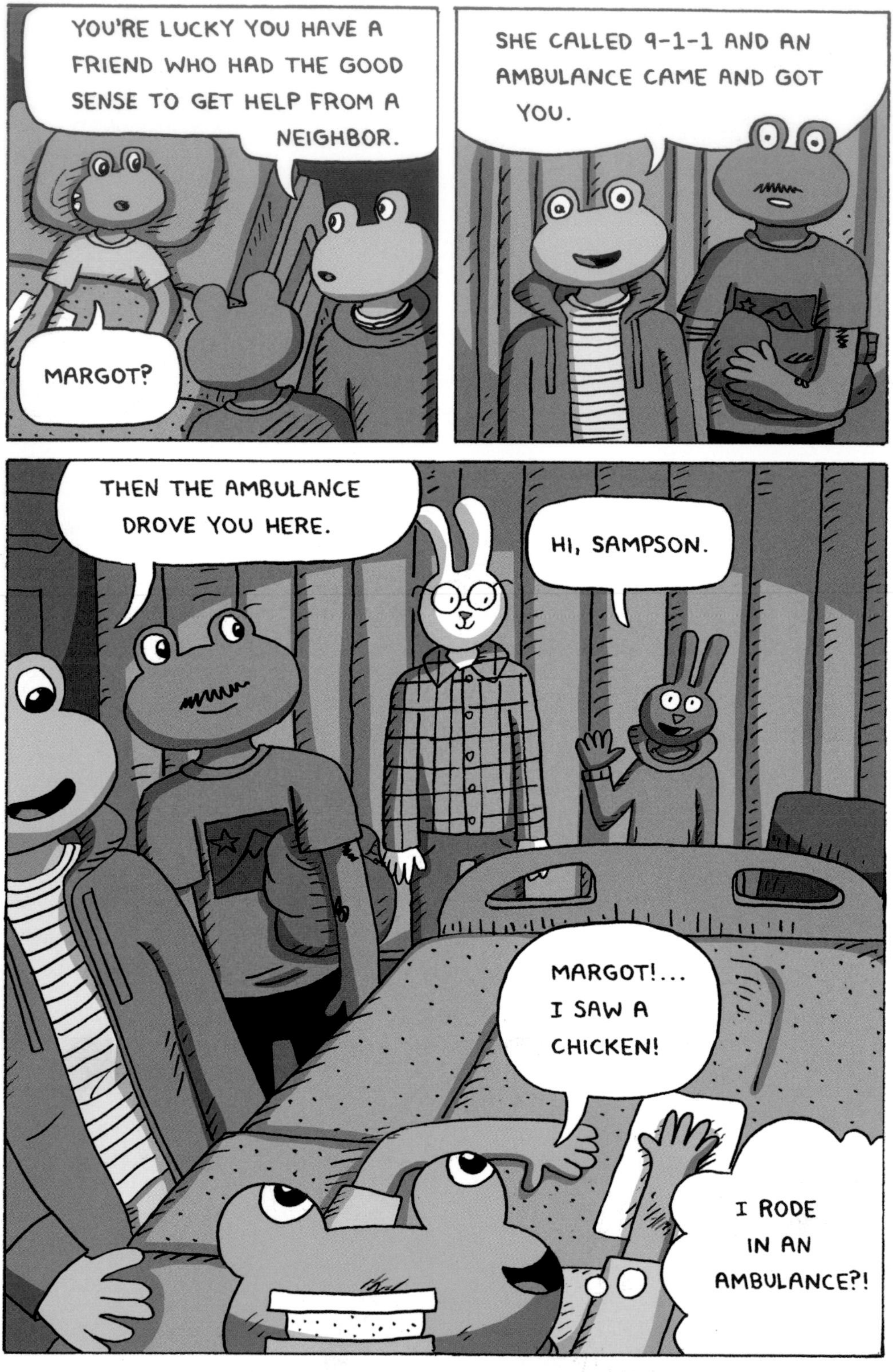
YOU'RE LUCKY YOU HAVE A FRIEND WHO HAD THE GOOD SENSE TO GET HELP FROM A NEIGHBOR.
MARGOT?
SHE CALLED 9-1-1 AND AN AMBULANCE CAME AND GOT YOU.
THEN THE AMBULANCE DROVE YOU HERE.
HI, SAMPSON.
MARGOT!... I SAW A CHICKEN!
I RODE IN AN AMBULANCE?!

YOU'VE BEEN ASLEEP FOR NEARLY AN HOUR.

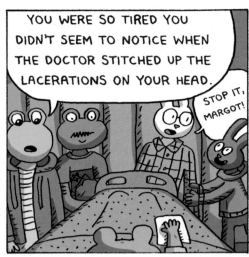

YOU WERE SO TIRED YOU DIDN'T SEEM TO NOTICE WHEN THE DOCTOR STITCHED UP THE LACERATIONS ON YOUR HEAD.

STOP IT, MARGOT!

YOU DIDN'T EVEN WAKE UP WHEN SHE SET YOUR ARM. YOU JUST CRIED OUT A LITTLE.

STOP.

SET MY ARM? YOU MEAN I BROKE MY ARM?!

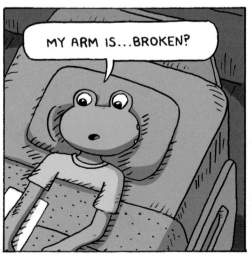

MY ARM IS...BROKEN?

WUH-HUH-HUH!

73

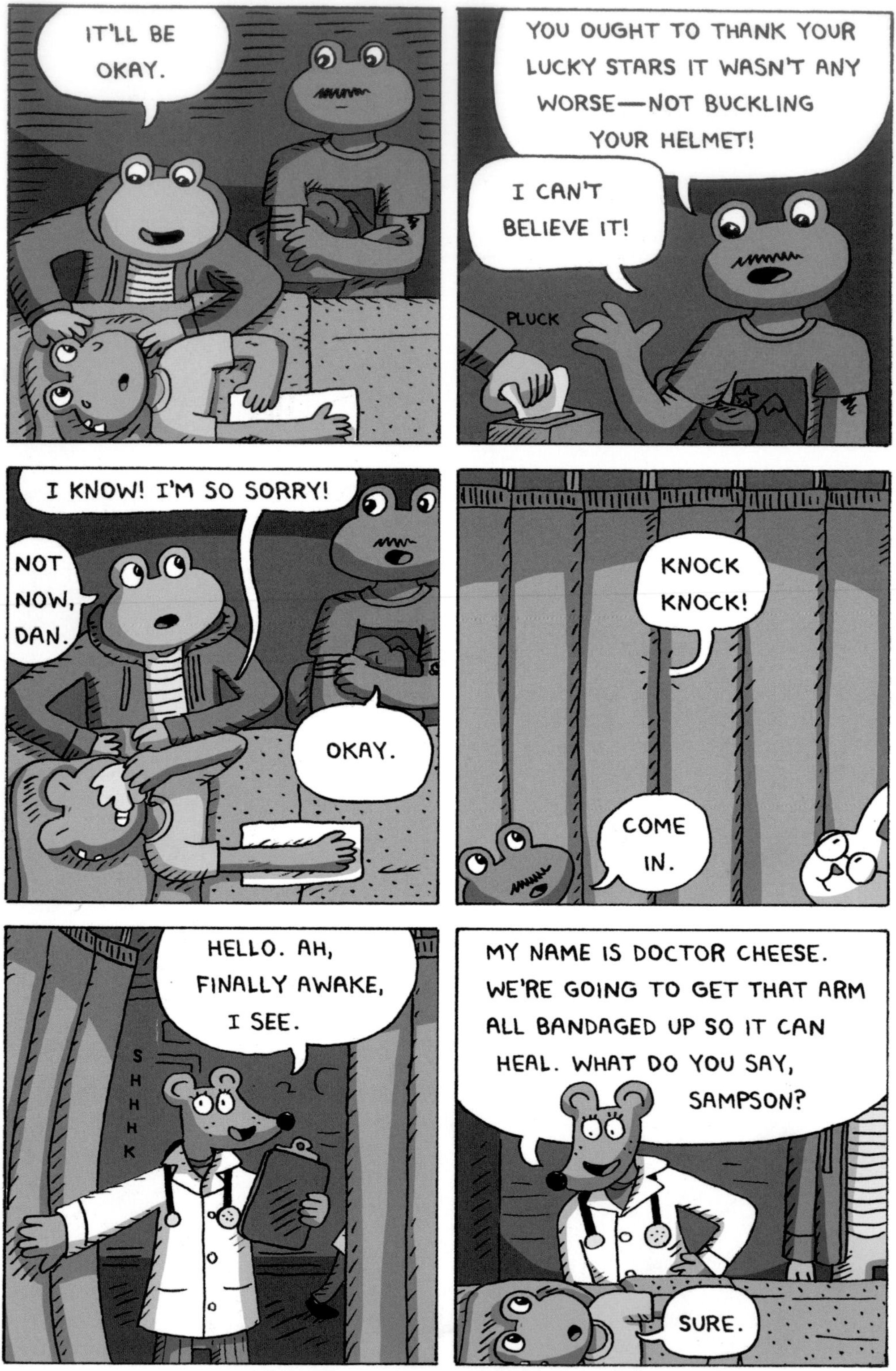
IT'LL BE OKAY.
YOU OUGHT TO THANK YOUR LUCKY STARS IT WASN'T ANY WORSE—NOT BUCKLING YOUR HELMET!
I CAN'T BELIEVE IT!
PLUCK
I KNOW! I'M SO SORRY!
NOT NOW, DAN.
OKAY.
KNOCK KNOCK!
COME IN.
HELLO. AH, FINALLY AWAKE, I SEE.
SHHHK
MY NAME IS DOCTOR CHEESE. WE'RE GOING TO GET THAT ARM ALL BANDAGED UP SO IT CAN HEAL. WHAT DO YOU SAY, SAMPSON?
SURE.

LET'S TAKE A LOOK AT YOUR X-RAYS.

MARGOT, WE SHOULD GET GOING.

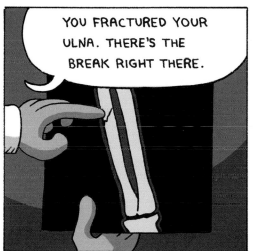

YOU FRACTURED YOUR ULNA. THERE'S THE BREAK RIGHT THERE.

BYE, SAMPSON. WE'VE GOTTA GO HOME.

MARGOT, THANK YOU FOR BEING BRAVE AND GETTING HELP FOR MY SAMMY.

WE'RE SO LUCKY THAT HE HAS YOU FOR A FRIEND.

YOU'RE WELCOME.

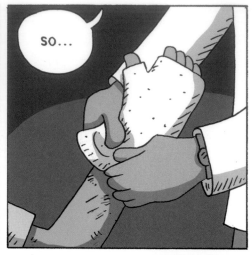

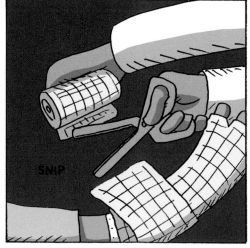

ARE YOU RIGHT- OR LEFT-HANDED?

DUNK

H_2O

RIGHT.

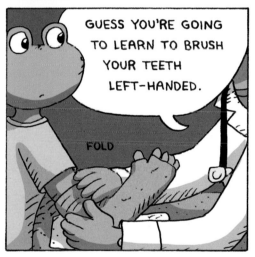

GUESS YOU'RE GOING TO LEARN TO BRUSH YOUR TEETH LEFT-HANDED.

FOLD

PICK HIS NOSE LEFT-HANDED IS MORE LIKE IT.

DAD! I DON'T DO THAT!

SMOOTH

I'M JUST TEASING.

OUCH! THAT HURTS!

THERE... ALL DONE.

JUST KEEP IT DRY AND IN A COUPLE OF MONTHS YOU'LL BE AS GOOD AS NEW.

THAT LONG?

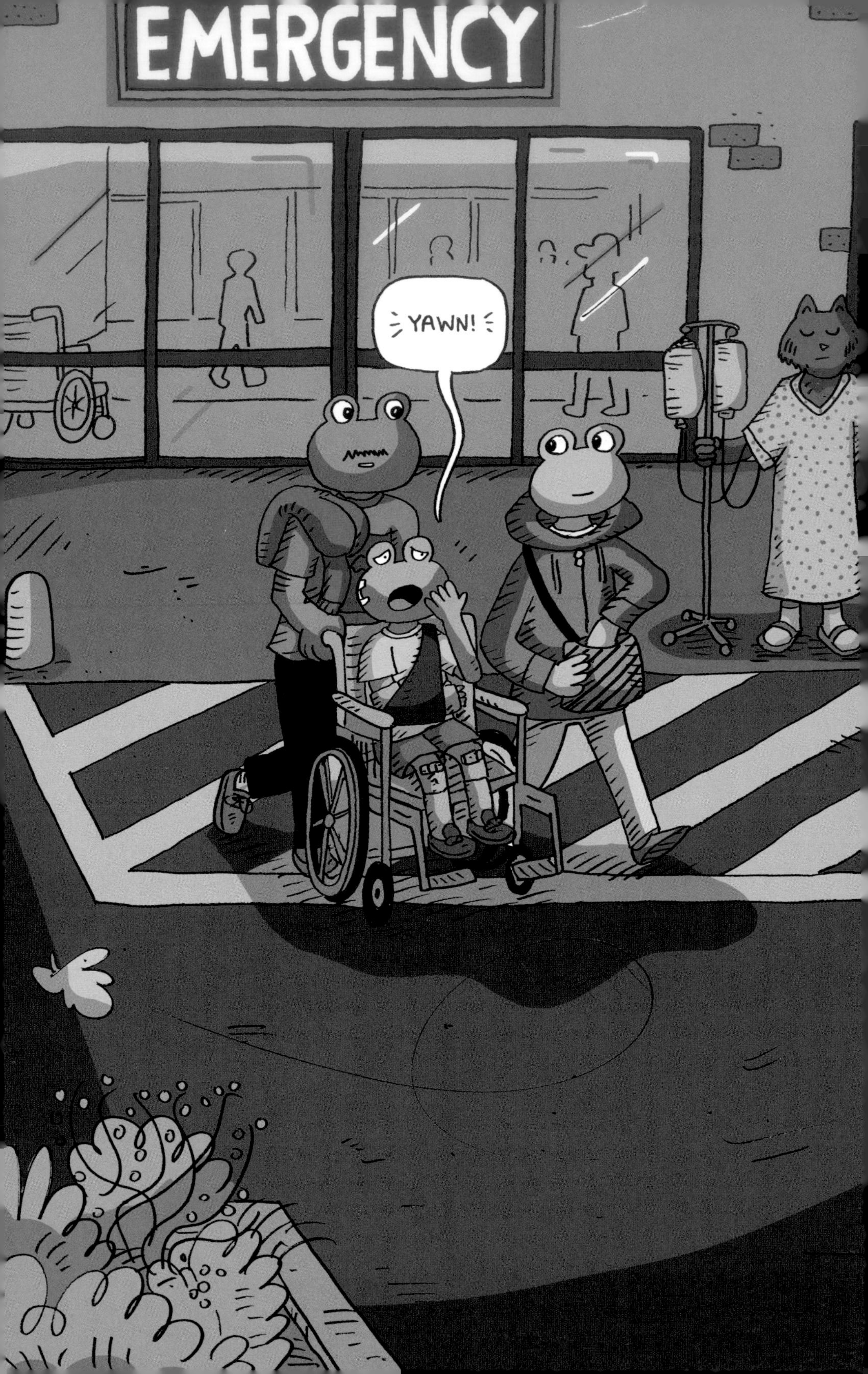
EMERGENCY
YAWN!

CHAPTER FIVE

The Day After

GOOD MORNING, HENRY! PLEASE TAKE THIS AND GET STARTED.

GOOD MORNING.

GOOD MORNING, LOLA.

MORNING.

ADDITION AND SUBTRACTION WORK...WHAT?!

MR. WOLF, EXCUSE ME, BUT WE LEARNED HOW TO DO THIS IN SECOND GRADE.

I THOUGHT SO, TOO, BUT I HAVE THE ASSESSMENTS THAT SHOW MANY OF US DO NOT REMEMBER HOW.

A LITTLE PRACTICE WON'T HURT.

BUT IF YOU THINK IT'S TOO EASY JUST RAISE YOUR HAND WHEN YOU'RE DONE AND I'LL COME AND MAKE IT HARDER FOR YOU.

...

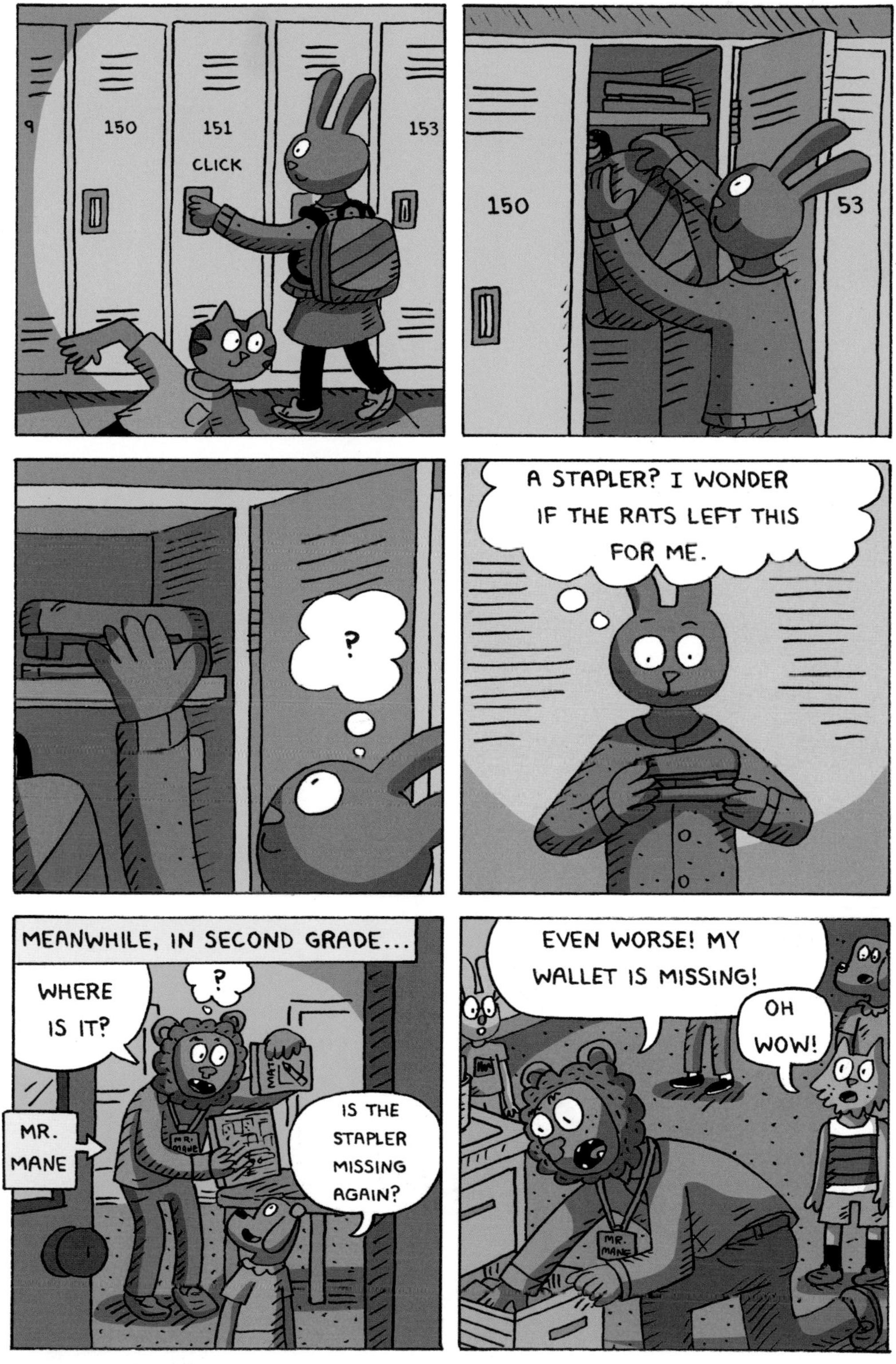
9
150
151
153
CLICK
150
53
?
A STAPLER? I WONDER IF THE RATS LEFT THIS FOR ME.
MEANWHILE, IN SECOND GRADE...
WHERE IS IT?
?
MR. MANE
IS THE STAPLER MISSING AGAIN?
EVEN WORSE! MY WALLET IS MISSING!
OH WOW!

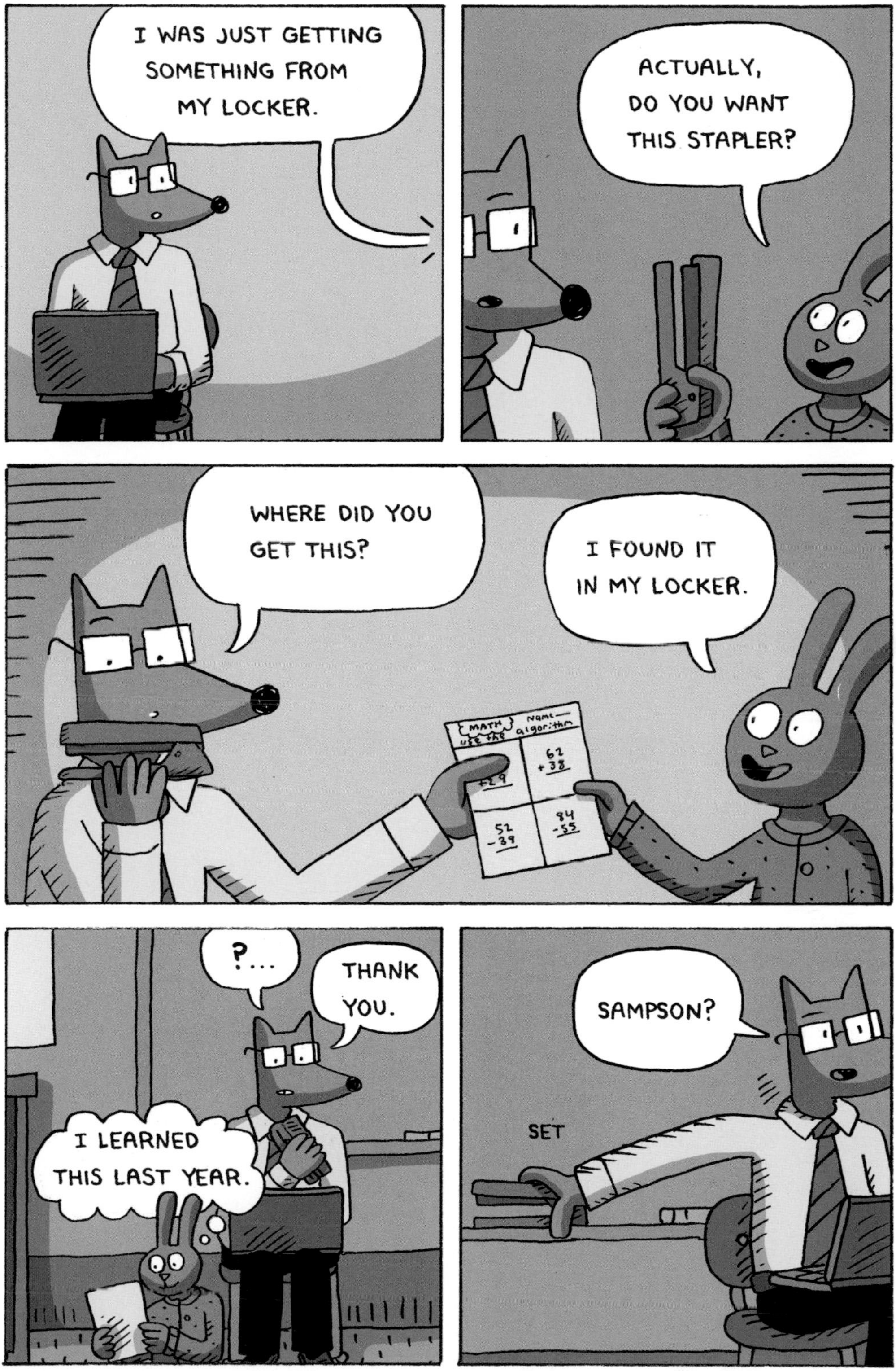
I WAS JUST GETTING SOMETHING FROM MY LOCKER.
ACTUALLY, DO YOU WANT THIS STAPLER?
WHERE DID YOU GET THIS?
I FOUND IT IN MY LOCKER.
MATH
Name
USE THE algorithm
62
+38
52
-39
84
-55
?...
THANK YOU.
I LEARNED THIS LAST YEAR.
SAMPSON?
SET

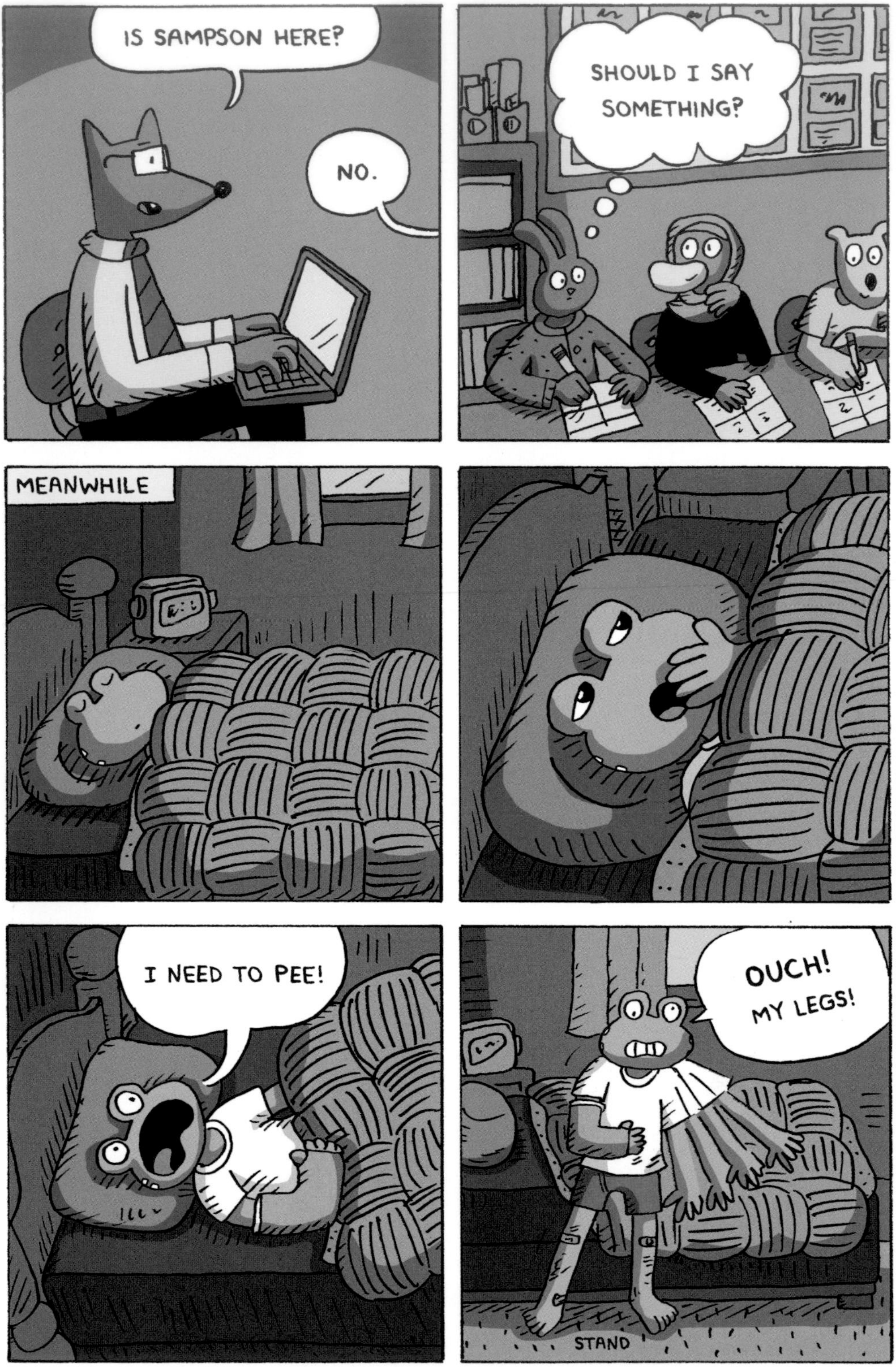
IS SAMPSON HERE?
NO.
SHOULD I SAY SOMETHING?
MEANWHILE
I NEED TO PEE!
OUCH! MY LEGS!
STAND

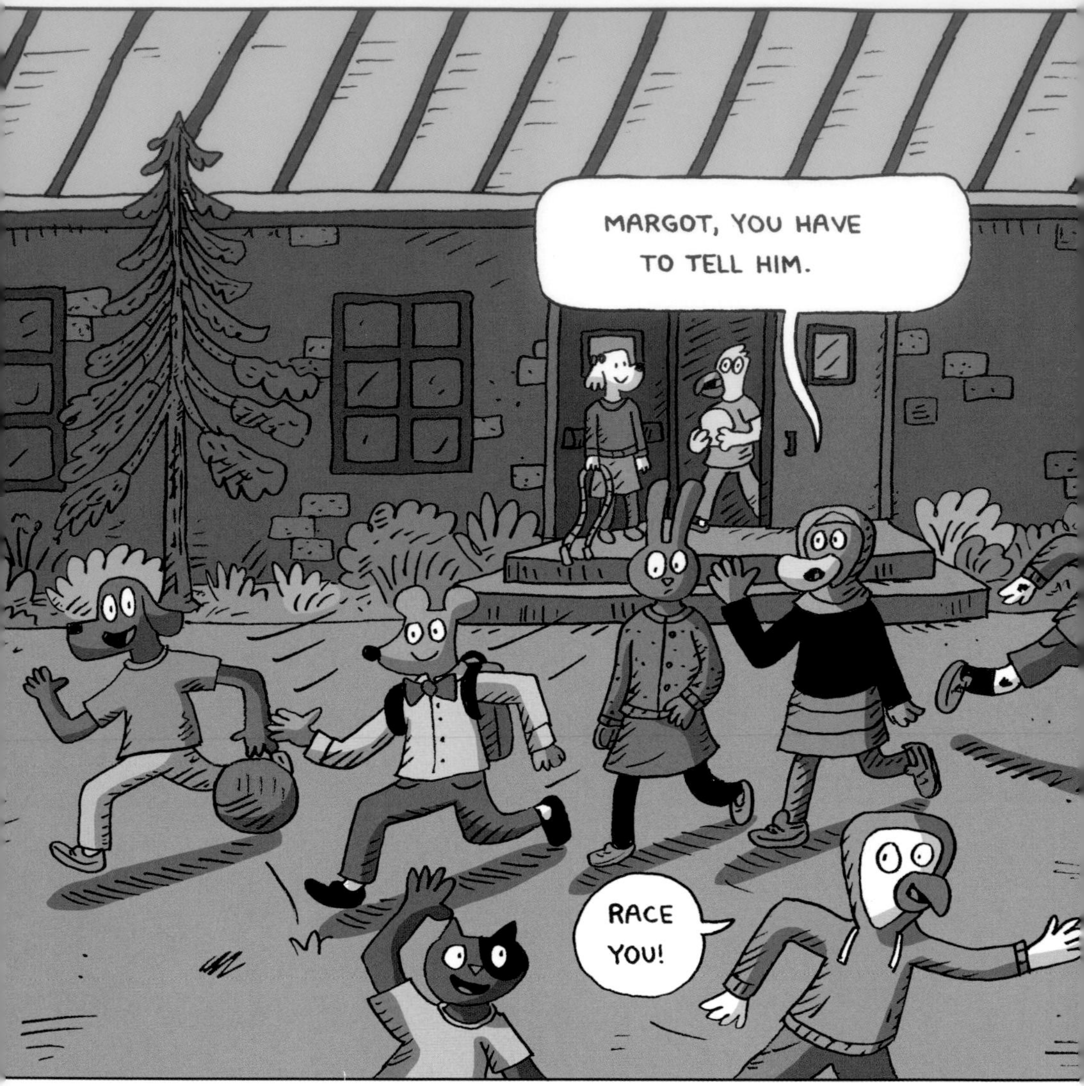
MARGOT, YOU HAVE TO TELL HIM.
RACE YOU!

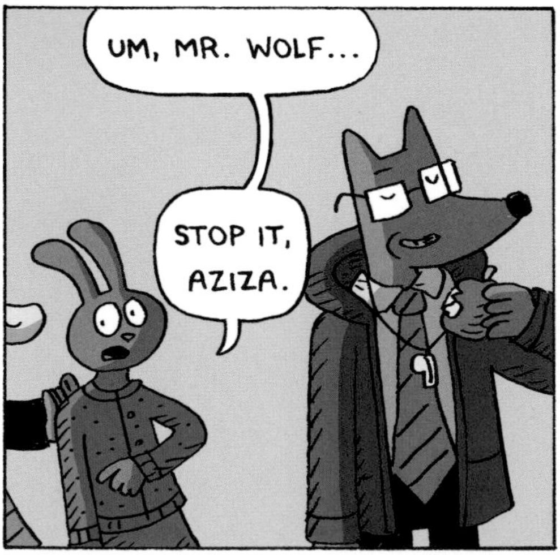
UM, MR. WOLF...
STOP IT, AZIZA.

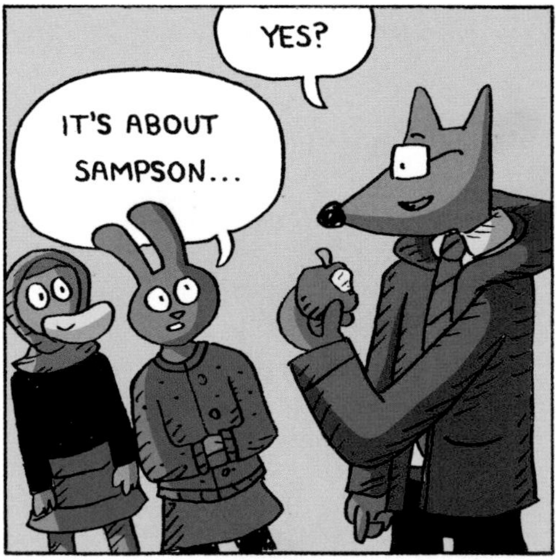
YES?
IT'S ABOUT SAMPSON...

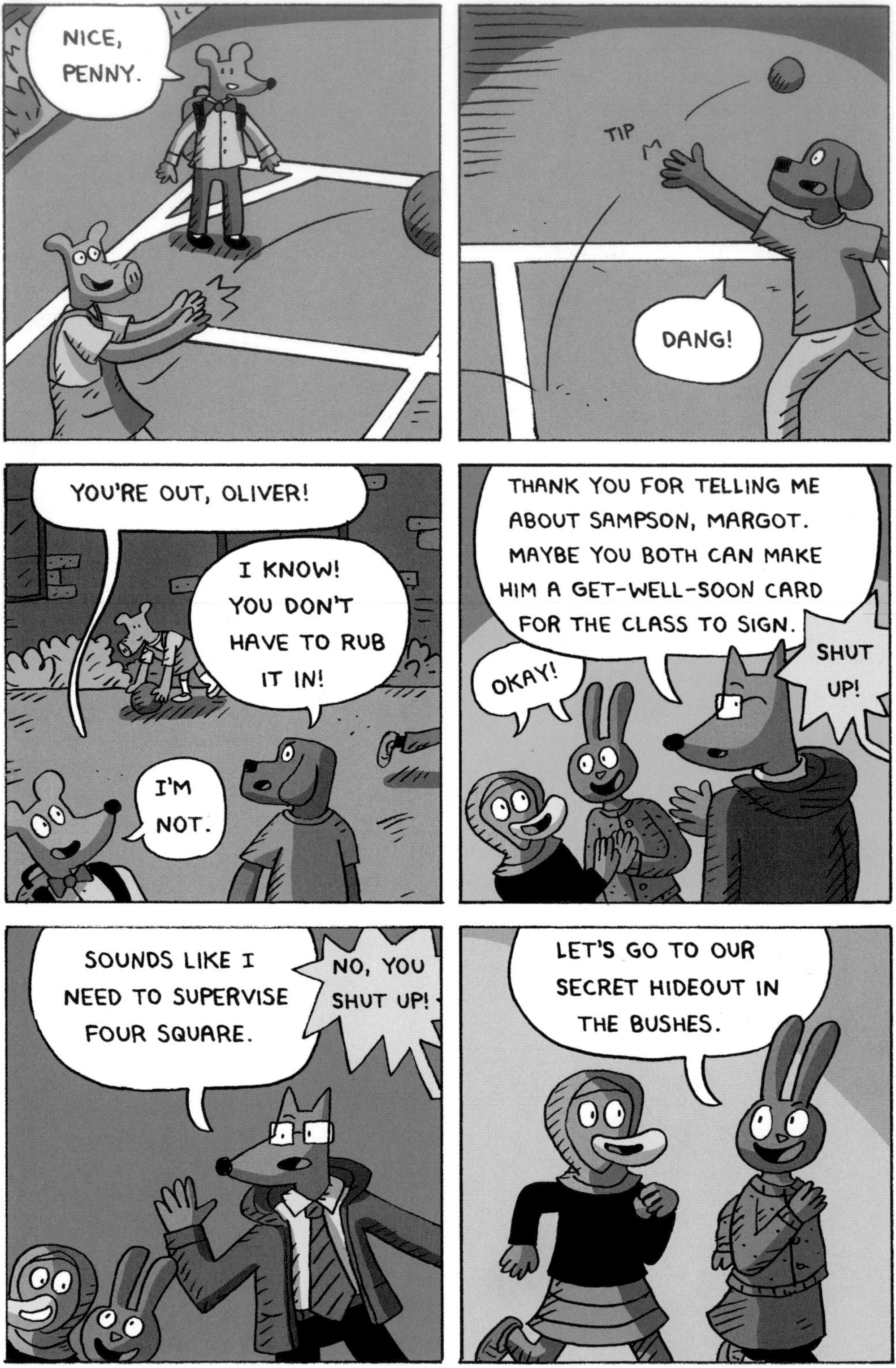
NICE, PENNY.
TIP
DANG!
YOU'RE OUT, OLIVER!
I KNOW! YOU DON'T HAVE TO RUB IT IN!
I'M NOT.
THANK YOU FOR TELLING ME ABOUT SAMPSON, MARGOT. MAYBE YOU BOTH CAN MAKE HIM A GET-WELL-SOON CARD FOR THE CLASS TO SIGN.
OKAY!
SHUT UP!
SOUNDS LIKE I NEED TO SUPERVISE FOUR SQUARE.
NO, YOU SHUT UP!
LET'S GO TO OUR SECRET HIDEOUT IN THE BUSHES.

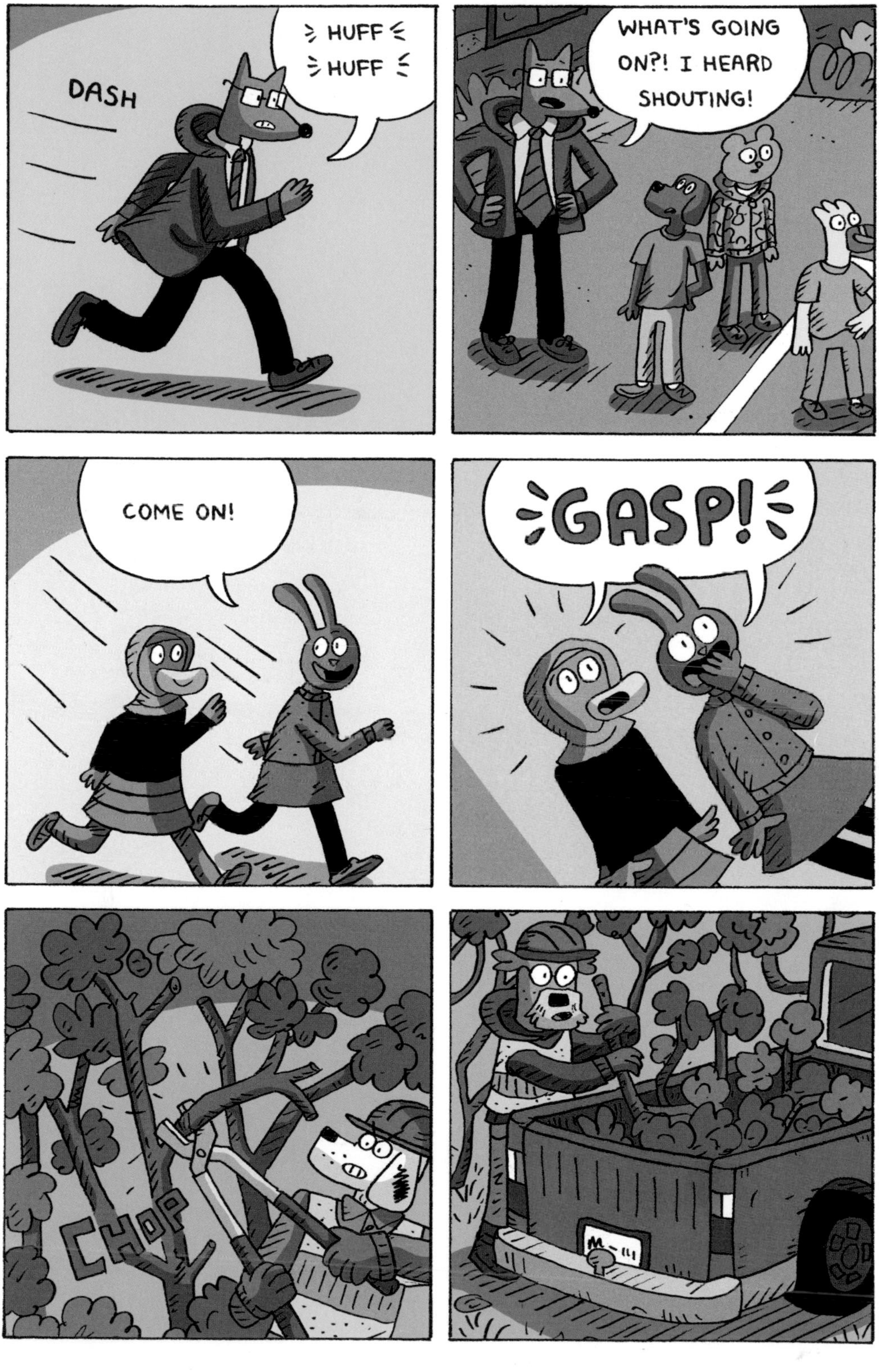
DASH
HUFF HUFF
WHAT'S GOING ON?! I HEARD SHOUTING!
COME ON!
GASP!
CHOP

VROOOOOOM

SNIP

CLIP

CLIP

OUR HIDEOUT!

IT'S RUINED!

PRINCIPAL WILCOX! PRINCIPAL WILCOX!

WHY ARE THOSE PEOPLE CUTTING DOWN OUR SECRET... I MEAN, THOSE BUSHES?

YEAH! WHY?

WE'RE JUST TRIMMING THEM BACK A BIT SO WE DON'T LOSE TRACK OF ANYONE.

THOSE BUSHES WERE A REAL HAZARD. WE DIDN'T KNOW WHAT KIDS WERE UP TO IN THERE.

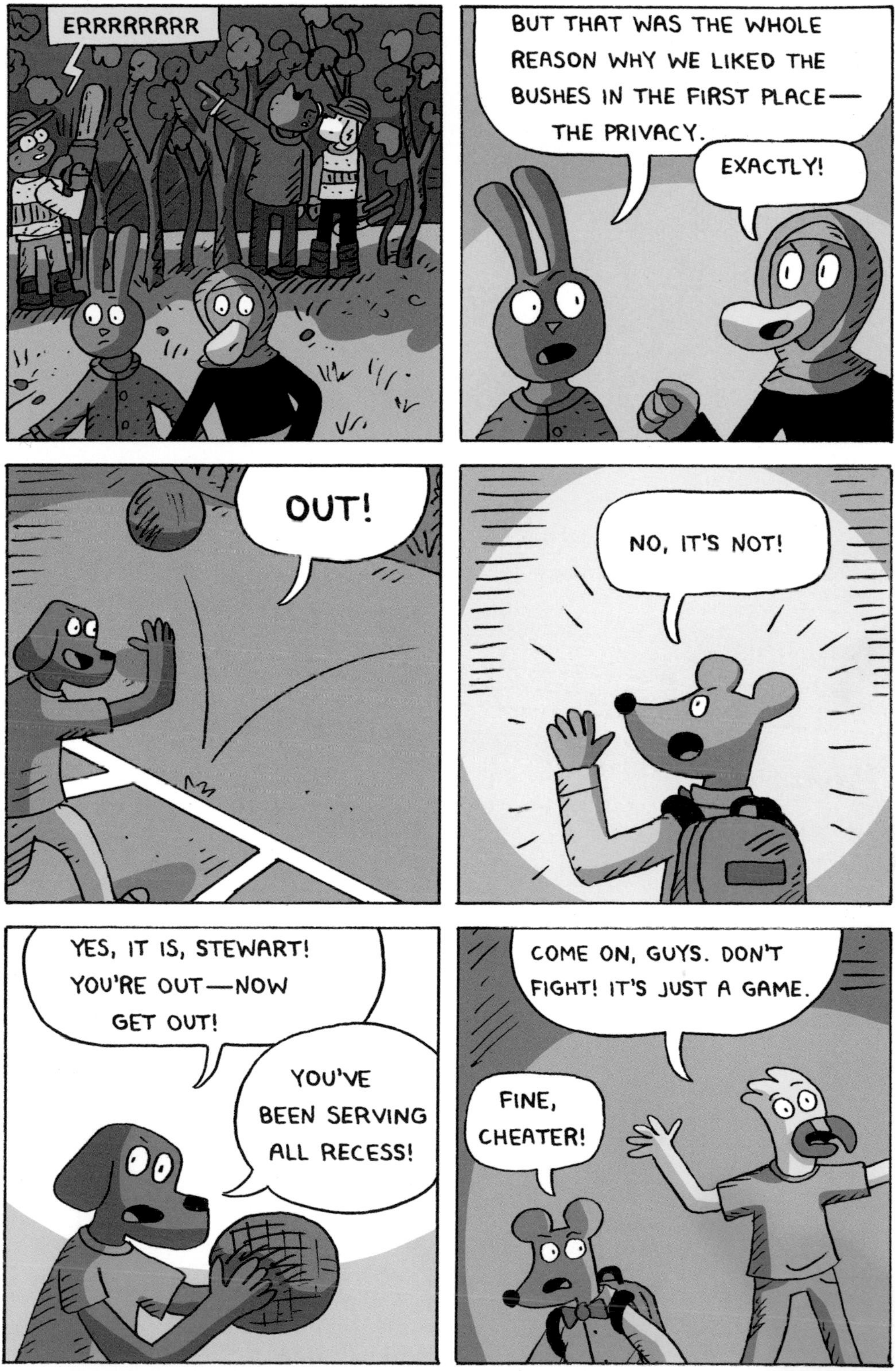
ERRRRRRRR
BUT THAT WAS THE WHOLE REASON WHY WE LIKED THE BUSHES IN THE FIRST PLACE— THE PRIVACY.
EXACTLY!
OUT!
NO, IT'S NOT!
YES, IT IS, STEWART! YOU'RE OUT—NOW GET OUT!
YOU'VE BEEN SERVING ALL RECESS!
COME ON, GUYS. DON'T FIGHT! IT'S JUST A GAME.
FINE, CHEATER!

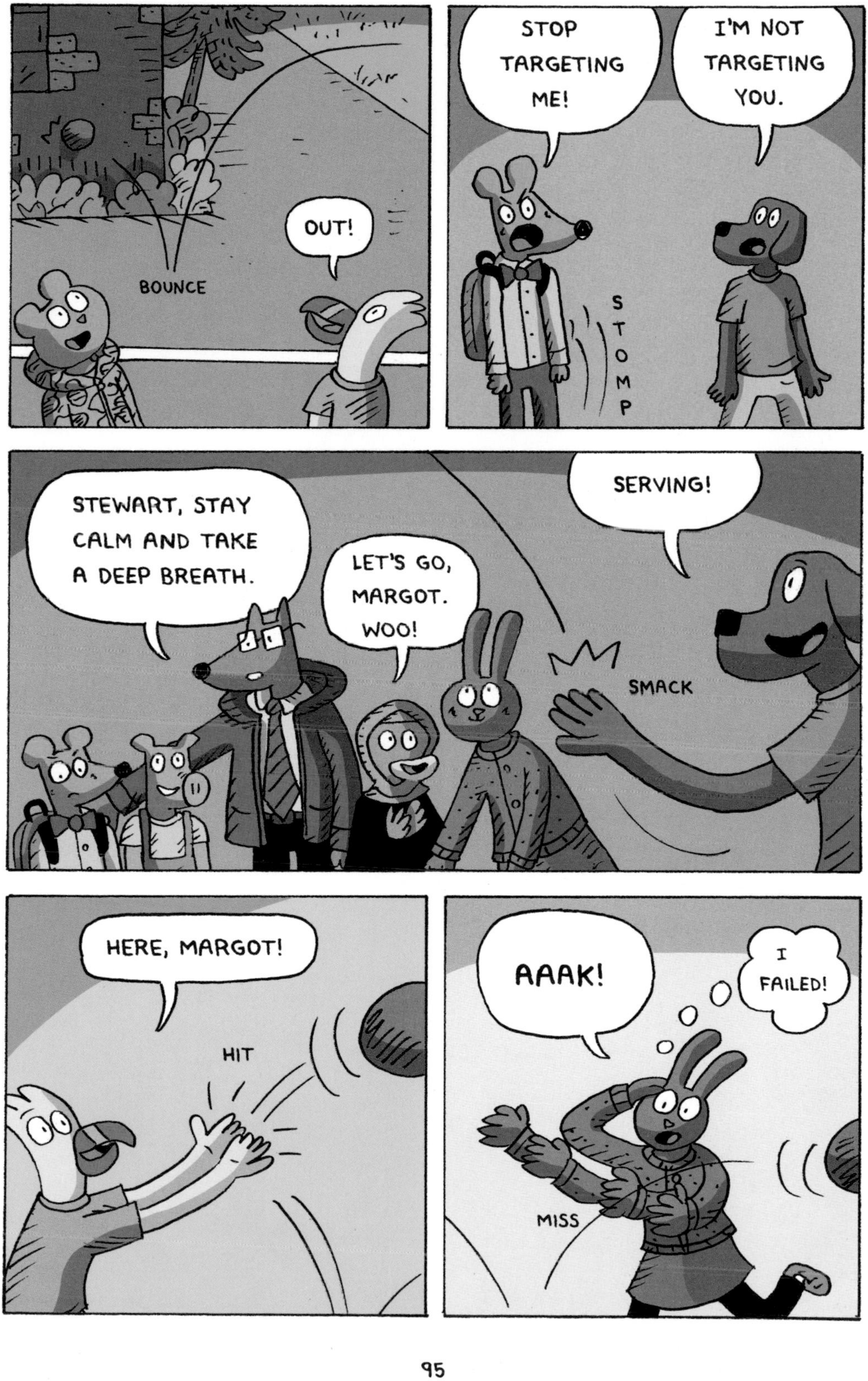
BOUNCE
OUT!
STOP TARGETING ME!
I'M NOT TARGETING YOU.
STOMP
STEWART, STAY CALM AND TAKE A DEEP BREATH.
LET'S GO, MARGOT. WOO!
SERVING!
SMACK
HERE, MARGOT!
HIT
AAAK!
I FAILED!
MISS

CHAPTER SIX
Noah's Tree Story

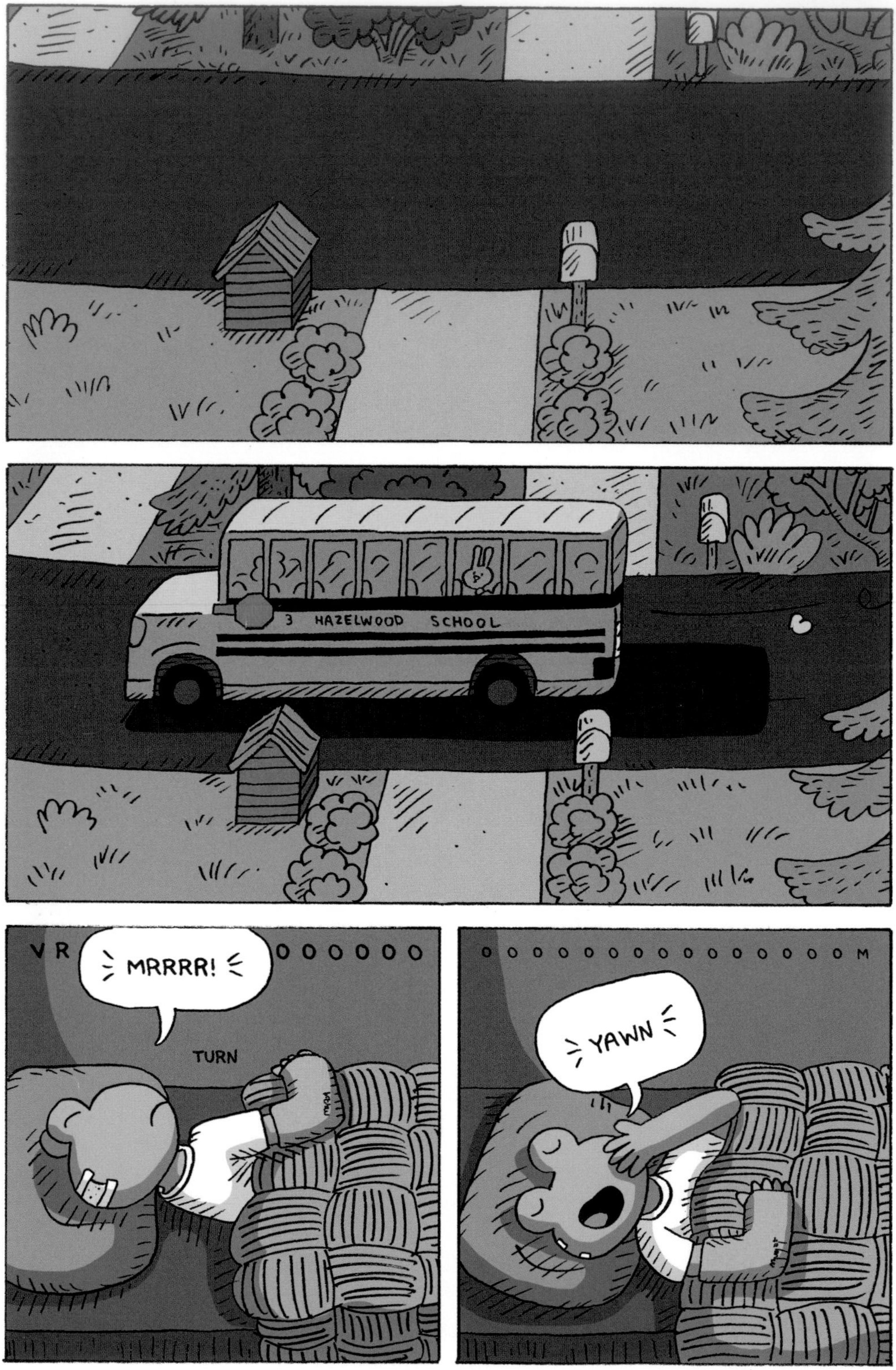
3 HAZELWOOD SCHOOL
VR
MRRRR!
OOOOOO
TURN
OOOOOOOOOOOOOOOOM
YAWN

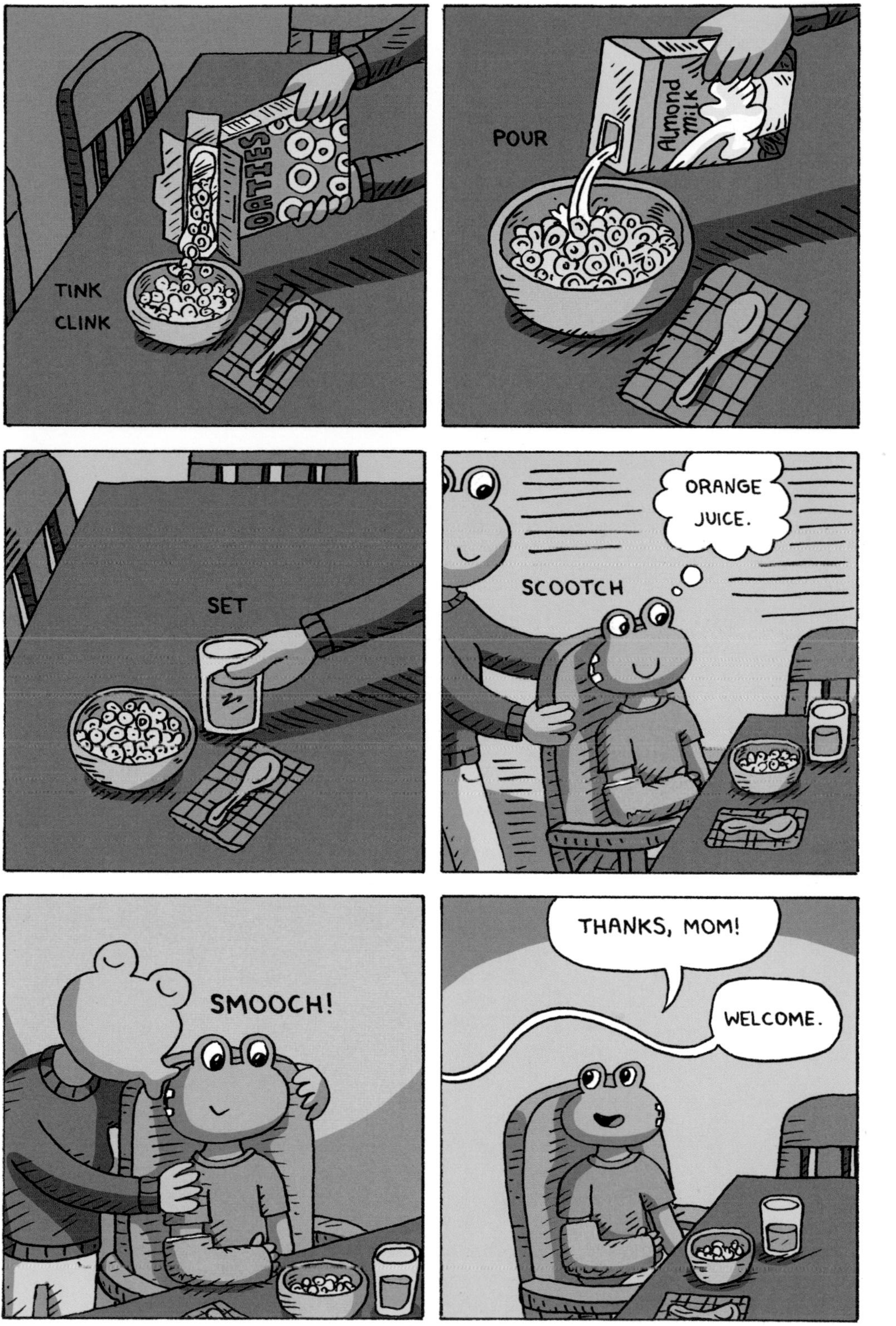
OATIES
TINK
CLINK
POUR
Almond milk
SET
ORANGE JUICE.
SCOOTCH
SMOOCH!
THANKS, MOM!
WELCOME.

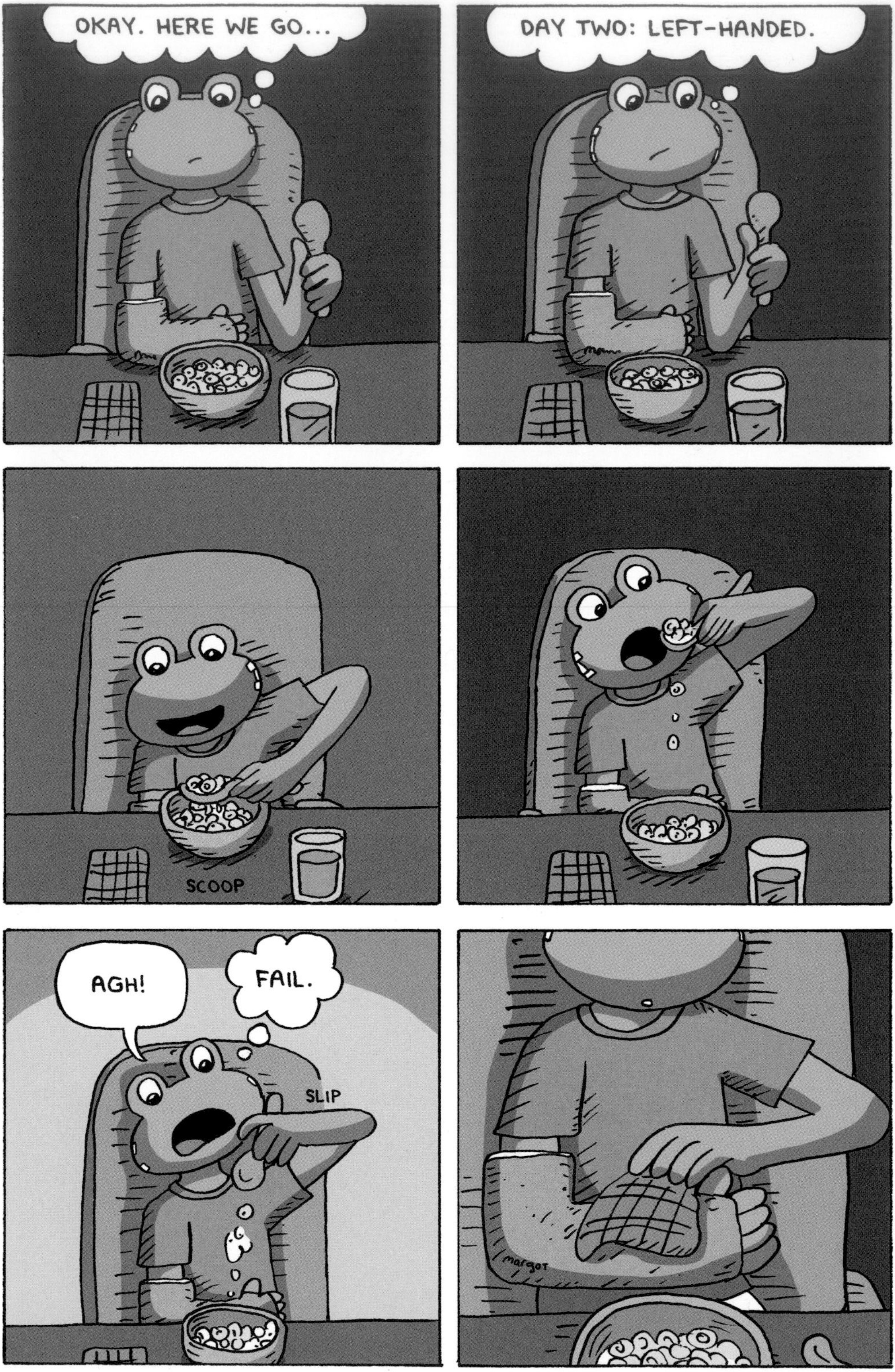
OKAY. HERE WE GO...
DAY TWO: LEFT-HANDED.
SCOOP
AGH!
FAIL.
SLIP
margot

110

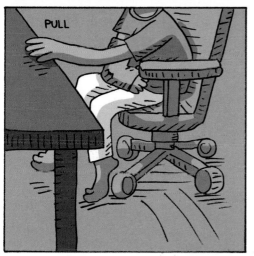

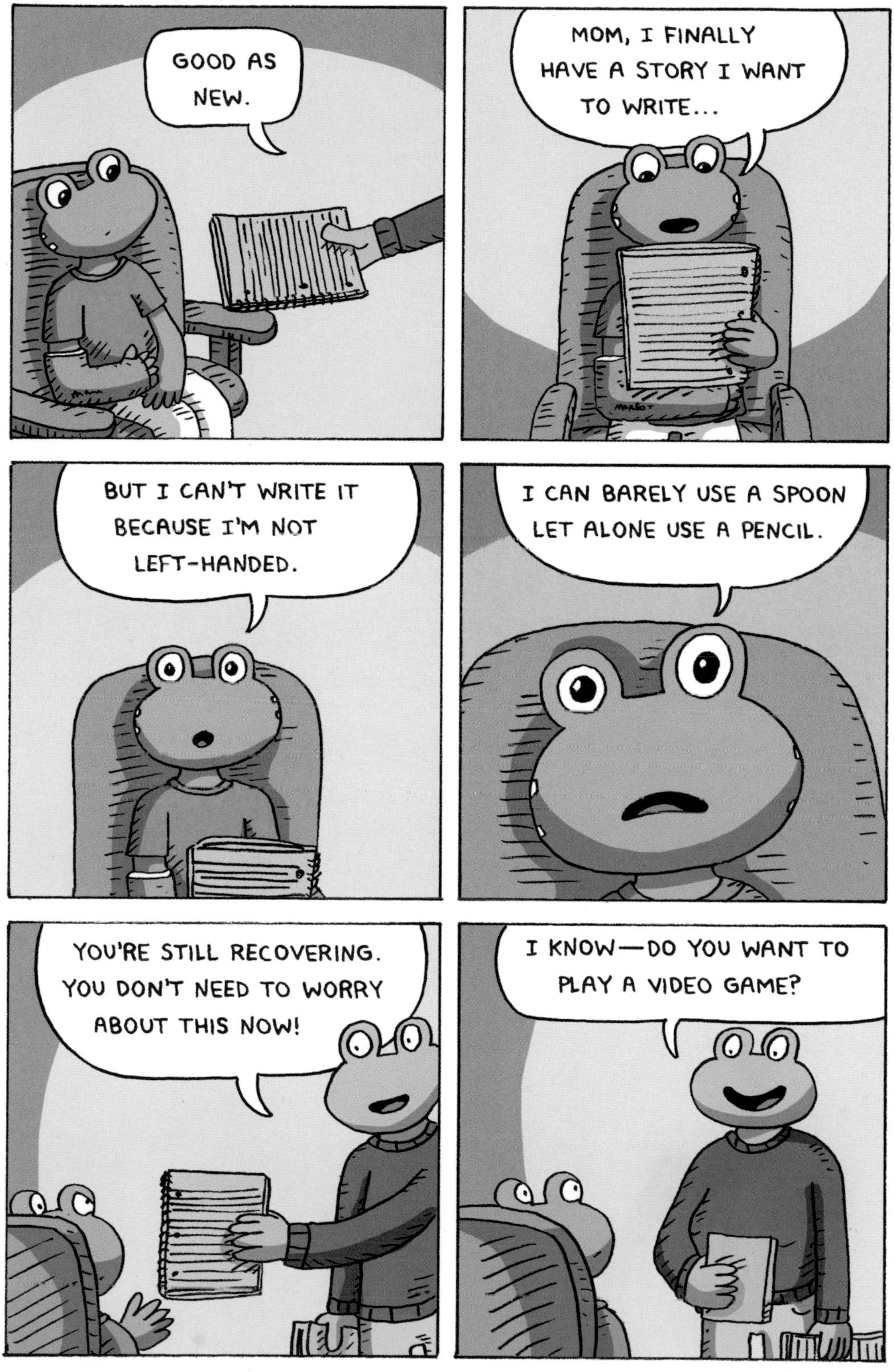
GOOD AS NEW.
MOM, I FINALLY HAVE A STORY I WANT TO WRITE...
BUT I CAN'T WRITE IT BECAUSE I'M NOT LEFT-HANDED.
I CAN BARELY USE A SPOON LET ALONE USE A PENCIL.
YOU'RE STILL RECOVERING. YOU DON'T NEED TO WORRY ABOUT THIS NOW!
I KNOW—DO YOU WANT TO PLAY A VIDEO GAME?

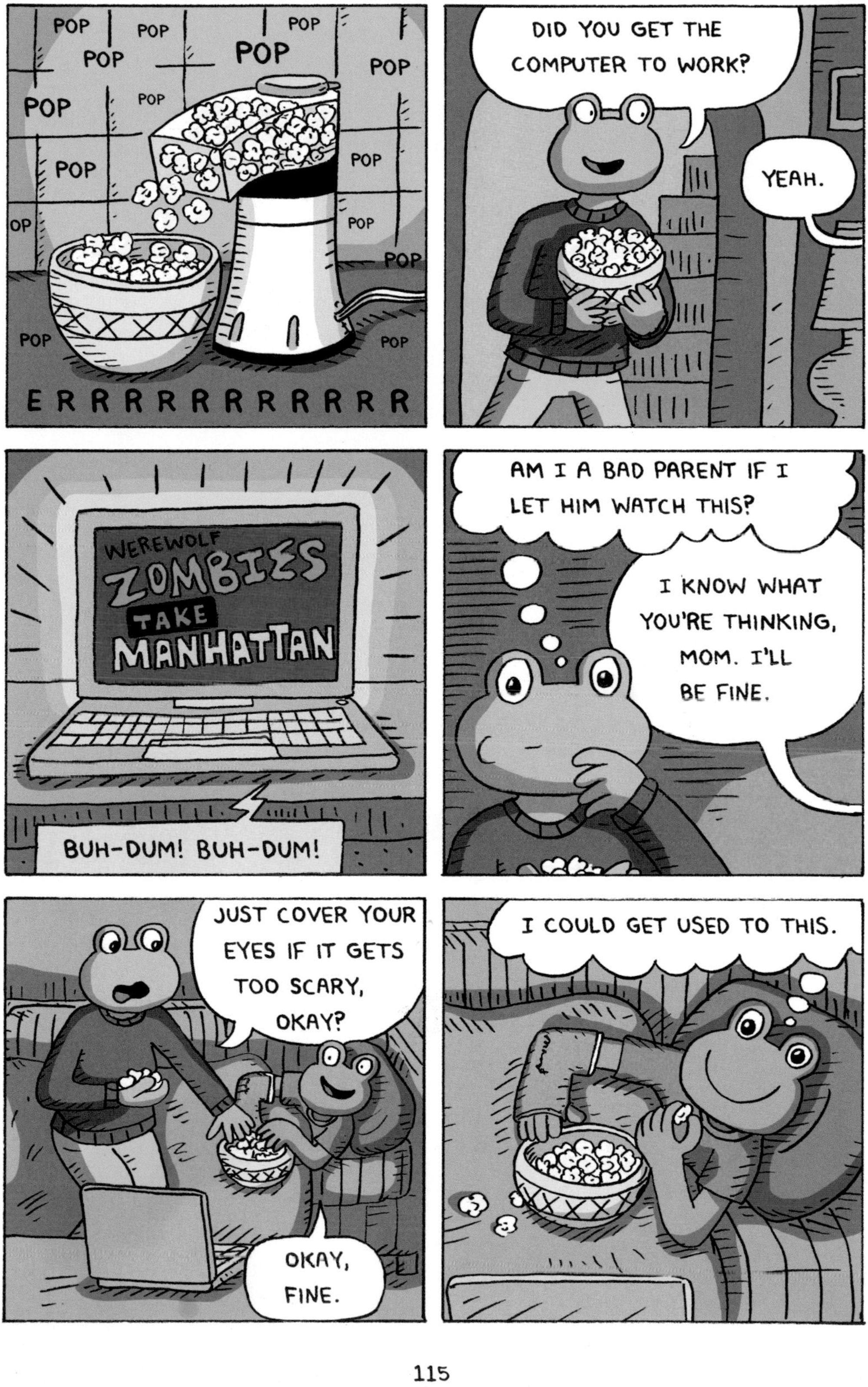
POP
POP
POP
POP
POP
POP
POP
POP
POP
OP
POP
POP
POP
POP
ERRRRRRRRRRR
DID YOU GET THE COMPUTER TO WORK?
YEAH.
WEREWOLF ZOMBIES TAKE MANHATTAN
BUH-DUM! BUH-DUM!
AM I A BAD PARENT IF I LET HIM WATCH THIS?
I KNOW WHAT YOU'RE THINKING, MOM. I'LL BE FINE.
JUST COVER YOUR EYES IF IT GETS TOO SCARY, OKAY?
OKAY, FINE.
I COULD GET USED TO THIS.

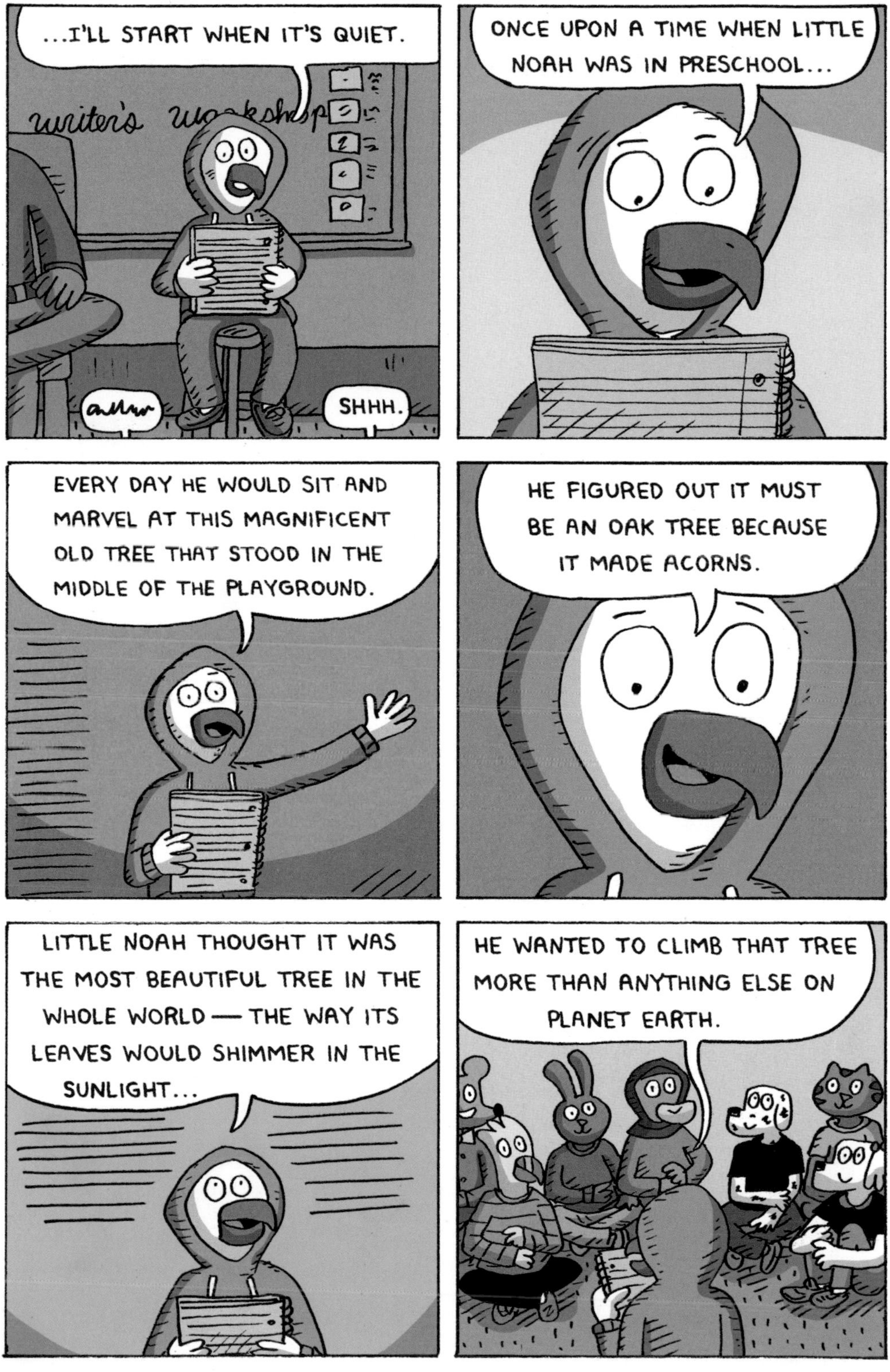
...I'LL START WHEN IT'S QUIET.
writer's workshop
SHHH.
ONCE UPON A TIME WHEN LITTLE NOAH WAS IN PRESCHOOL...
EVERY DAY HE WOULD SIT AND MARVEL AT THIS MAGNIFICENT OLD TREE THAT STOOD IN THE MIDDLE OF THE PLAYGROUND.
HE FIGURED OUT IT MUST BE AN OAK TREE BECAUSE IT MADE ACORNS.
LITTLE NOAH THOUGHT IT WAS THE MOST BEAUTIFUL TREE IN THE WHOLE WORLD — THE WAY ITS LEAVES WOULD SHIMMER IN THE SUNLIGHT...
HE WANTED TO CLIMB THAT TREE MORE THAN ANYTHING ELSE ON PLANET EARTH.

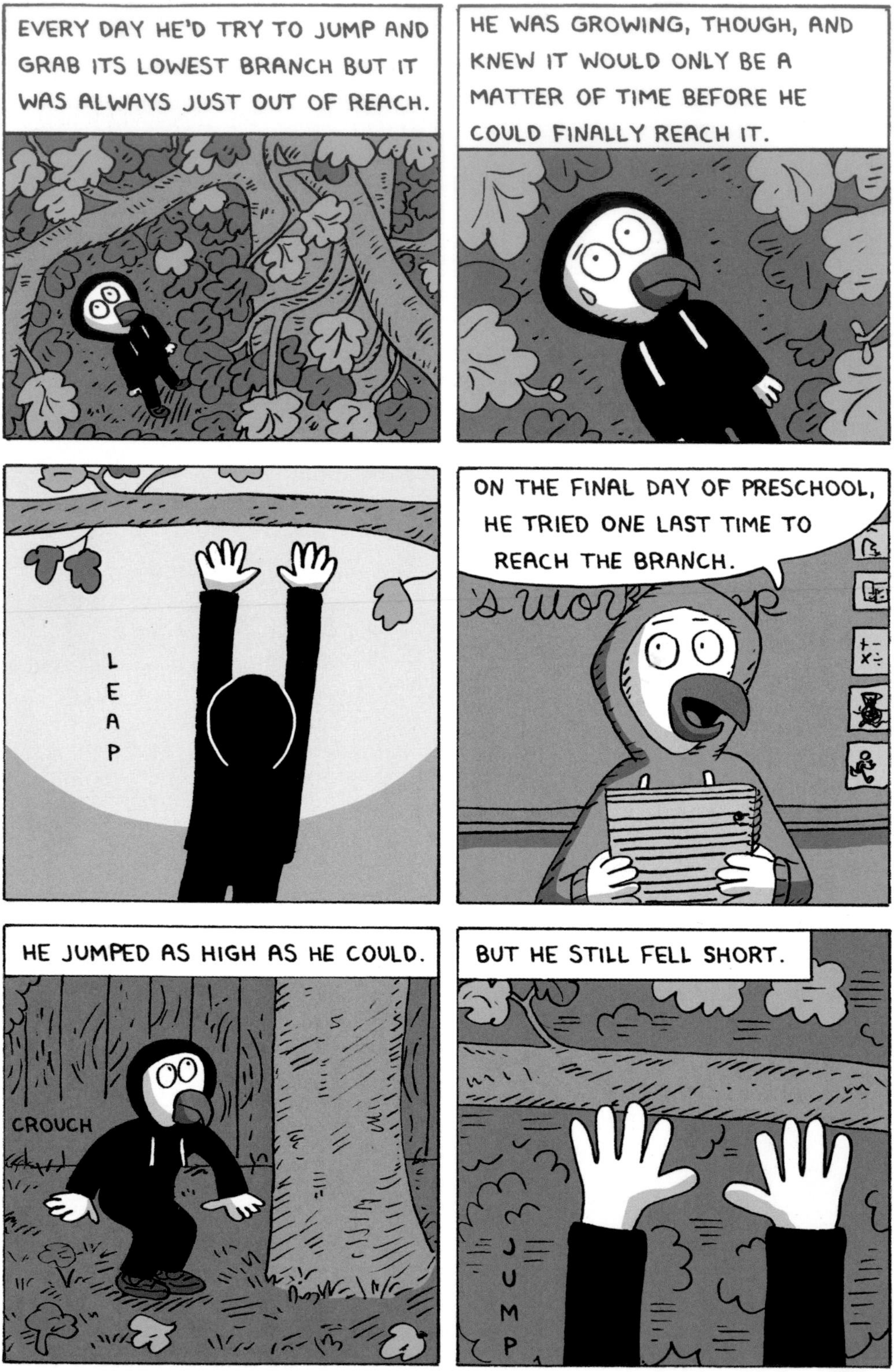
EVERY DAY HE'D TRY TO JUMP AND GRAB ITS LOWEST BRANCH BUT IT WAS ALWAYS JUST OUT OF REACH.
HE WAS GROWING, THOUGH, AND KNEW IT WOULD ONLY BE A MATTER OF TIME BEFORE HE COULD FINALLY REACH IT.
LEAP
ON THE FINAL DAY OF PRESCHOOL, HE TRIED ONE LAST TIME TO REACH THE BRANCH.
HE JUMPED AS HIGH AS HE COULD.
CROUCH
BUT HE STILL FELL SHORT.
JUMP

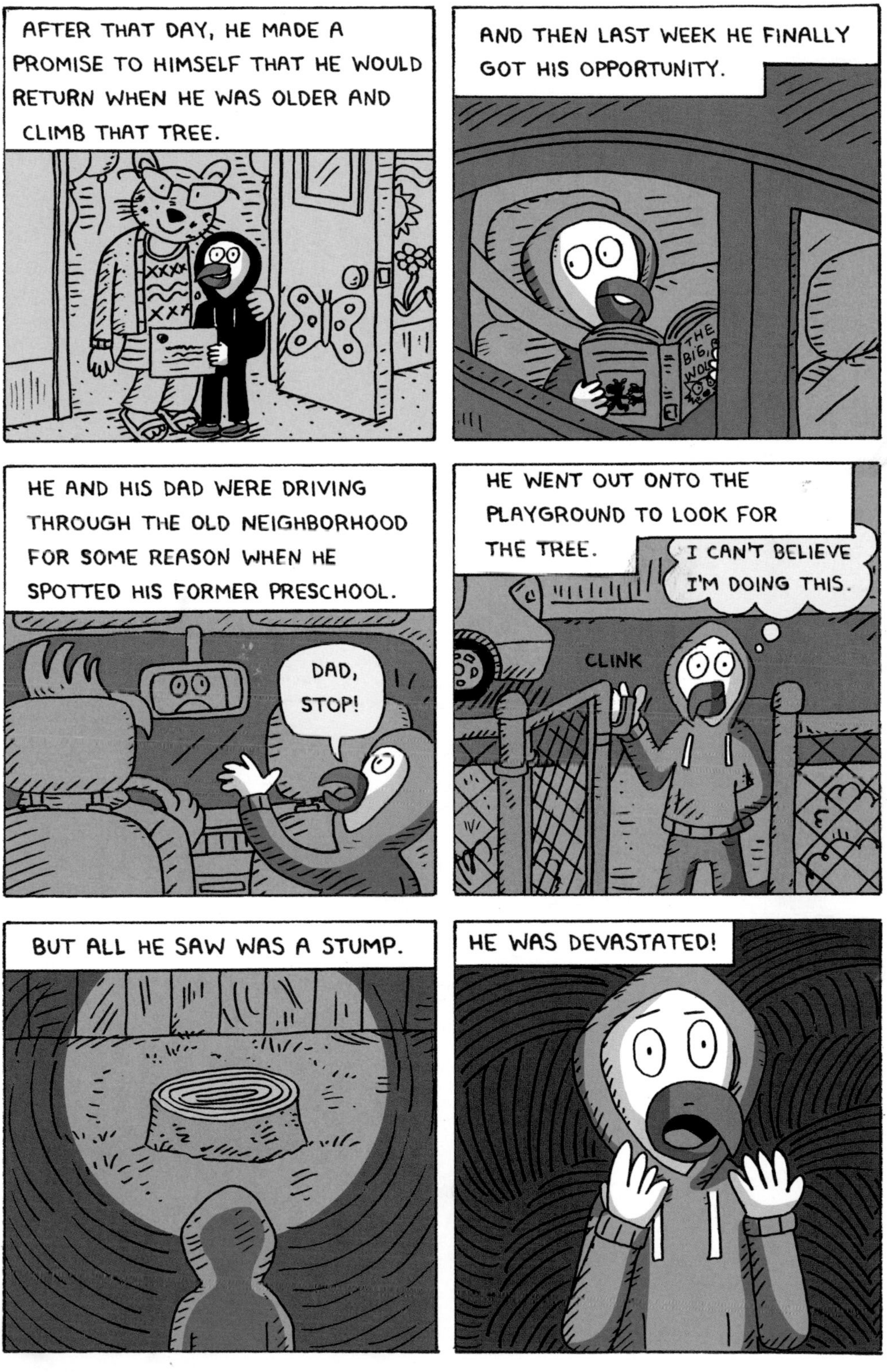
AFTER THAT DAY, HE MADE A PROMISE TO HIMSELF THAT HE WOULD RETURN WHEN HE WAS OLDER AND CLIMB THAT TREE.
AND THEN LAST WEEK HE FINALLY GOT HIS OPPORTUNITY.
HE AND HIS DAD WERE DRIVING THROUGH THE OLD NEIGHBORHOOD FOR SOME REASON WHEN HE SPOTTED HIS FORMER PRESCHOOL.
DAD, STOP!
HE WENT OUT ONTO THE PLAYGROUND TO LOOK FOR THE TREE.
I CAN'T BELIEVE I'M DOING THIS.
CLINK
BUT ALL HE SAW WAS A STUMP.
HE WAS DEVASTATED!

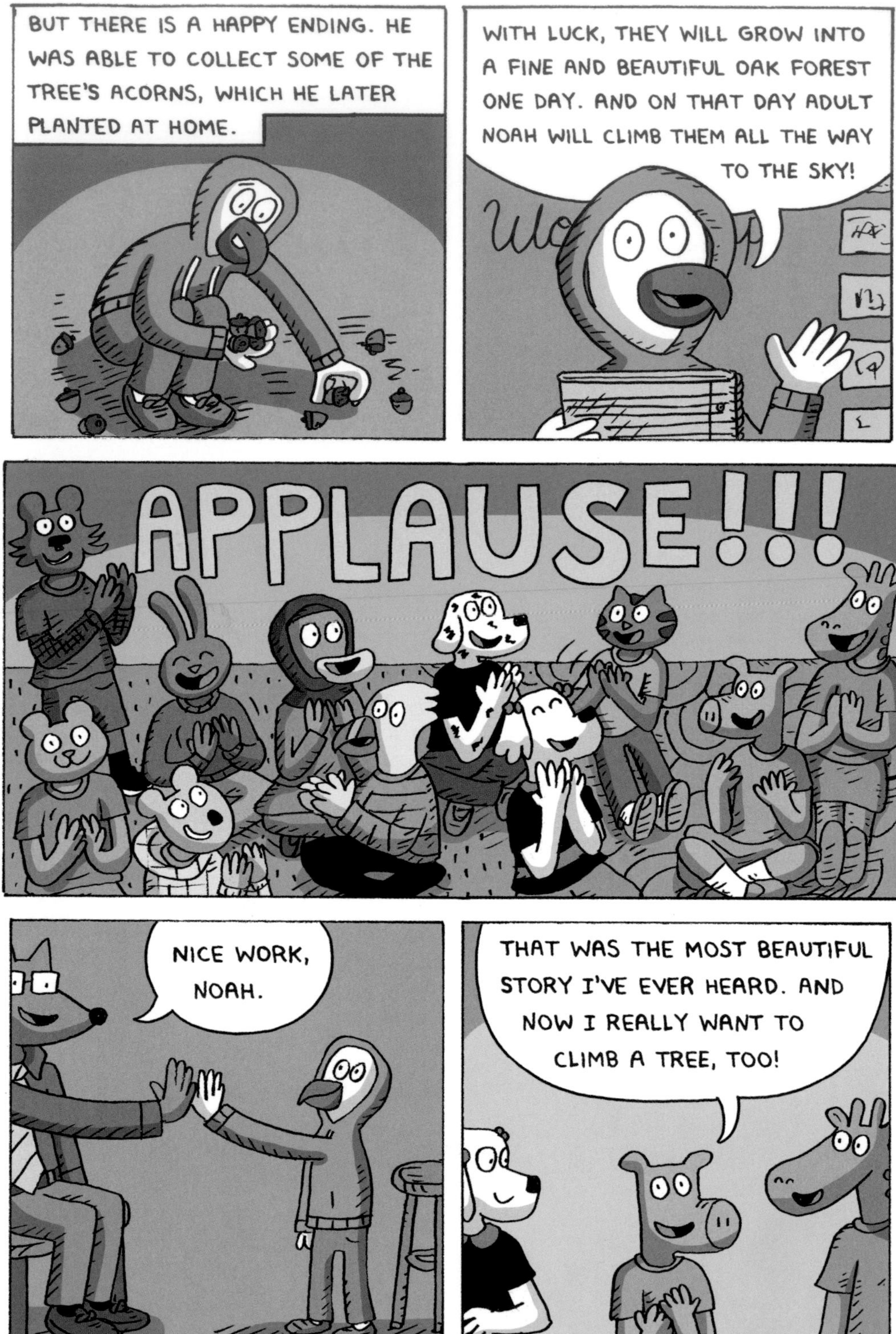
BUT THERE IS A HAPPY ENDING. HE WAS ABLE TO COLLECT SOME OF THE TREE'S ACORNS, WHICH HE LATER PLANTED AT HOME.
WITH LUCK, THEY WILL GROW INTO A FINE AND BEAUTIFUL OAK FOREST ONE DAY. AND ON THAT DAY ADULT NOAH WILL CLIMB THEM ALL THE WAY TO THE SKY!
APPLAUSE!!!
NICE WORK, NOAH.
THAT WAS THE MOST BEAUTIFUL STORY I'VE EVER HEARD. AND NOW I REALLY WANT TO CLIMB A TREE, TOO!

CHAPTER SEVEN

A New Perspective

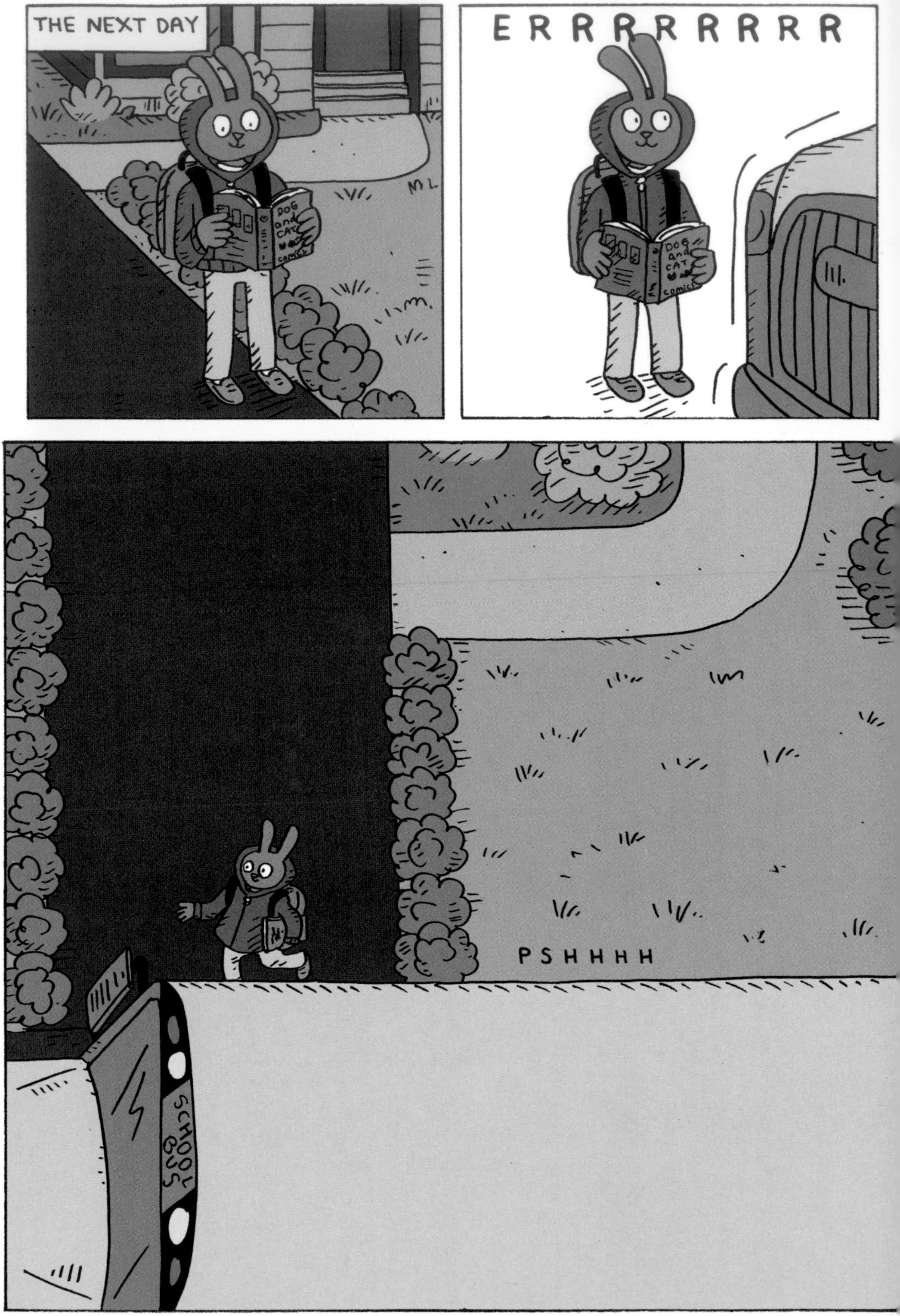
THE NEXT DAY
ERRRRRRRR
PSHHHH
SCHOOL BUS

123

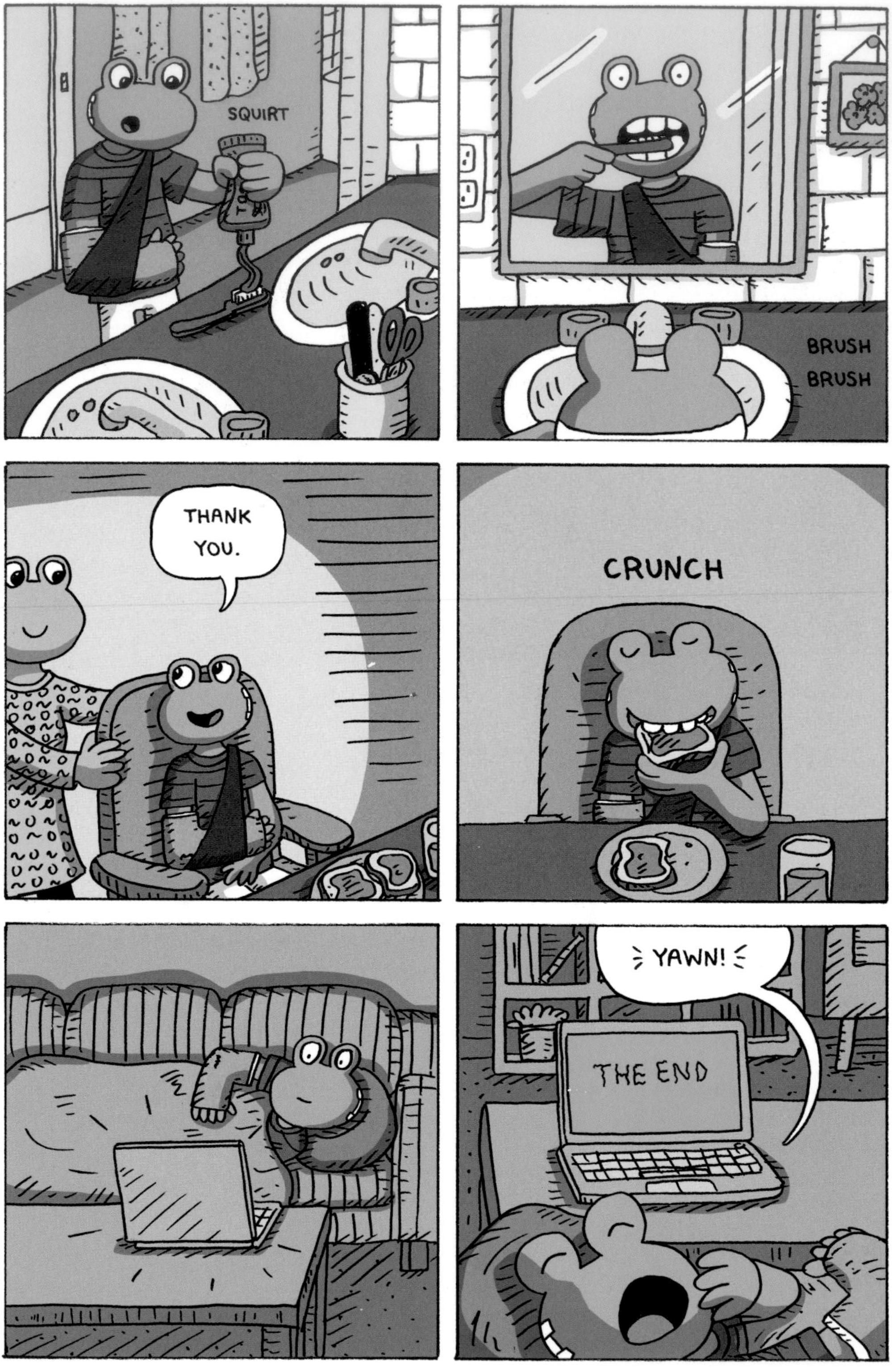
SQUIRT
BRUSH
BRUSH
THANK YOU.
CRUNCH
YAWN!
THE END

MOM, CAN I WATCH ANOTHER ONE?

NO, I THINK YOU'VE WATCHED ENOUGH.

FINE.

CLOSE

THEN WHAT SHOULD I DO?

I'M BORED!

ARE YOU WELL ENOUGH TO GO BACK TO SCHOOL?

NO.

NOT YET.

I THINK.

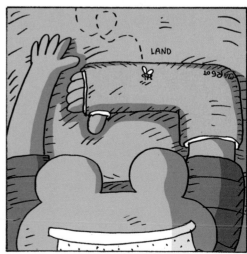

LAND

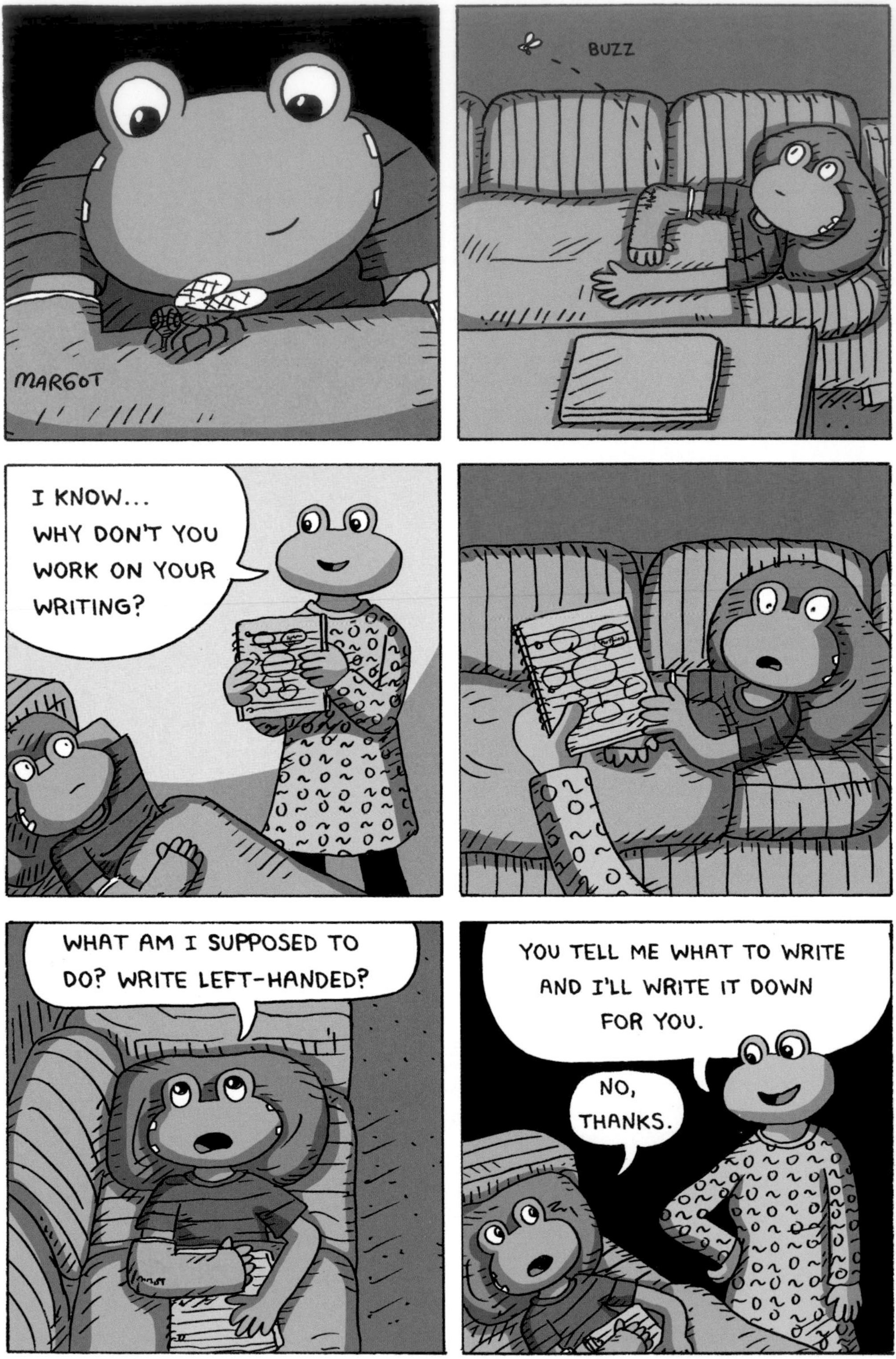
MARGOT
BUZZ
I KNOW... WHY DON'T YOU WORK ON YOUR WRITING?
WHAT AM I SUPPOSED TO DO? WRITE LEFT-HANDED?
YOU TELL ME WHAT TO WRITE AND I'LL WRITE IT DOWN FOR YOU.
NO, THANKS.

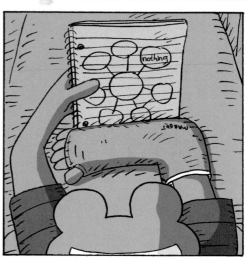

MAYBE I CAN WRITE LEFT-HANDED. MAYBE I'M THE BEST LEFT-HANDED WRITER IN THE WHOLE WORLD.

I'LL NEVER KNOW IF I NEVER TRY.

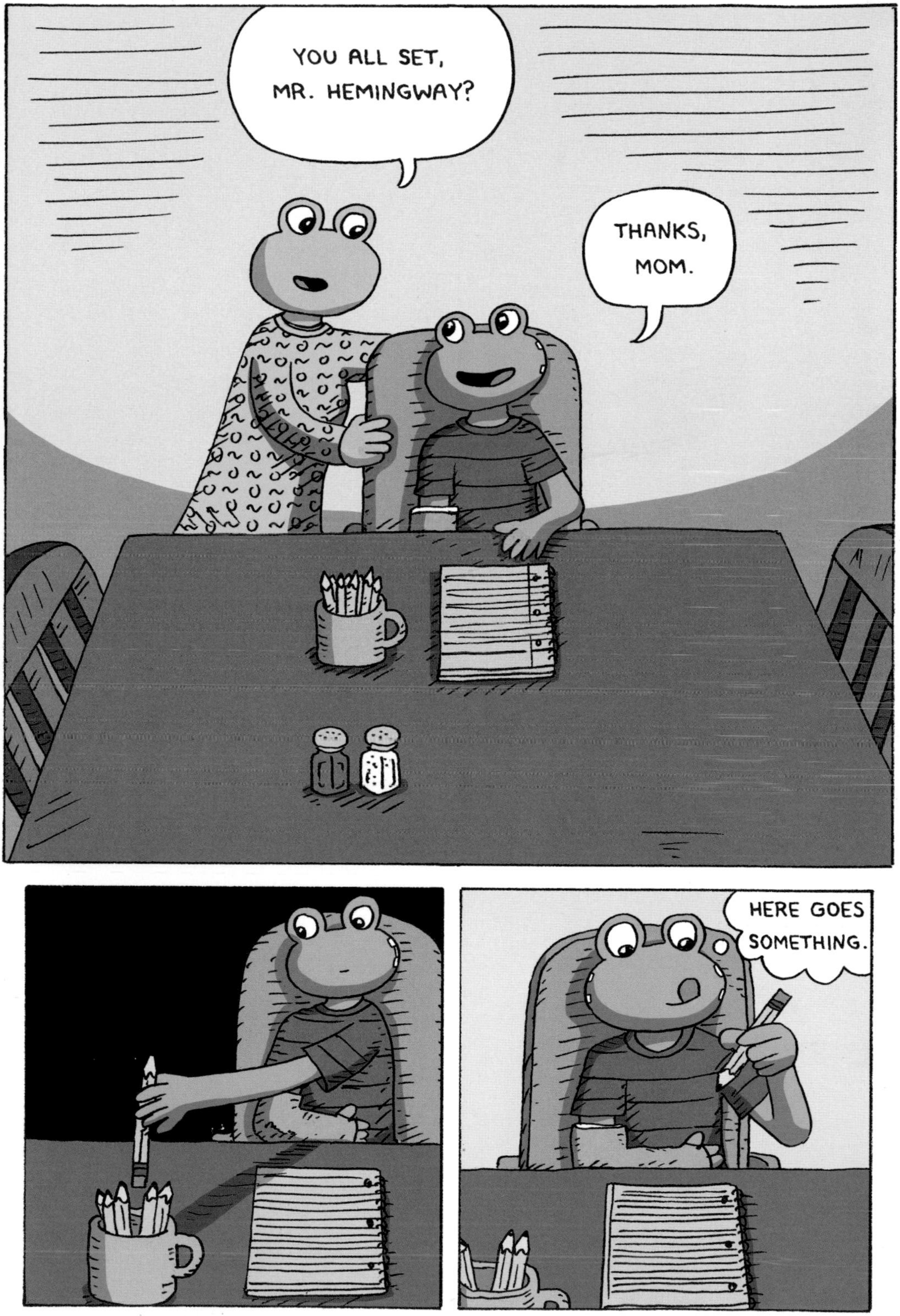
YOU ALL SET, MR. HEMINGWAY?
THANKS, MOM.
HERE GOES SOMETHING.

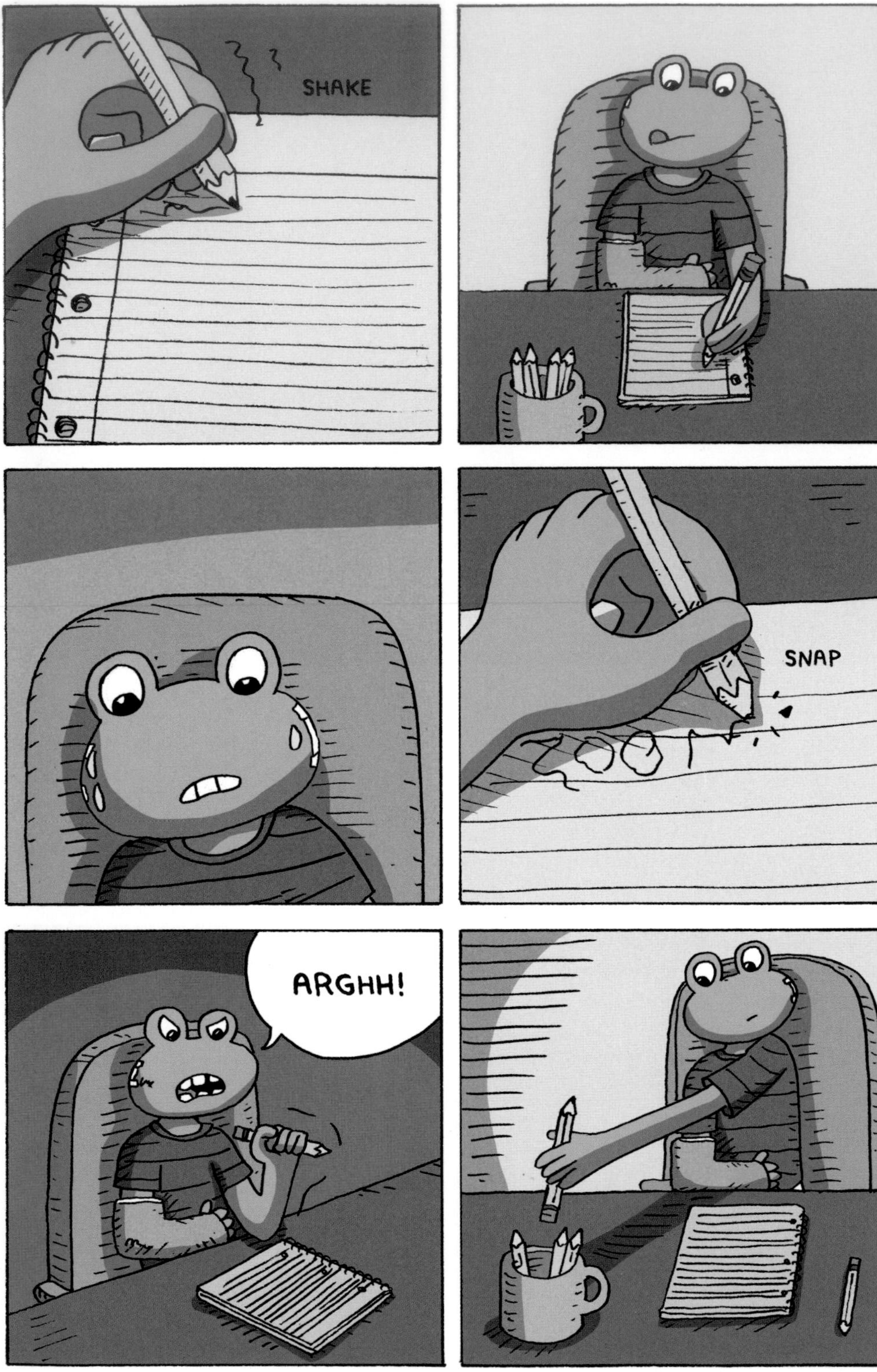
SHAKE
SNAP
ARGHH!

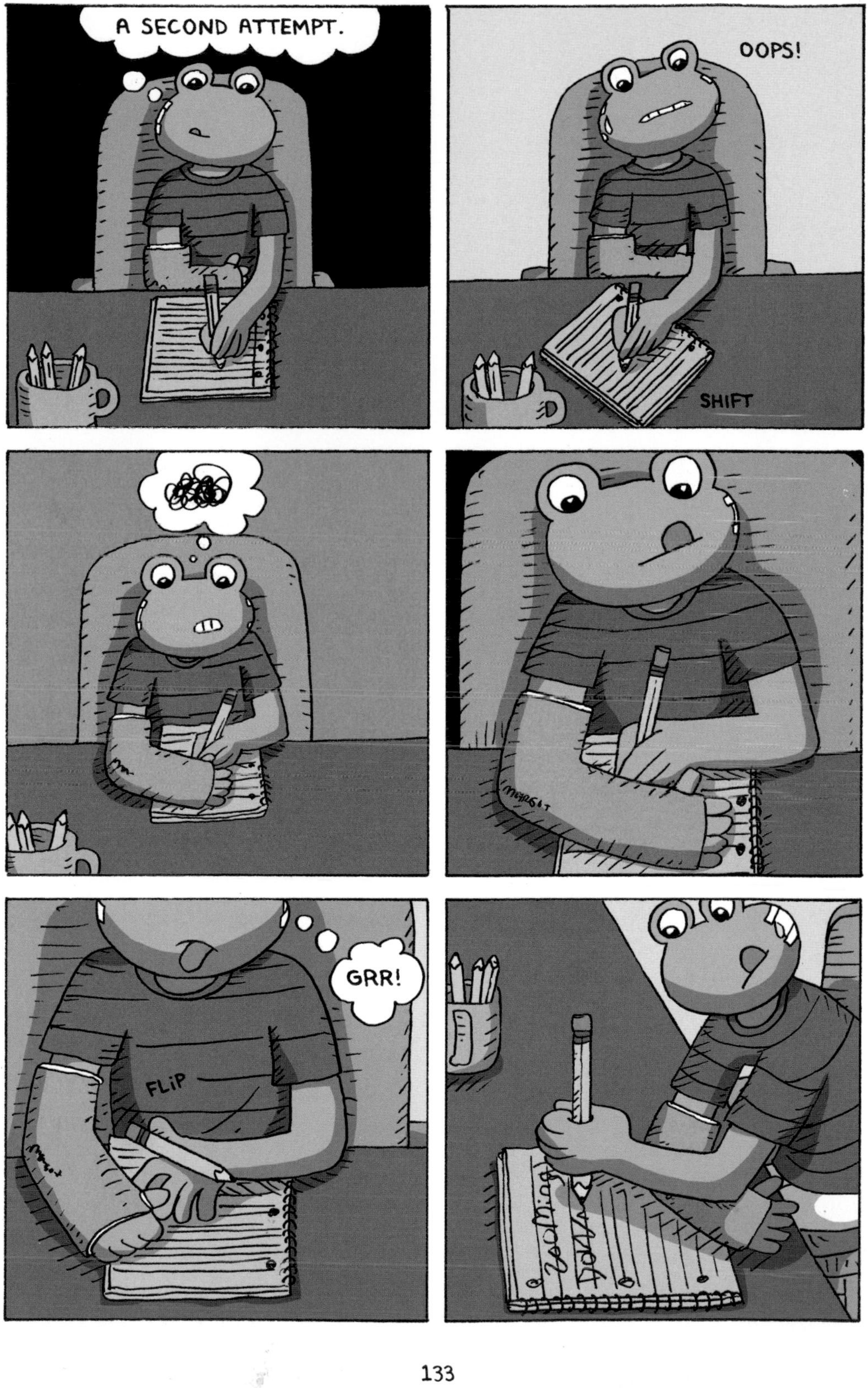
A SECOND ATTEMPT.
OOPS!
SHIFT
FLIP
GRR!

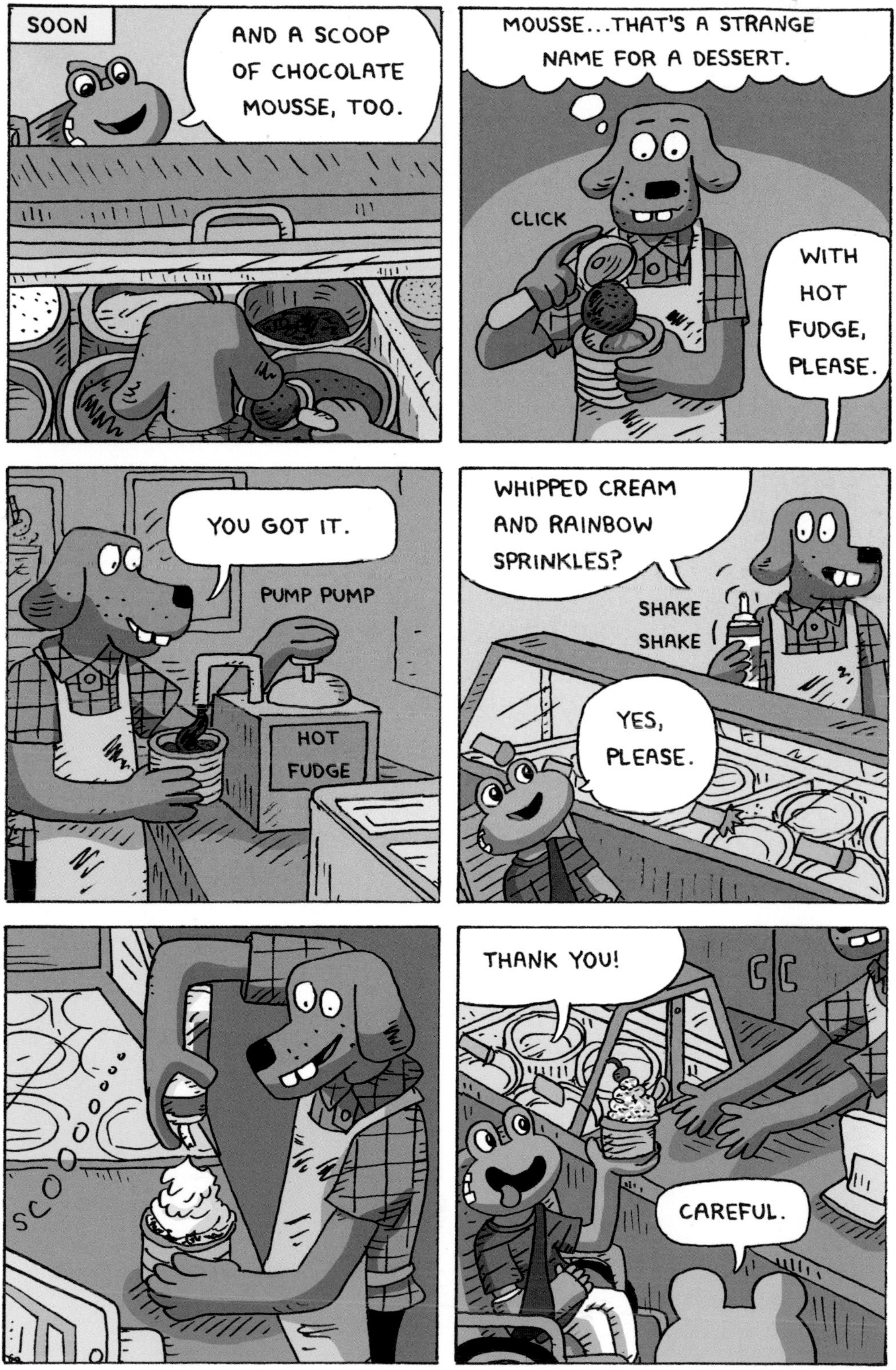
SOON
AND A SCOOP OF CHOCOLATE MOUSSE, TOO.
MOUSSE...THAT'S A STRANGE NAME FOR A DESSERT.
CLICK
WITH HOT FUDGE, PLEASE.
YOU GOT IT.
PUMP PUMP
HOT FUDGE
WHIPPED CREAM AND RAINBOW SPRINKLES?
SHAKE SHAKE
YES, PLEASE.
THANK YOU!
CAREFUL.

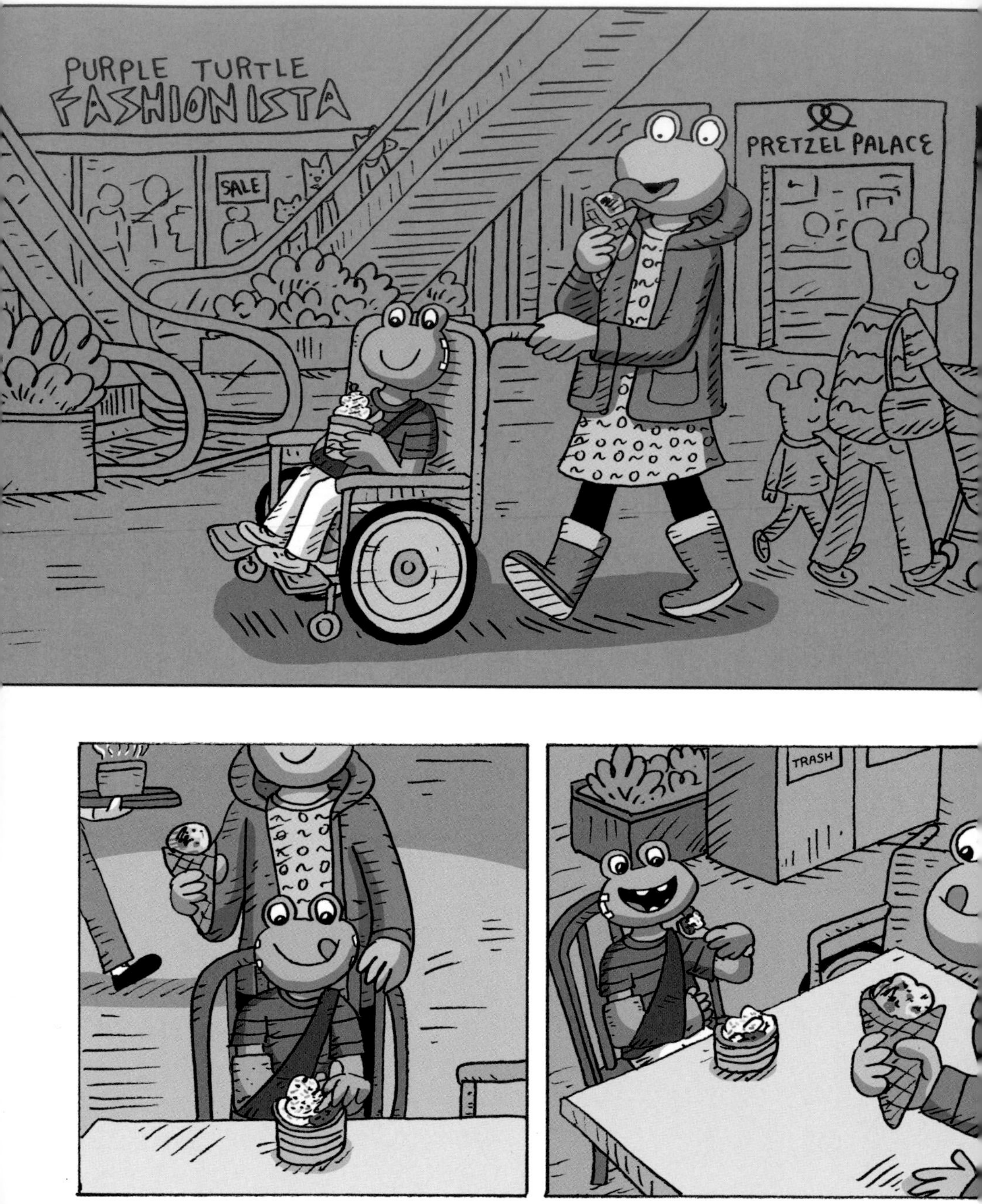
PURPLE TURTLE
FASHIONISTA
SALE
PRETZEL PALACE
TRASH

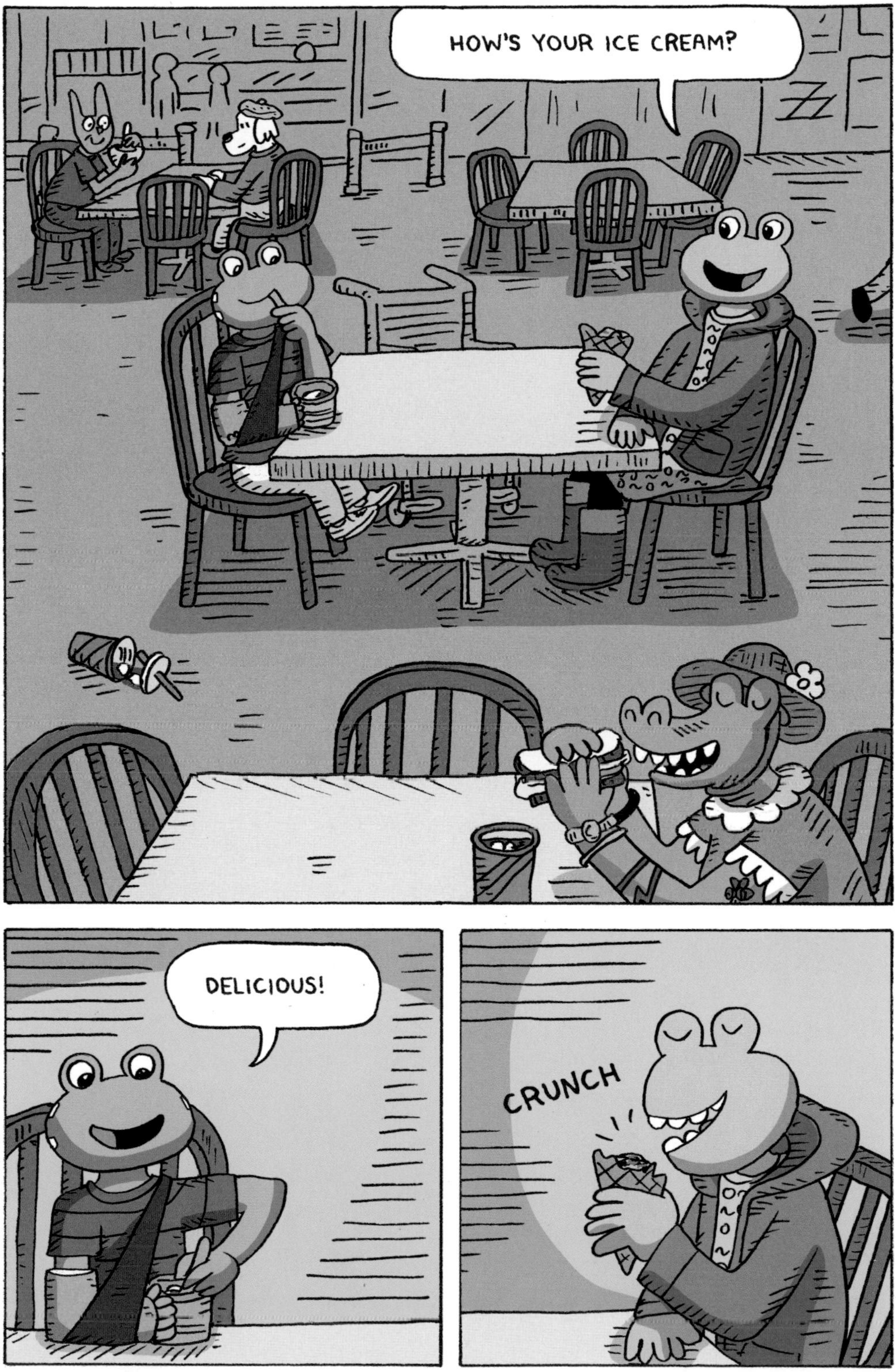
HOW'S YOUR ICE CREAM?
DELICIOUS!
CRUNCH

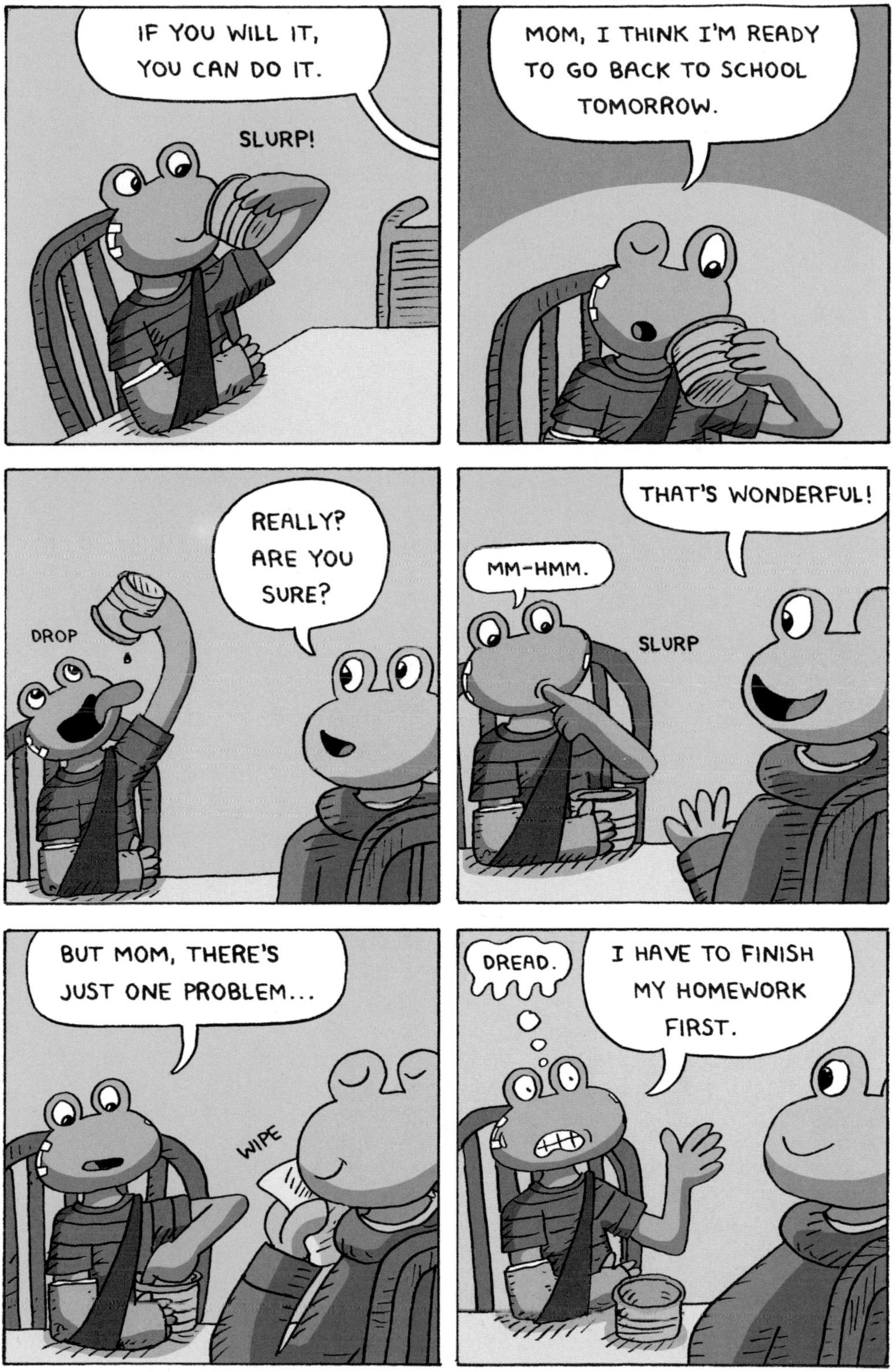
IF YOU WILL IT, YOU CAN DO IT.
SLURP!
MOM, I THINK I'M READY TO GO BACK TO SCHOOL TOMORROW.
DROP
REALLY? ARE YOU SURE?
MM-HMM.
SLURP
THAT'S WONDERFUL!
BUT MOM, THERE'S JUST ONE PROBLEM...
WIPE
DREAD.
I HAVE TO FINISH MY HOMEWORK FIRST.

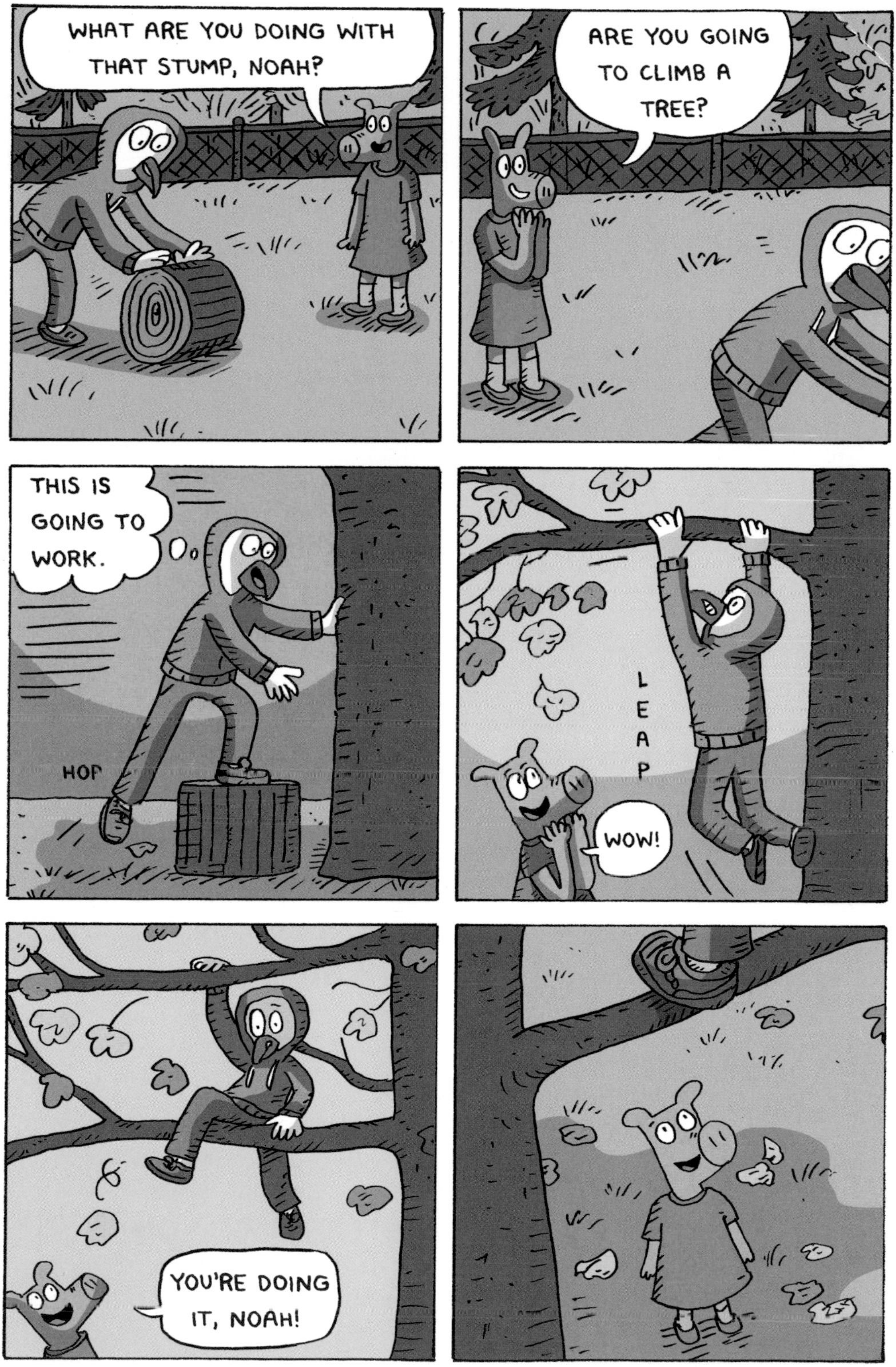
WHAT ARE YOU DOING WITH THAT STUMP, NOAH?
ARE YOU GOING TO CLIMB A TREE?
THIS IS GOING TO WORK.
HOP
LEAP
WOW!
YOU'RE DOING IT, NOAH!

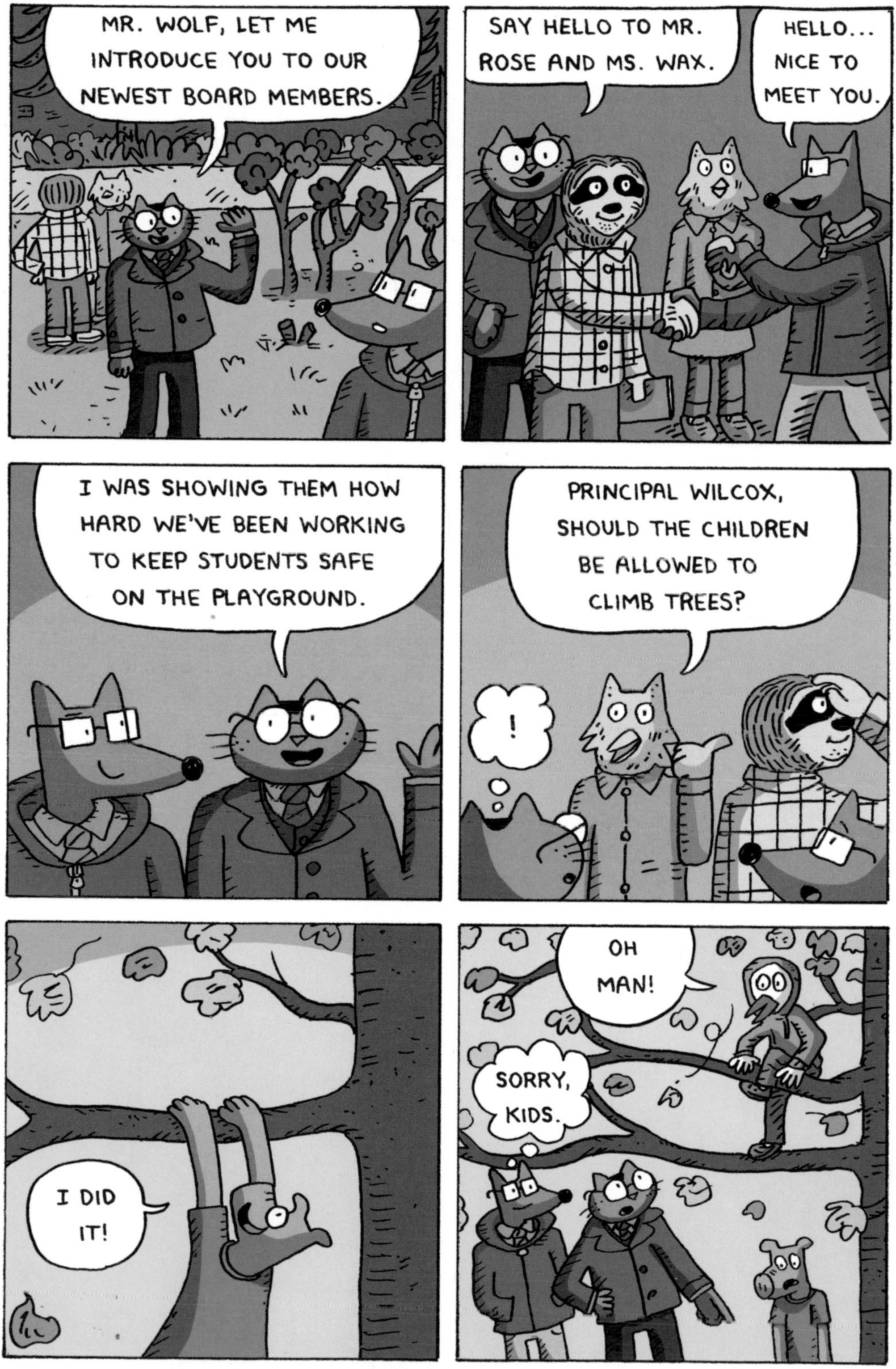
MR. WOLF, LET ME INTRODUCE YOU TO OUR NEWEST BOARD MEMBERS.
SAY HELLO TO MR. ROSE AND MS. WAX.
HELLO... NICE TO MEET YOU.
I WAS SHOWING THEM HOW HARD WE'VE BEEN WORKING TO KEEP STUDENTS SAFE ON THE PLAYGROUND.
PRINCIPAL WILCOX, SHOULD THE CHILDREN BE ALLOWED TO CLIMB TREES?
!
I DID IT!
OH MAN!
SORRY, KIDS.

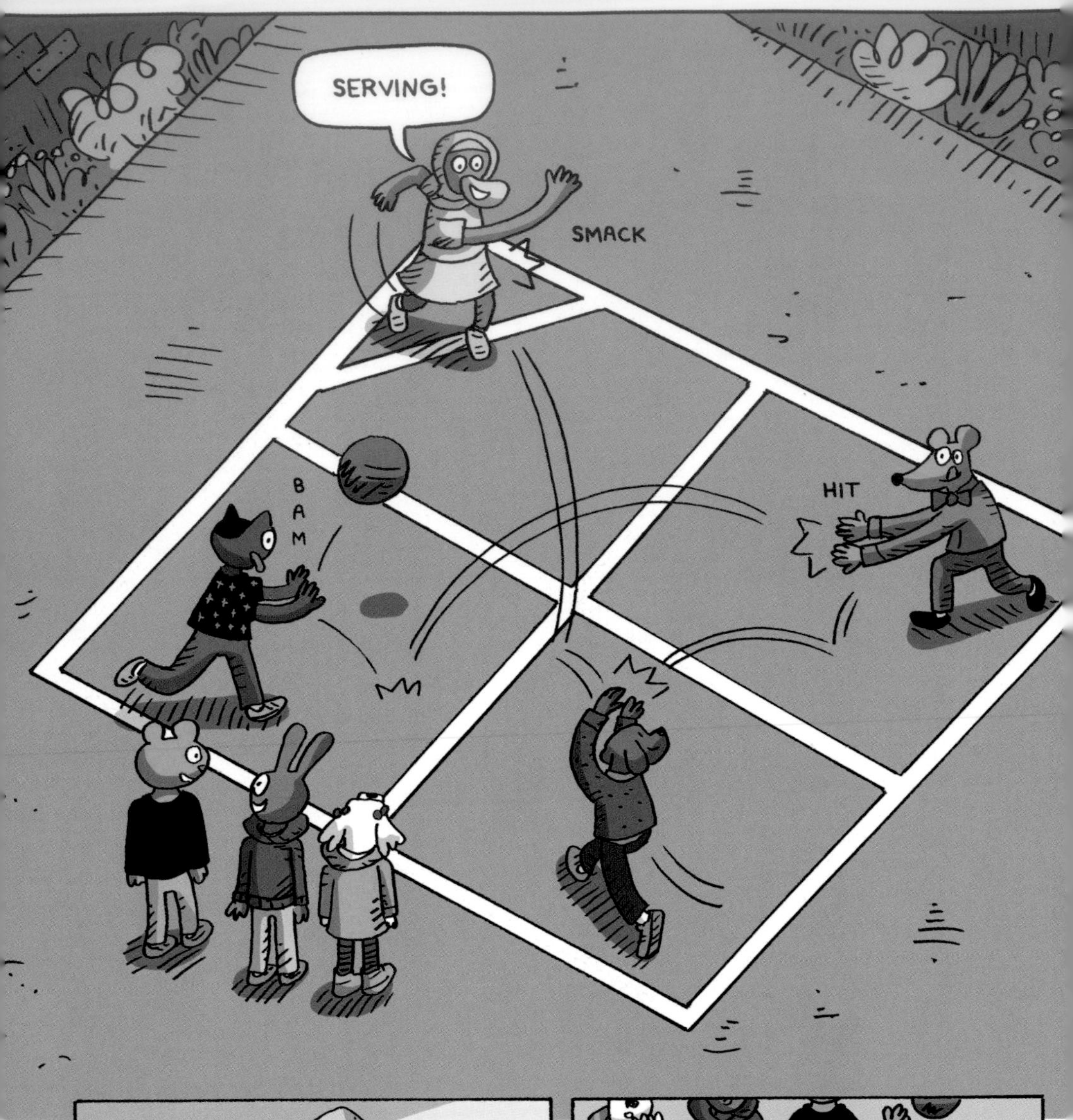
SERVING!
SMACK
BAM
HIT

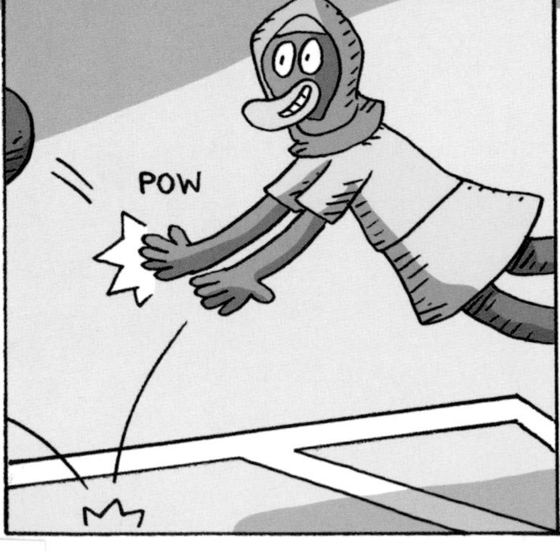
POW

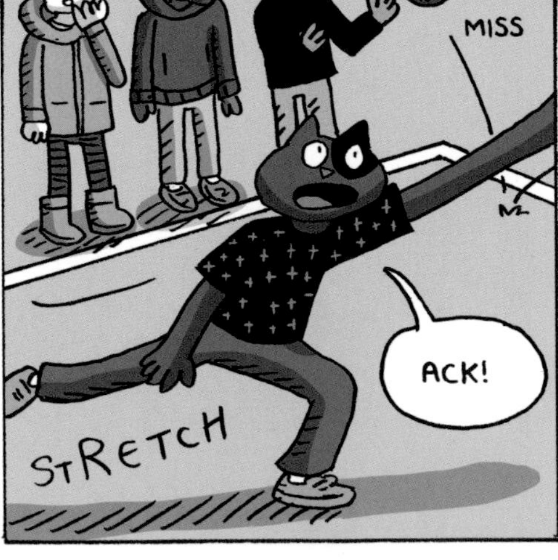
MISS
ACK!
STRETCH

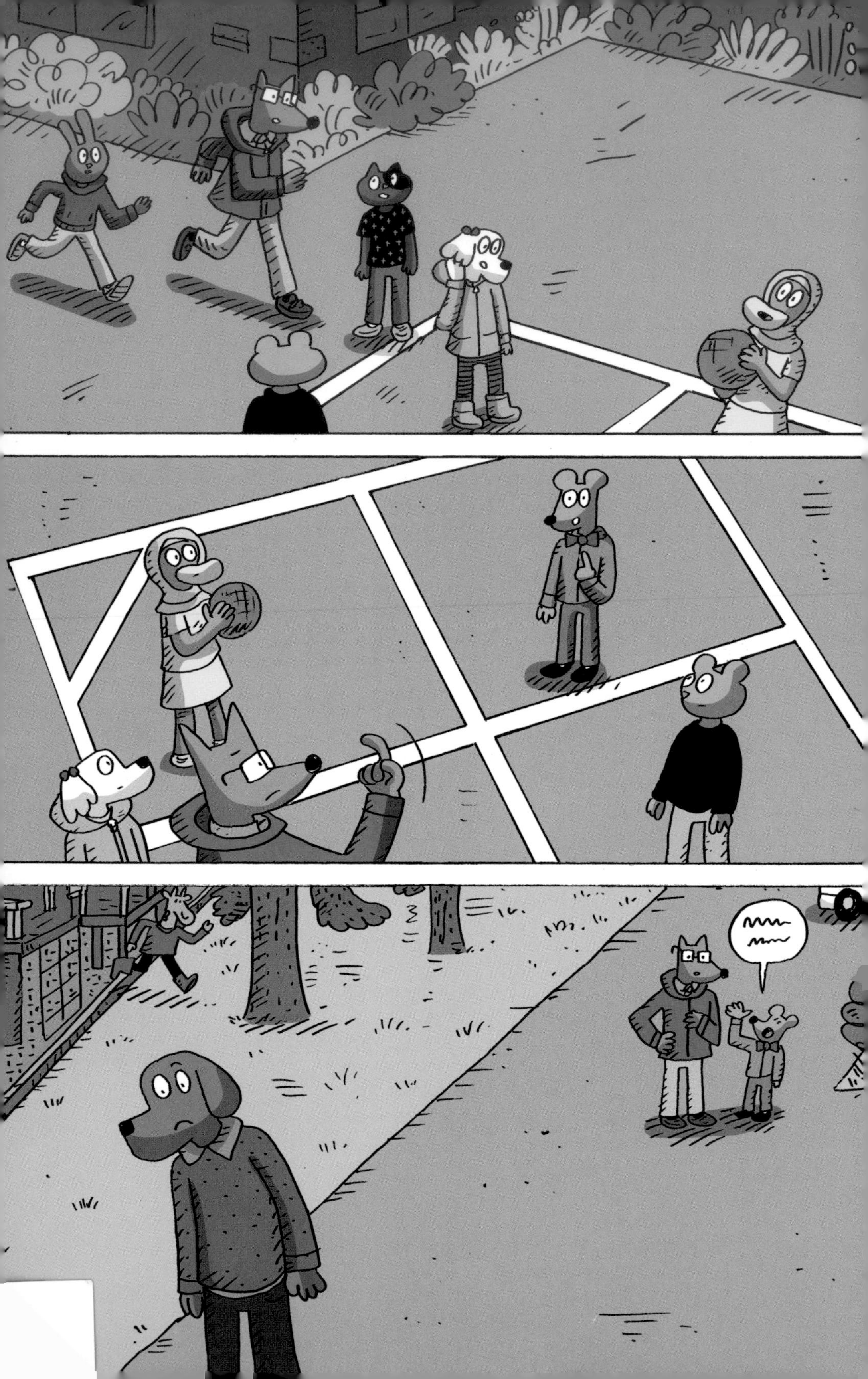

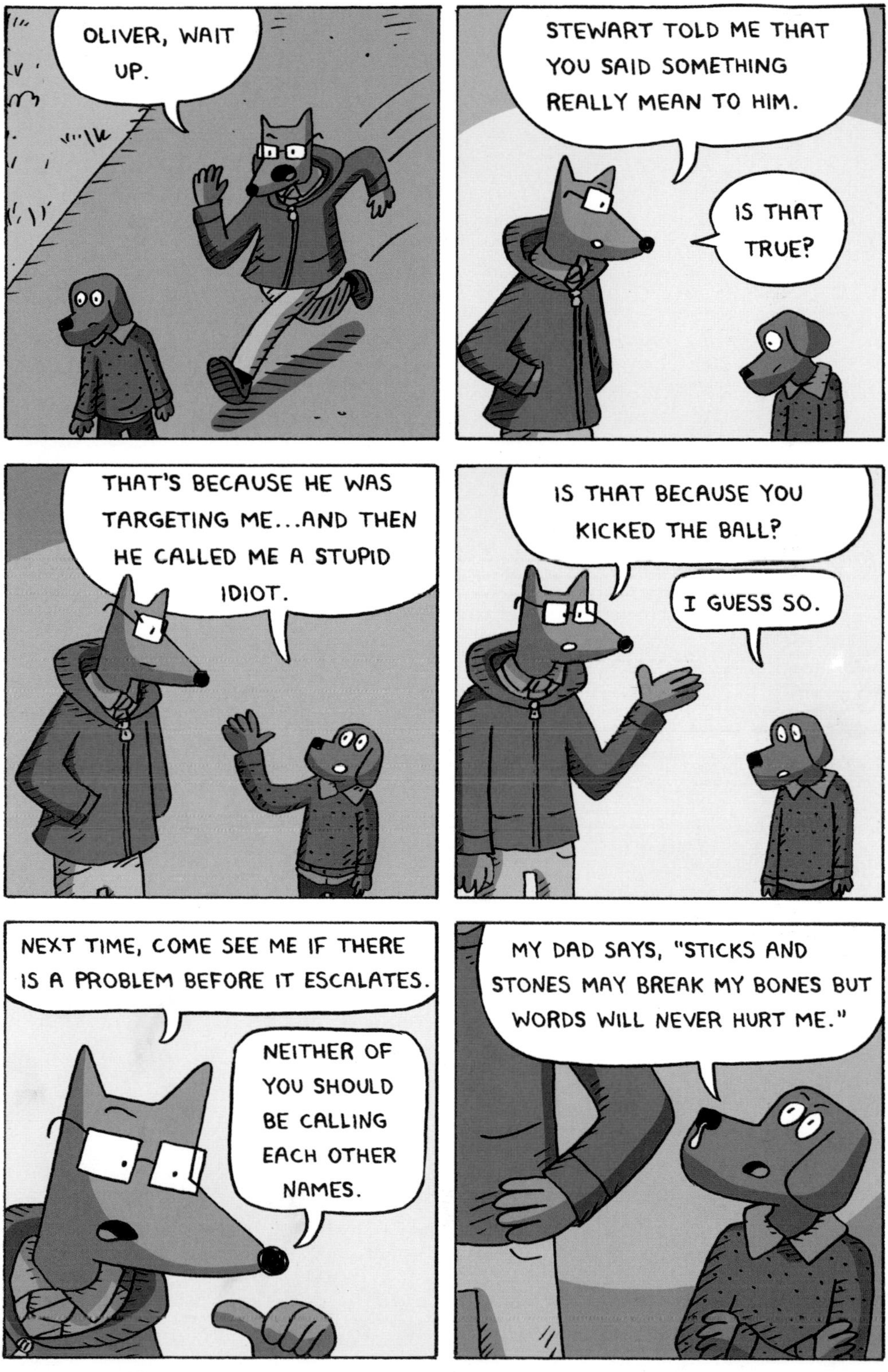
OLIVER, WAIT UP.
STEWART TOLD ME THAT YOU SAID SOMETHING REALLY MEAN TO HIM.
IS THAT TRUE?
THAT'S BECAUSE HE WAS TARGETING ME...AND THEN HE CALLED ME A STUPID IDIOT.
IS THAT BECAUSE YOU KICKED THE BALL?
I GUESS SO.
NEXT TIME, COME SEE ME IF THERE IS A PROBLEM BEFORE IT ESCALATES.
NEITHER OF YOU SHOULD BE CALLING EACH OTHER NAMES.
MY DAD SAYS, "STICKS AND STONES MAY BREAK MY BONES BUT WORDS WILL NEVER HURT ME."

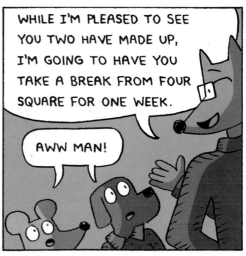

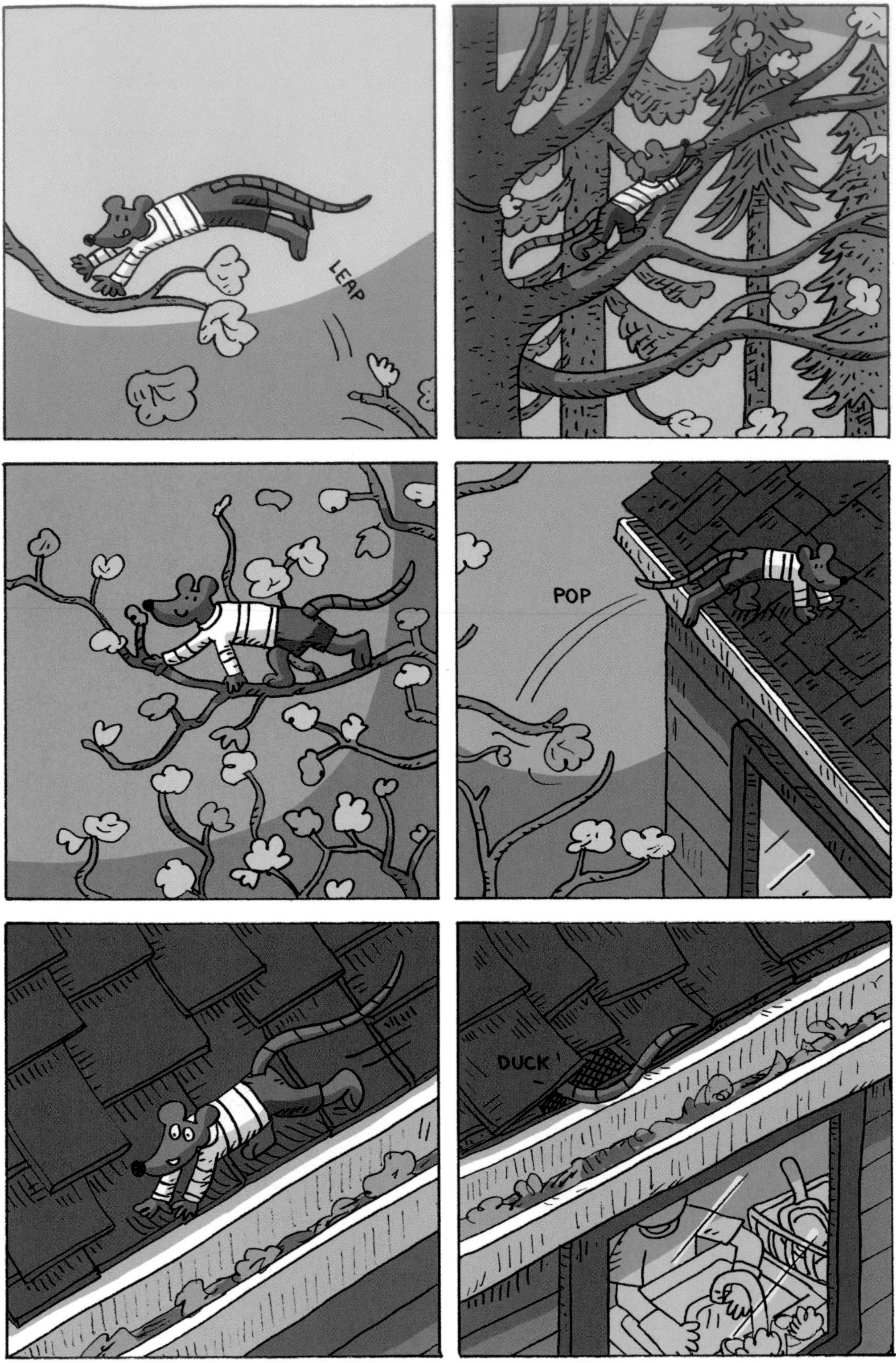
LEAP
POP
DUCK

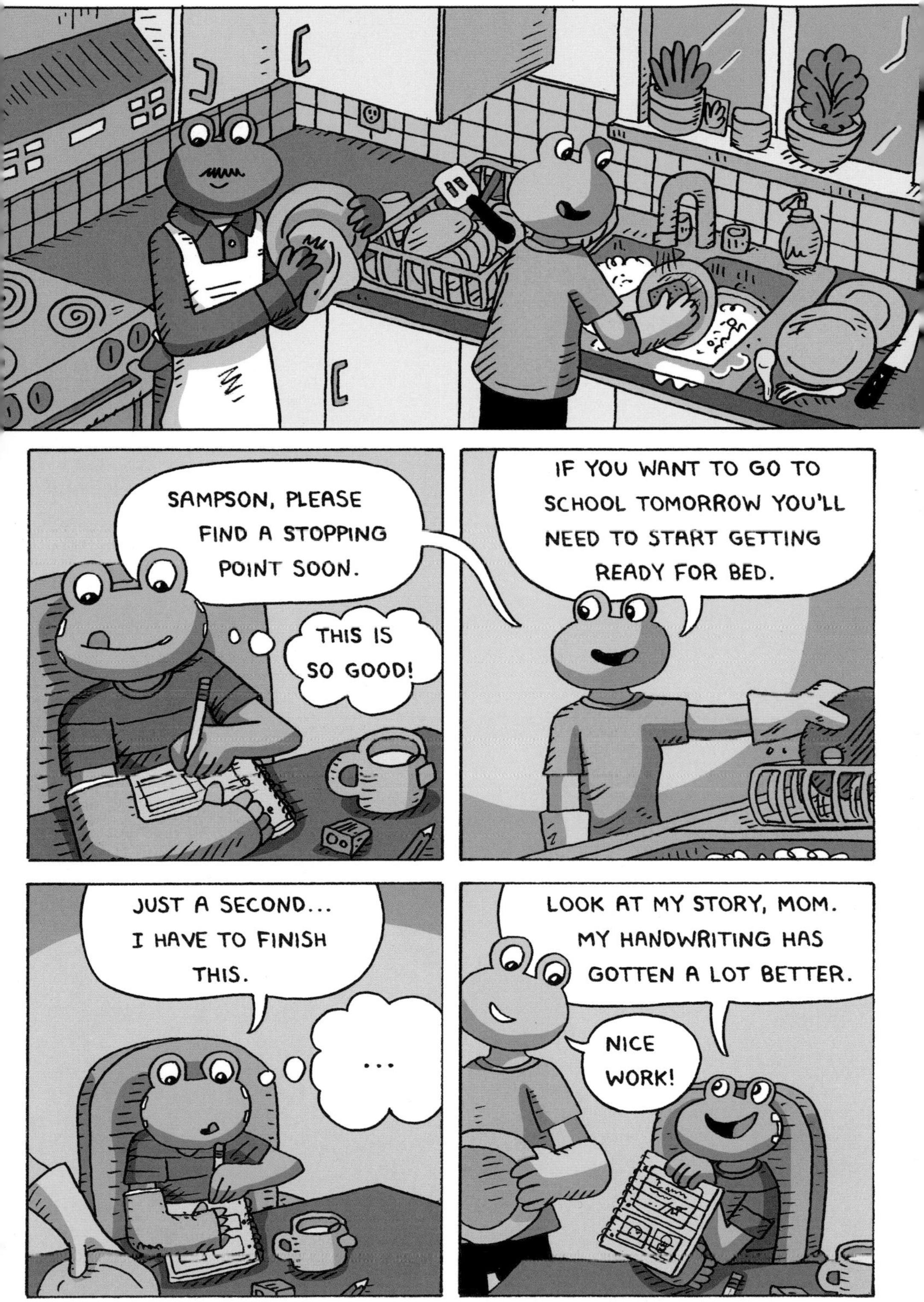

SAMPSON, PLEASE FIND A STOPPING POINT SOON.
THIS IS SO GOOD!
IF YOU WANT TO GO TO SCHOOL TOMORROW YOU'LL NEED TO START GETTING READY FOR BED.
JUST A SECOND... I HAVE TO FINISH THIS.
...
LOOK AT MY STORY, MOM. MY HANDWRITING HAS GOTTEN A LOT BETTER.
NICE WORK!

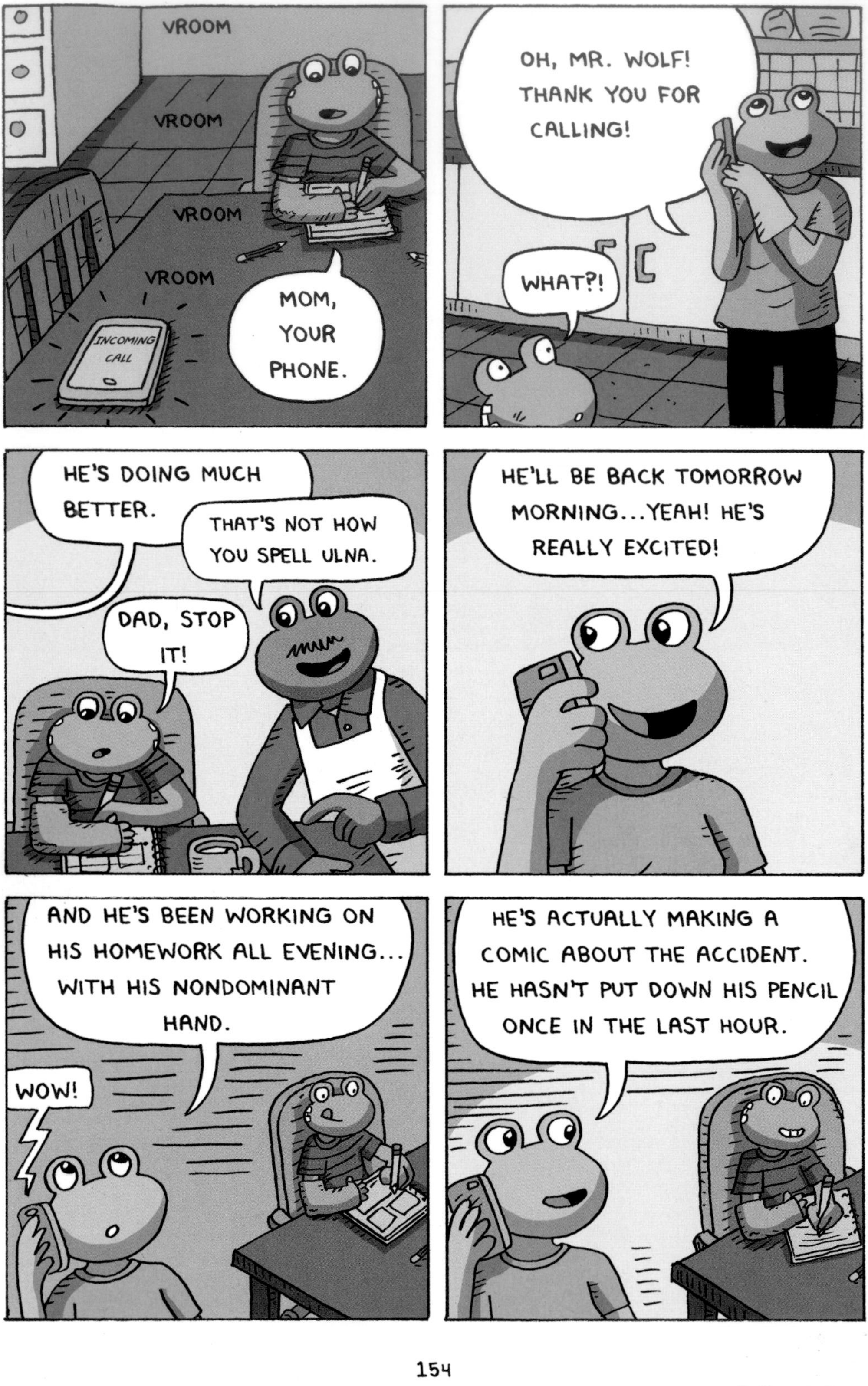
VROOM
VROOM
VROOM
VROOM
INCOMING CALL
MOM, YOUR PHONE.
OH, MR. WOLF! THANK YOU FOR CALLING!
WHAT?!
HE'S DOING MUCH BETTER.
THAT'S NOT HOW YOU SPELL ULNA.
DAD, STOP IT!
HE'LL BE BACK TOMORROW MORNING...YEAH! HE'S REALLY EXCITED!
AND HE'S BEEN WORKING ON HIS HOMEWORK ALL EVENING... WITH HIS NONDOMINANT HAND.
WOW!
HE'S ACTUALLY MAKING A COMIC ABOUT THE ACCIDENT. HE HASN'T PUT DOWN HIS PENCIL ONCE IN THE LAST HOUR.

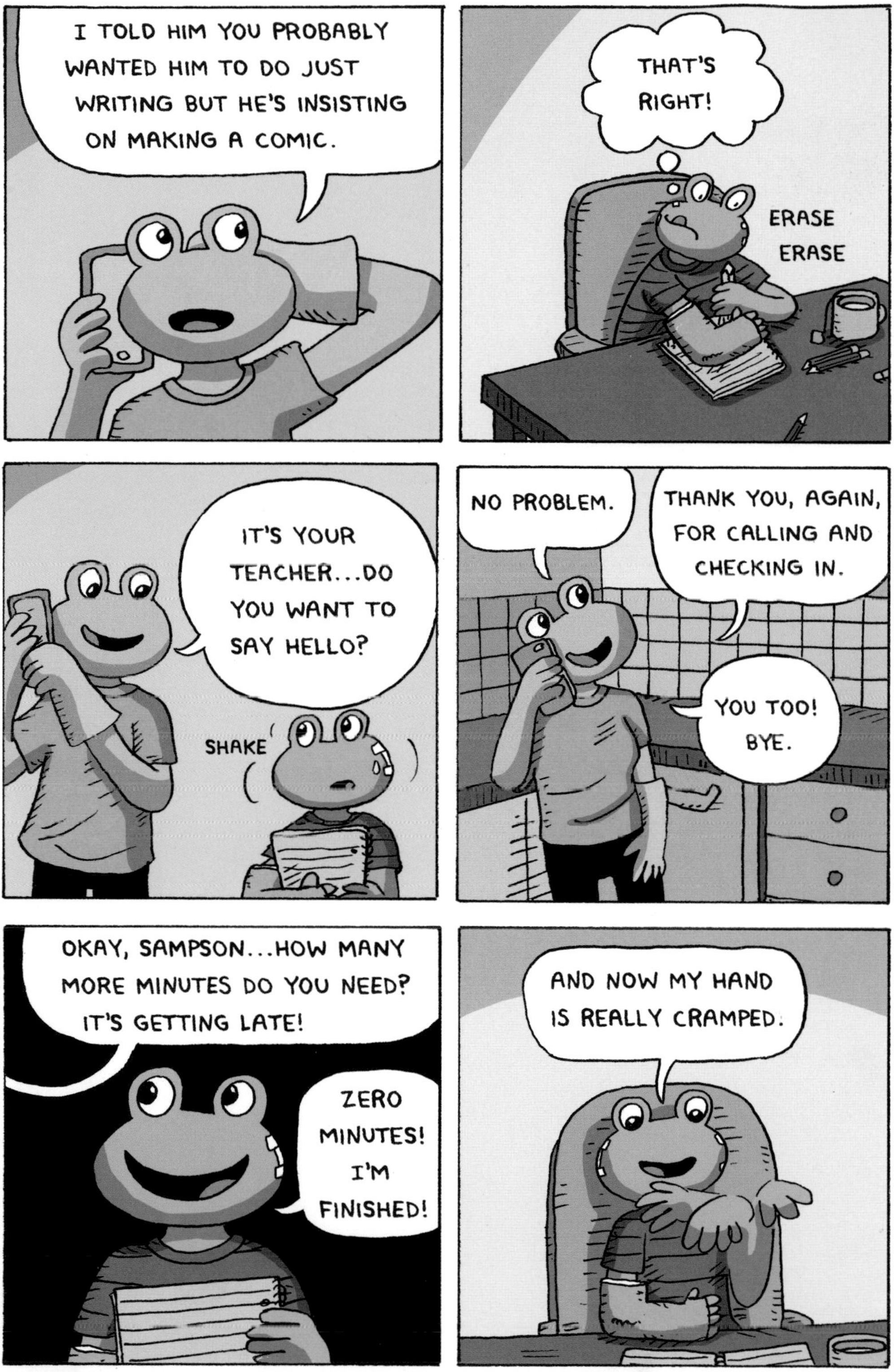
I TOLD HIM YOU PROBABLY WANTED HIM TO DO JUST WRITING BUT HE'S INSISTING ON MAKING A COMIC.
THAT'S RIGHT!
ERASE ERASE
IT'S YOUR TEACHER...DO YOU WANT TO SAY HELLO?
SHAKE
NO PROBLEM.
THANK YOU, AGAIN, FOR CALLING AND CHECKING IN.
YOU TOO! BYE.
OKAY, SAMPSON...HOW MANY MORE MINUTES DO YOU NEED? IT'S GETTING LATE!
ZERO MINUTES! I'M FINISHED!
AND NOW MY HAND IS REALLY CRAMPED.

CHAPTER EIGHT
Sampson's Return

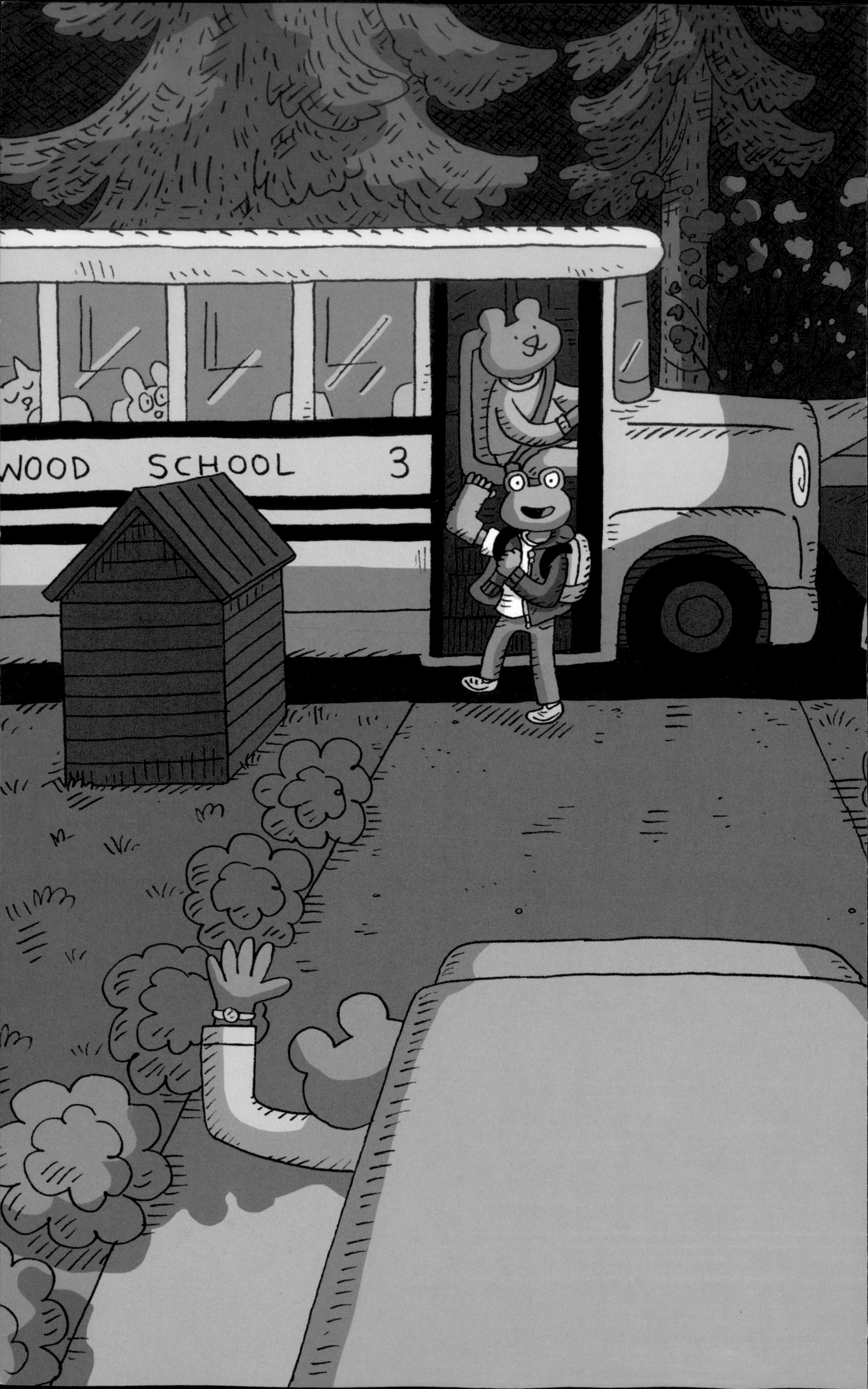
WOOD SCHOOL 3

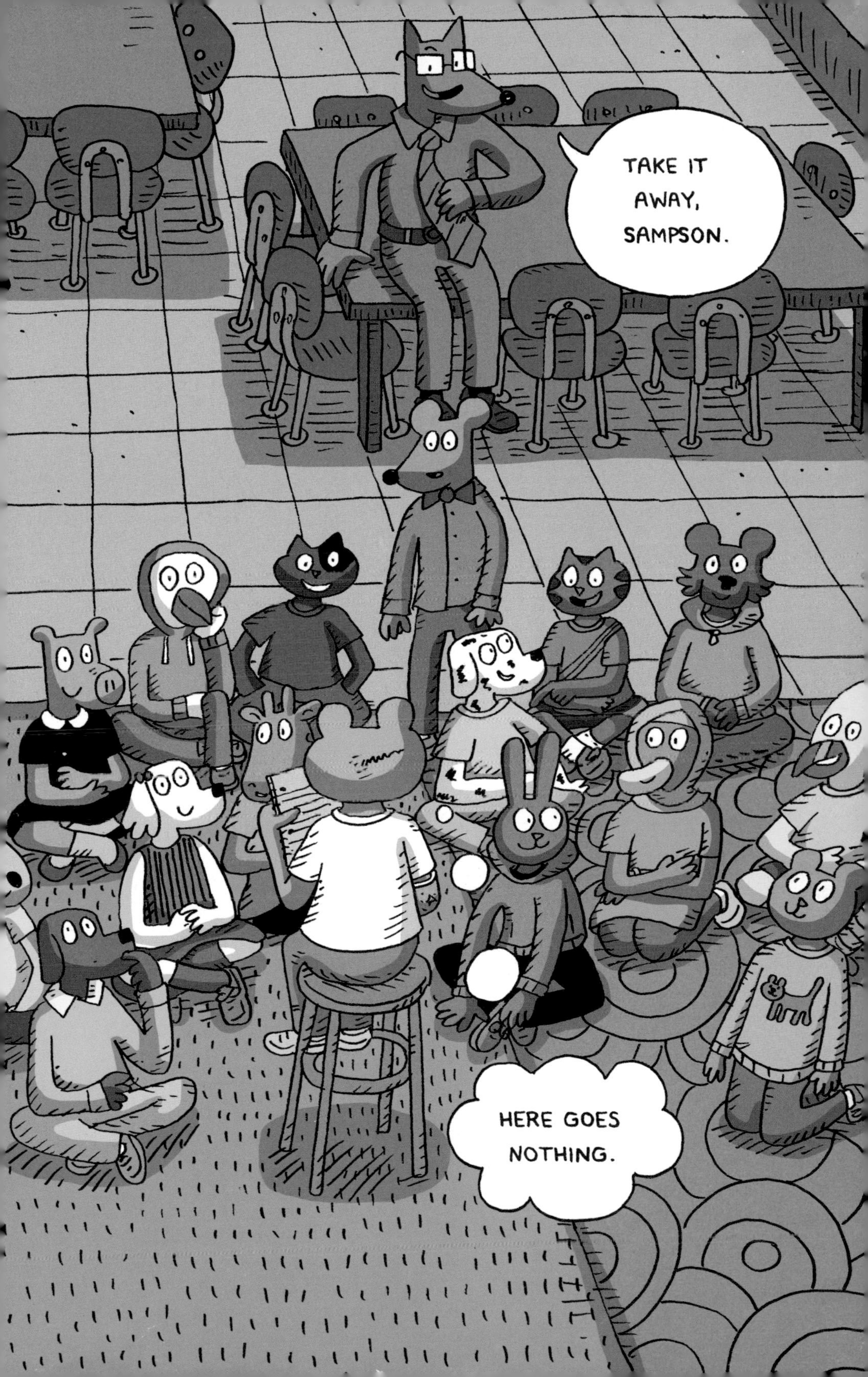
TAKE IT AWAY, SAMPSON.
HERE GOES NOTHING.

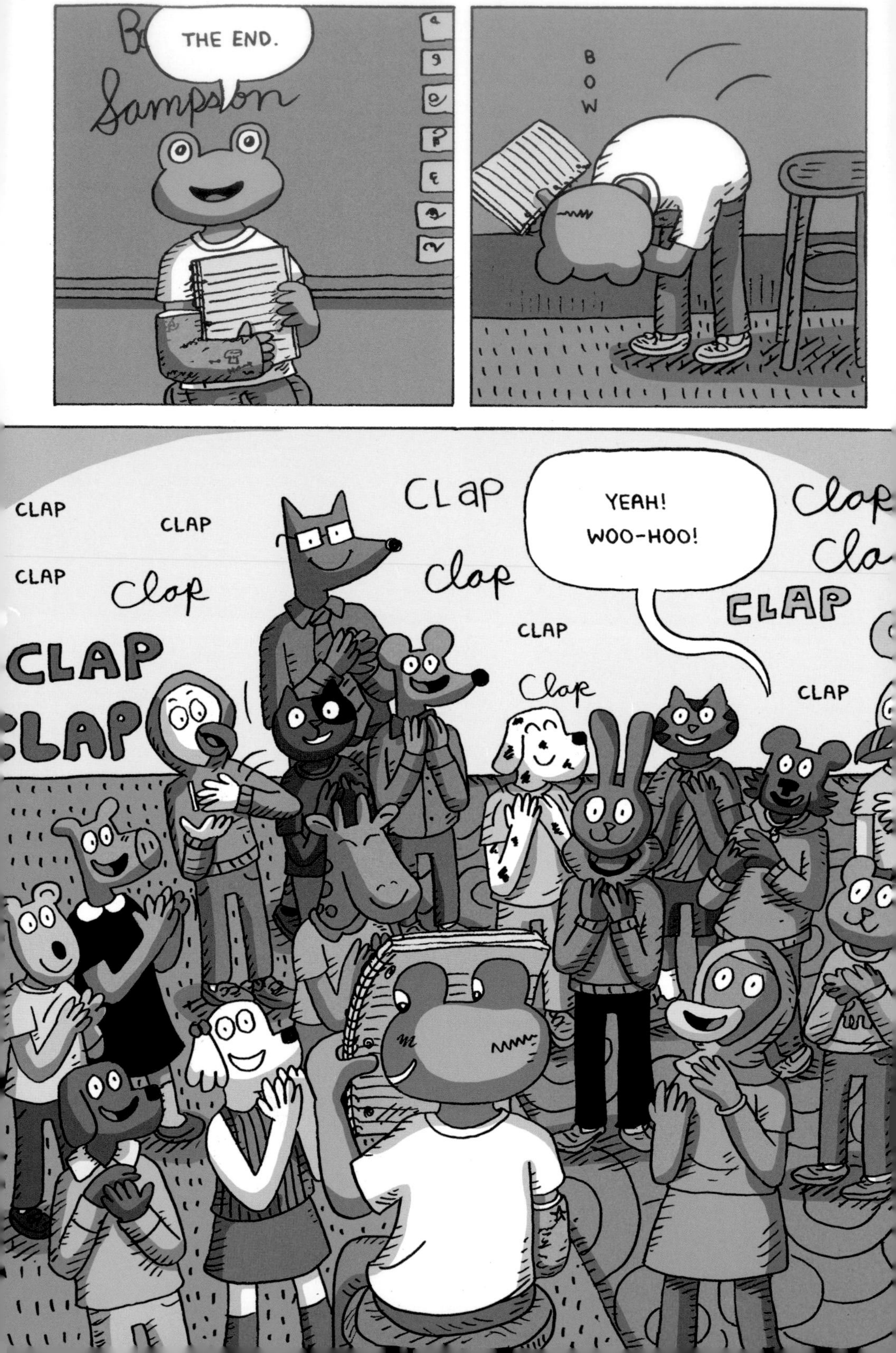
Sampson
THE END.
BOW
CLAP
CLAP
CLAP
Clap
CLAP
CLap
Clap
CLAP
Clap
YEAH!
WOO-HOO!
Clap
CLAP
CLAP

166

167

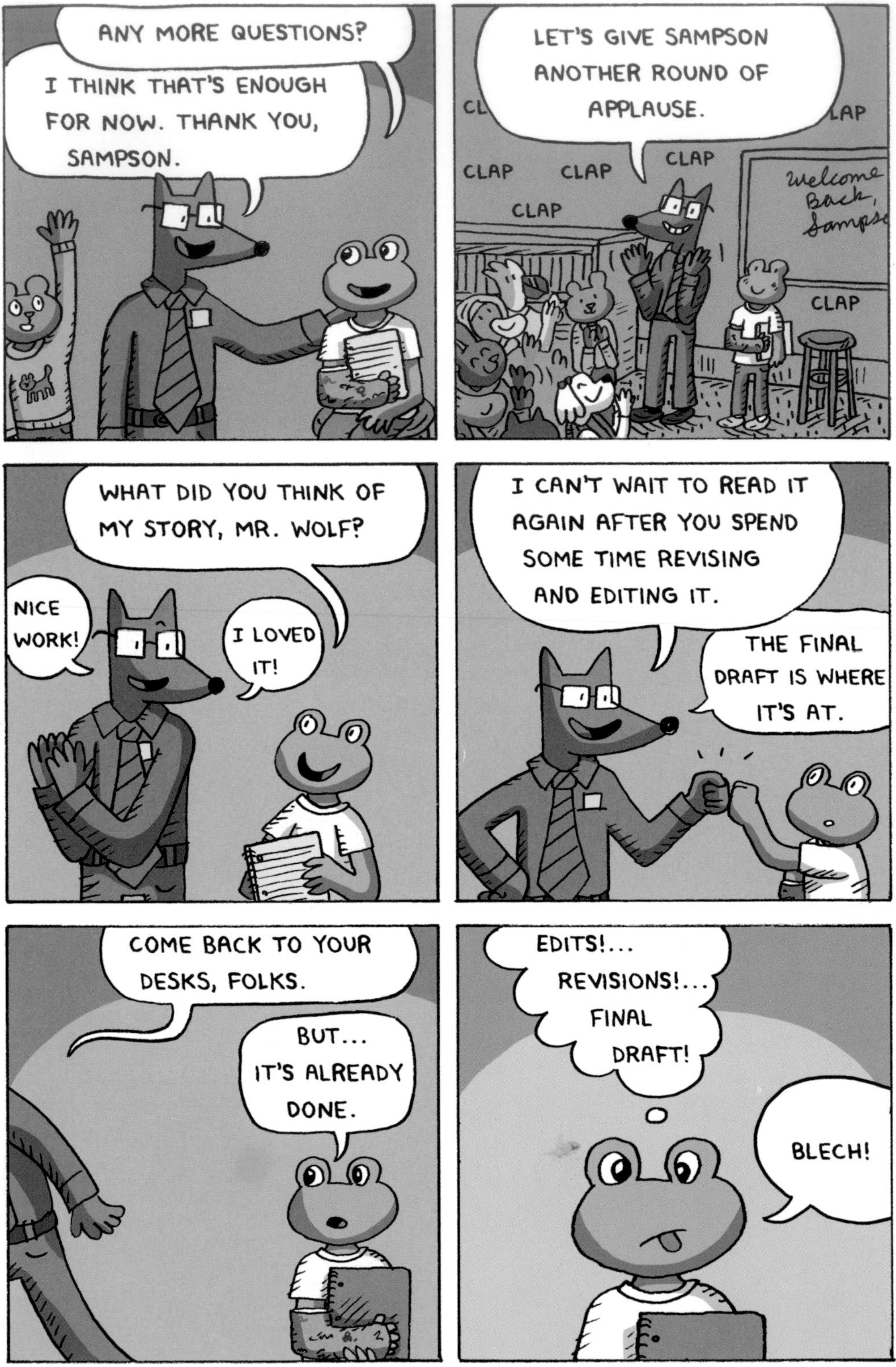
ANY MORE QUESTIONS?
I THINK THAT'S ENOUGH FOR NOW. THANK YOU, SAMPSON.
LET'S GIVE SAMPSON ANOTHER ROUND OF APPLAUSE.
CLAP CLAP CLAP CLAP CLAP
Welcome Back,
WHAT DID YOU THINK OF MY STORY, MR. WOLF?
NICE WORK!
I LOVED IT!
I CAN'T WAIT TO READ IT AGAIN AFTER YOU SPEND SOME TIME REVISING AND EDITING IT.
THE FINAL DRAFT IS WHERE IT'S AT.
COME BACK TO YOUR DESKS, FOLKS.
BUT... IT'S ALREADY DONE.
EDITS!... REVISIONS!... FINAL DRAFT!
BLECH!

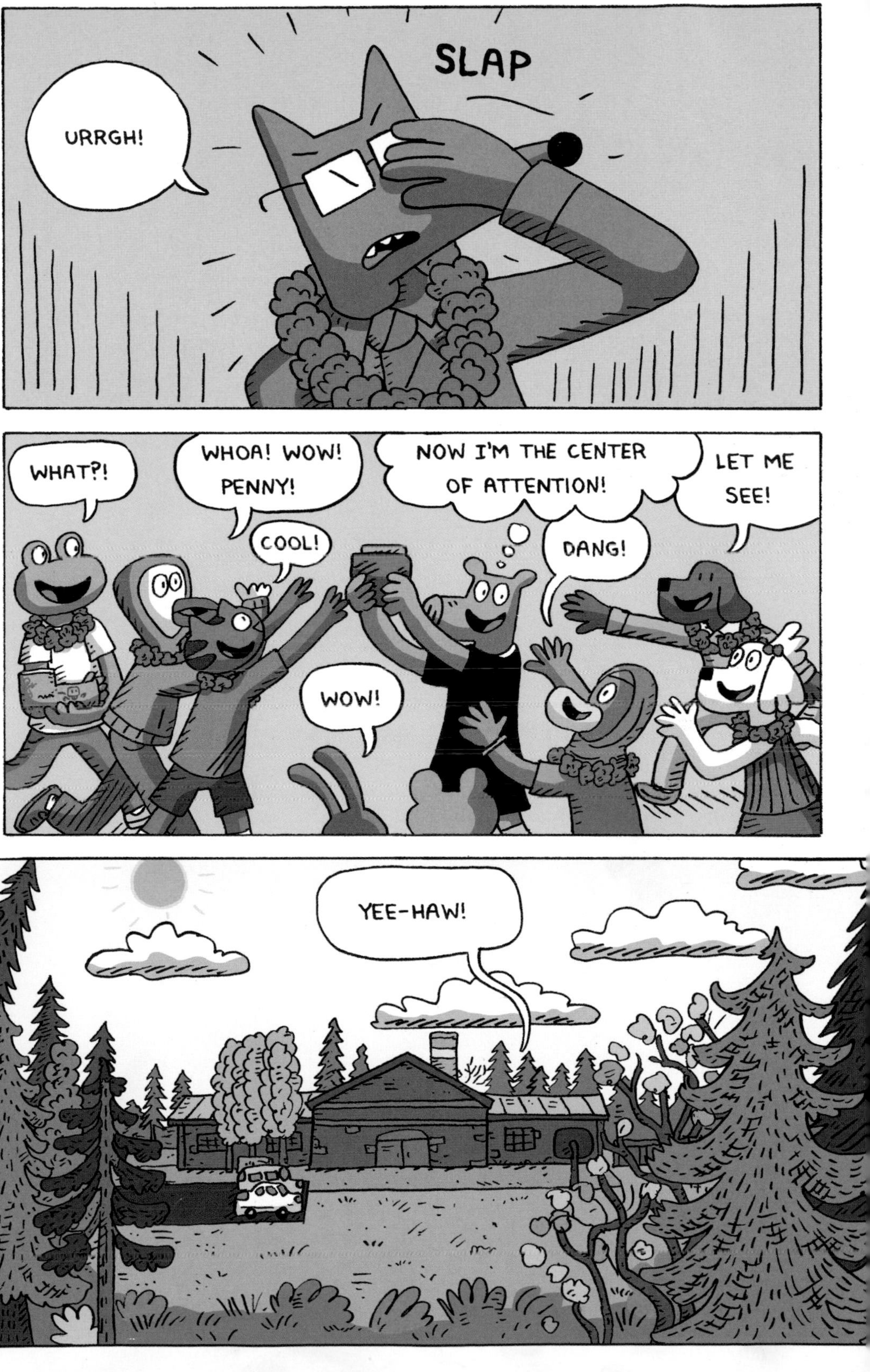
URRGH!
SLAP
WHAT?!
WHOA! WOW! PENNY!
COOL!
NOW I'M THE CENTER OF ATTENTION!
LET ME SEE!
DANG!
WOW!
YEE-HAW!

Thank you to . . .

Judy Hansen, Cassandra Pelham Fulton, Phil Falco, David Saylor, Jordana Kulak, Emily Heddleson, Judy Newman, Matt Poulter, Michael Strouse, and everyone at Scholastic and Graphix who helped this book make it into your hands.

To Ariel, Marlen, Don, Alona, Lisa, David, Ed, and the rest of my family.

To my students, who always surprise me year after year with their creativity, curiosity, and compassion.

To Alex Chiu, Barry Deutsch, Jonathan Hill, Lark Pien, Raina Telgemeier, Jarrett Krosoczka, Andy Runton, Alec Longstreth, Kate Messner, John Schu, Michael Ring, Greg Means, and Gene Luen Yang for your help and support.

Thank you to all of the small and independent bookstores that have supported me throughout the years, as well as a huge thank-you to school and community librarians who are doing the good work.

To Inez, Jack, Finn, Viola, Connor, and all the kids on the block.

And of course, thank you, dear reader, for spending time in Mr. Wolf's class.

Author photo by Renée Lopez

Aron Nels Steinke is the Eisner Award–winning creator of the Mr. Wolf's Class series, and is the illustrator and coauthor, with Ariel Cohn, of *The Zoo Box*. One summer day back in 1988 when Aron was seven years old, he had a bad bike accident that left him with a broken arm and unable to walk for two weeks. He wasn't wearing a helmet and considers himself very lucky that his injuries weren't more serious. Once they had healed, he quickly got back on his bike and hasn't stopped riding since. If you're in Portland, Oregon, you might find him riding his bike to his other job, where he teaches fourth and fifth graders.

Don't miss the other adventures in Mr. Wolf's class!

From the Eisner Award-winning author
ARON NELS STEINKE
MR. WOLF'S CLASS

From the Eisner Award-winning author
ARON NELS STEINKE
MR. WOLF'S CLASS
MYSTERY CLUB

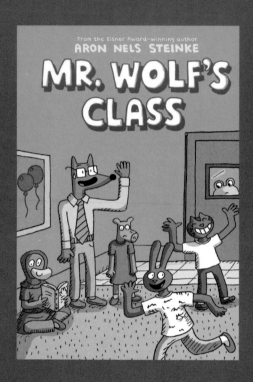

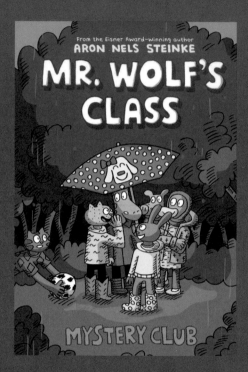